DONOVAN'S WAR

A MILITARY THRILLER

W.J. LUNDY

Tom
Thank you for your
Service Brother, Lets
Get Together for B-2ues

DONOVAN'S WAR

WJ LUNDY © 2017

V10.11.2017

COPYRIGHT

The Toyota Land Cruiser pulled through the factory gates. A lone streetlight cast an eerie glow over a gravel lot filled with idling military trucks of all shapes and sizes. Exhaust fumes hung in the cold air like mist. Soldiers clad in dark-green uniforms moved along the roadway with flashlights, directing an olive-drab bus and longer eighteen wheelers into a single line. From an open warehouse, civilians overburdened with luggage were approaching the transports, guards checking papers as they boarded.

Four men sat concealed behind the tinted glass of the Toyota, performing a last round of weapons and communications checks. With their broad shoulders, shaggy hair, and trimmed beards, they could have been clones, all cut from the same cloth in Uncle Sam's sewing shop. These men weren't designed for farm life or working in cubicles; they were warriors. A thousand years earlier, they would have found their places behind axes or at the grip of the sword. Even dressed in khakis and polo shirts, there was no mistaking who they were.

Soldiers down to their DNA, they found their way into service and were eventually selected for their military backgrounds and training. That is where their association with conventional military service ended. Off the books of any government agency, they worked alone, outside the lines, doing things in the shadows. Members of the clandestine Ground Division, a branch of the CIA, they now shared more in common with private contractors and cutthroat mercenaries than any formal branch of the armed forces.

As the driver cut the headlights, the men made last-minute preparations. In his seat behind the driver, Tommy flexed his cramped legs. The Heckler & Koch UMP45 that was pressed under his left arm ground against his ribs with every movement. The air conditioner running on high did little to prevent the sweat that ran down his back. Tommy watched the armed Iraqi soldiers moving just to his front. Shivers went down his neck, heightening his senses as he felt the tension of how close they were to their enemy.

Tommy Donovan was a soldier through and through. This was his life, his purpose—a weapon in his hand and an enemy in front of him. Not even twenty-five years old and just a few short years out of the Rangers, Tommy was already a formidable force. He stood out among his peers in the battalion and had gone to Special Forces Selection, but he was pulled from the ranks early during the process and moved to a secluded location where he was briefed on other possibilities for his future. Always one to take a task head on, he accepted the offer and soon found himself in the clandestine Ground Division. The next years were spent training until he was an expert in desert, jungle, mountain, and arctic survival. Finally, out of school and assigned to an operational unit, he was one of two junior members on their first mission with plenty to prove.

"You sure about this, boss?" Tommy asked.

Jack Conway was a beast of a man with combat experience in Afghanistan and, before that, Central and South America. He looked back at Tommy from the front passenger seat and forced a smile. "I haven't been sure of anything since we crossed the border. Just stay cool and we'll be drowning in pints at a pub in Germany before you know it."

This was a four-man expedition into enemy territory on the eve of the ground invasion into Iraq. Posing as French aid workers with all the proper papers, they had been able to move freely from Jordan to this small desert border town located just inside Iraq. Nobody bought their cover; four men built like lumberjacks pretending to be aid workers had turned the eye of every customs agent who heard their story. But the papers were legit and stamped by the highest authority, so their travel wasn't delayed, their persons and vehicles never searched. Everything they wore had been sanitized, the clothing all purchased in Germany, and the weapons picked up from a dealer in Jordan. Even the radios were Japanese, bought through a street dealer in Kuwait.

James, the team's youngest member, sat beside Tommy in the back seat. He was Tommy's closest friend in the Ground Division. Tommy had even attended the kid's wedding a year earlier during a break in their training. They were close, but not out of any commonality. James was a rich kid with well-connected parents, while Tommy had grown up an orphan having to find his own way. The two men had become friends out of necessity, the way many military friendships begin. They had both been recruited at the same time and developed a bond during their schooling, amidst the struggle to get through each day.

Shooting a smile at Tommy, James racked the slide of a Walther PPK and slid it into an ankle holster strapped just above his right boot.

Tommy shook his head. "What is it with you and all the James Bond bullshit? You really think you're ever going to use an ankle holster?"

James shrugged. "I don't know, man, but this has got to be some of the most whack shit I've ever done. Can't hurt to pack some extra iron."

Elias "Papa" Beda, the oldest veteran of the team, chuckled from the driver's seat. "Welcome to Ground Division, boys, where everything is whack shit," he said, turning off the ignition. A solid gun fighter, Papa had been with the Ground Division team longer than there had been a team. Before joining the division, he'd been a Marine and had done years with recon, working his way up the ranks. Loaned out to the CIA after 9/11, the agency quickly learned the value of adding paramilitary forces to their ranks.

Papa had officially retired from the Marine Corps in early 2000, but had been called back after 9/11. Even though all the men spoke Arabic, only Papa had the perfect dialect and could easily blend in as a local, because technically he was one. His parents lived in Syria and even though he immigrated to the United States as a boy he still held a dual citizenship. His background and Arabic language skills made him a vital part of any mission. He had more time on the ground, in and out of every third-world toilet, than the rest of the men combined. Everywhere Elias went, he seemed to have a connection with the local population. He had a way with people, making strangers feel like they'd been friends for years.

"You see any of your brothers out there?" Jack asked, running a coiled wire into his right ear.

Papa scowled and pushed a hand-rolled cigarette into the corner of his mouth. "Screw you. I'm not an Iraqi—you, dickhead."

"What's the difference? Palestinian mother, Syrian father—just different flavors of the same," Jack taunted. He looked up and spotted a fat man with a thick, black Saddam Hussein mustache approaching. Jack snapped his fingers and signaled with his chin. "Show time, boys. Looks like we got the Hyena's attention."

"What the hell—who names a kid Hyena?" Tommy whispered. "What is he, some kind of cop?"

Jack grunted and shook his head. "No. Syrian Special Police, secret service type. Real asshole from what I read in his file. He runs a special unit they call the Badawi Brigade. It's like the Iraqi's Republican Guard—only for homicidal maniacs. And, allegedly, this guy likes to pick up the scraps of others, hence the code name. File says he's an opportunist, so let's keep our distance and we'll be fine."

The fat man wore olive-green coveralls and enough flashy stitching on his collars to indicate he was in charge.

He paused, squinting to look through the tinted glass, then approached the vehicle, smiling from ear to ear. Before he could reach the front, the Land Cruiser's doors clicked open and the men exited. With James close by his side, Tommy moved to the back and opened the cargo hatch. In the back was a dark-brown Pelican case. Inside were two tight bundles of orange-fabric Combat Identification Panels. Tommy took one bundle while James took the other and closed the hatch. When Tommy had moved to the front of the vehicle, Papa was finishing words with the Hyena.

Papa turned toward him and pointed to the panels in their arms. In perfect Arabic, he explained, "Make sure each vehicle has a panel securely fastened on the hood."

The Hyena grinned with crooked teeth and nodded before turning on his heels, shouting commands. Two young Iraqi soldiers ran from the back, taking the bundles. Tommy moved to the side and watched as the men followed the instructions on fastening the materials to the hoods of the vehicles. They were identification panels that would hopefully prevent coalition aircraft from targeting and destroying the vehicles once they entered the open desert on the road toward the Syrian border.

Tommy stepped away from the vehicle with James still by his side. Even though not always apparent, the men were constantly covering each other's blind spots. They worked in pairs, Tommy supporting James as Jack and Papa did the same. Tommy continued scanning for threats, letting the weight of his concealed weapons comfort him. Iraqis scrambled up and down the line of vehicles, loading cargo and emptying cans of fuel into the vehicles' tanks.

He looked back toward their own vehicle and could see that Jack and Papa were still talking with the Hyena, the conversation now joined by an Iraqi and a Syrian military officer. Tommy moved farther away and stood in the shadows, watching the loading and positioning of the vehicles. James nudged him with an elbow and signaled toward two large semi-trucks being loaded from the back with fork trucks. The cargo consisted of wooden crates with obscure bio-hazard markings. Someone had attempted to paint over them, but in the right light, the markings still reflected through.

"What the fuck are we doing here?" James whispered. "Iraqis, Syrians. This is bad."

Tommy dipped his chin and scowled then turned toward the school busses being loaded with families. "You were at the same briefing I was. We're helping high-level foreign nationals safely exit the country before the invasion."

"That explains the busses, but not those trucks, bro. That ain't luggage and household goods they're packing up."

Jack and Papa approached them from behind. Jack moved close, and the men instinctively shifted positions to create another protective bubble. Jack turned back to the front and said, "You boys are looking just a little too hard at the cargo; you're going to make someone nervous."

James shrugged his shoulders and let his eyes drift away. "Nasty shit they're loading, boss. Does the homestead know what we got here? Isn't that what this whole war is all about?"

"Doesn't matter if it's bubble gum or the zombie apocalypse. You read the order. We escort this convoy to Syria and make sure the Air Force don't blow it to shit. In exchange, Assad promises not to rain down hate on Israel for attacking his Arab brother to the east."

James shook his head. "Like I said, this is some whack shit."

"Hey, boys, you've all played dominoes. If we don't get Assad on board and he bombs Israel, then the Israelis strike back, and suddenly Iran gets a wild hair in their ass to hit the Jewish State. Then instead of a world coalition against Iraq, we got ourselves a Middle Eastern shit sandwich and we all get to take a bite."

"So, basically, make this work?" Tommy grunted.

Jack grinned. "Yeah, make it work."

Shrugging, Tommy turned his attention back to the front as diesel engines came to life, the previously low idles now roaring and coughing blue exhaust from rusted tail pipes. A blue and white Mazda sedan with police emblems pulled up beside them. The window rolled down and the Hyena shot the team a big smile and thumbs up. Jack watched intently while Papa and the Hyena exchanged words before the window closed and the vehicle moved to the head of the convoy. Papa turned back toward them. He dropped a cigarette and crushed it under his boot. "It's time to go."

Tommy stood, trying to resist the temptation to adjust the submachine gun under his jacket. Everything about the mission felt wrong, and his senses were tingling on high alert. Jack pointed to the Land Cruiser, and he followed the others. He returned to his seat in the Toyota and unslung the submachine gun from his armpit then placed it between his knees. The Toyota started and Papa edged the vehicle forward. The Iraqi soldiers shone flashlights on them and directed their vehicle into the center of the convoy.

"You know, I just realized something. We aren't escorts," Tommy said. "We're human shields."

"Not likely," Jack replied without looking back. "To be an effective shield someone has to know we're here, and then that someone would have to give a shit."

James sighed. "Some whack shit, man."

Jack opened a center console and removed a dark-gray steel box with a stubby, black antenna. He flipped a switch on the base of the case, which illuminated an LED light at the top. It flashed red several times then locked to green to let the men know they were being tracked by coalition aircraft. "This gives our location to the birds over our head, letting them know we're friendly."

"Can we talk to them with it?" Tommy asked.

Jack shook his head. "Nope." He popped open the glove box and removed a tiny olive-colored tactical beacon (TACBE). "But I have a couple of these."

They were old and phased out by most armies, but the best they could get while maintaining their cover. The radio would be good for making and receiving emergency calls and had a twenty-four-hour battery. In theory, all coalition aircraft would be listening to the frequency, so if they got into trouble, they could fire it up for a quick rescue. Also, as a last resort, it could be used to call off an airstrike if for some reason a NATO aircraft didn't pick up on the orange panels and the friend-or-foe, gray box transponder.

It was less than a hundred miles to the border, and the convoy hardly slowed as the vehicles crossed over it. The Syrians knew they were coming and had the gates wide open for their approach. As the convoy sped past, Tommy looked out of his window and saw the armed border guards standing on the shoulder of the road at attention, presenting salutes to the vehicles.

"What the hell is that all about?" he mumbled.

Papa turned his head from the driver's seat. "The bus —it's full of dignitaries, high-level families, stuff like that. Important people."

"Damn," James said from his seat. He looked out at the dark terrain of the wide-open desert that had the same appearance as the surface of the moon. "I don't know who they were, but I don't like the thought of going into this place, man."

"Hold it together, boys. We rendezvous up here, and then we all go our own way."

"It can't come soon enough. I feel like I have my ass hanging out back here. We are so far from friendlies, we're hosed if shit goes sideways," Tommy said.

Papa slapped the side of the wheel with his open palm. "Man, you two cherries need to calm the fuck down. It's bad juju to be talking shit like this on an op."

Tommy leaned back into the seat, suddenly embarrassed. "I'm sorry—you're right."

"Don't be sorry," Papa scorned. "Get your ass back on point. You ain't back there to lick the damn windows. Keep your eyes open."

The vehicles moved onward through the desert. The

terrain changed and the road with it, from a dusty trail to a wide, black-top highway. Soon they were crossing over mountains and through small villages that grew larger the farther they got from the border. Tommy watched the terrain pass by his open window, listening to the buzzing of the tires against the pavement. He caught himself nodding off and reached into his shirt pocket for a blister pack of nicotine gum. He didn't smoke, but he used the gum to help stay focused on long missions. He popped out two pieces and stuffed them in his mouth before passing the rest of the pack off to James.

"We're stopping," Papa said.

Jack was already upright in his seat, leaning forward to see what was happening. The convoy was at a wide intersection. The busses loaded with civilians were being directed north, escorted away by Syrian police cars. The loaded trucks turned south, guided by military vehicles. That left only the Ground Division team, the Hyena, and his men in the two remaining Range Rovers. Papa pulled the vehicle up and to the center of the road where the Syrian Secret Service man was standing with his men. Papa rolled down the window, and the fat, mustached man approached the vehicle with a big smile. He extended his hand and Papa reached out, returning the handshake.

"This was a very successful day, gentlemen," the Hyena said in broken English.

Papa laughed and replied in Arabic, "Yes, indeed. So that's it? We are complete?"

The Hyena grinned and nodded, his expression revealing that he caught the point Papa had made by not responding in English. The team was still on the job, and poor cover or not, they had to maintain it. The man walked closer to the vehicle and put his hands on the roof then leaned down, looking inside. He spoke calmly. "You all must be very tired. We will escort you to your hotel and say our farewells." With a smile, he took two steps back and returned to his vehicle.

"That cat is weird," James said. "He looks like a seventies porn star with that mustache."

Jack laughed. "I can do weird, let's just hold it together a bit longer and get this done." He pulled a paper map from his lap and tried to make sense of it, matching it to the GPS coordinates from a device in his left hand. "No idea where this joker is taking us. The street data and this map must be from the 1950s. This highway isn't even on here."

Papa chuckled. "It's the third world. Updating Garmin probably isn't a priority."

The vehicles pulled back onto the road with Papa following the Hyena's blue police car. The two olive-green Range Rovers with military markings stayed close behind them. They were led down a highway and into a city. The sun was coming up when they exited onto a narrow road then turned onto even tighter streets. The police car to the front slowed then turned with the others following. Soon it stopped on a dead-end street in front of a tall warehouse. Jack stiffened in his seat. "This doesn't look like a hotel," he whispered.

Papa looked in the rearview mirror and spoke softly. "Those Rovers behind us are blocking us in, boys."

Tommy looked over his shoulder and could see that the vehicles had turned out, making a classic roadblock shape. The blue car to their front was still stopped, the red brake lights glowing back at them. Tommy reached down between his knees and readied the submachine gun. He could see that the other men were doing the same. Jack's voice was calm and matter-of-fact. "I don't know where this is going, boys, but they don't take any of us. If they try to disarm us—it's on. Does everyone understand?"

The men mumbled their acknowledgement and held their breath as they watched the door of the blue vehicle open and the Hyena exit, walking away from the car and stepping onto the sidewalk in front of the warehouse building. Papa again looked in the mirror and said, "I got two moving up on us from the rear."

"We fighting or talking, boss?" Tommy said, gripping the weapon, ready to lunge out and take down the armed men.

Jack took in a deep breath, his chest expanding, then exhaled loudly. "Let's show these fuckers we got teeth, but no shooting unless I give the word or they fire first." With that, he flung open his door and stepped into the street with his rifle up and aimed at the head of the Hyena. The other men did the same, exiting the vehicle quickly and finding targets of their own.

"Talk to him, Papa, before I bust his skull wide open," Jack shouted, this time in English for effect.

The fat man was smiling, his hands in the air as if it was all a misunderstanding. He took a step forward before Jack intensified his grip on the rifle. "Stay where you're at, tough guy," Jack ordered. "I'd hate to ruin that finely groomed mustache of yours."

"You have no worries, we are just changing vehicles. No worries, friends, no worries."

Tommy watched the men to the rear take aggressive steps closer, both armed with AK-47 rifles. Others still in the Range Rovers were exiting and taking up firing positions at the back. "Fuck that noise, boss. I got six to eight shooters back here," Tommy shouted. "This is a takedown if I ever did see one. Let me loose."

"No, no, friends, it's okay, it's okay," the Hyena said again, maintaining his smile.

Papa moved around the front of the Land Cruiser, his rifle up. He looked at the Hyena and back to the front toward the blue car in the dead-end street. "What the hell is going on here, Abdul? We had a deal," he said, using the man's first name.

"Your deal is still good, there will just be delays. Now, I insist you drop your weapons and surrender to my men."

"Not going to happen," Jack said as he spun and put his weapon on the men moving up from the rear, realizing the greater threat. "We're not about to become your bounty."

Papa did the same, taking cover over the door. Bolts locked on rifles, chambering rounds. Tommy could see the Badawi Brigade soldiers were in cover with their rifles up and in good positions. The team would be cut down in the center of the street if they resisted now. He flexed his shoulders and leaned into the submachine gun, slowly taking the slack out of the trigger, ready to light them up as soon as the word was given.

James was looking at the same thing and knew a fight couldn't be won. "Wait," he said, stepping away from the Toyota. "Just hold up." He held his rifle over his head.

"What the hell are you doing? Get back to your position, James," Jack ordered.

"Nah, hell with that. Look at 'em, there's too many. We ain't getting out of this alive." James shook his head and laid his rifle on the roof of the Toyota then lifted his arms into the air.

"He said it's just a delay, right?" James said, looking to the Hyena, who was smiling again.

The fat man nodded. "Yes, of course, just a delay. I talk to your State Department and you will all be home in no time. Big strong men, they'll pay for you."

"See?" James moved away from the Toyota with his hands still up, and closer to the Hyena. "Let's just listen to what the guy has to say."

Jack shook his head and relaxed his grip on the rifle, not knowing what to do. Papa did the same. In the back, Tommy could see that the soldiers were coming out of cover and closing in on them.

"It's okay, boys. Let's just trust this guy," James said, still walking toward the Hyena, now only paces away.

Tommy looked to his friend and shook his head. "Don't."

James stared at him and winked. "It's better to live to fight another day."

The Badawi soldiers, now feeling confident, came out of cover and closed in around them. James moved to the sidewalk and dropped to his knees with his hands over his head. The Hyena looked down at the surrendering man with a pleased expression. "Now, please, we can do all of this peacefully, if you just follow the lead of your friend."

Shaking his head, Jack spit on the ground and took

his rifle off his shoulder. Tommy eased his finger off the trigger and pushed back as the enemy soldiers closed in on him. As all attention was on the three armed Americans, James rolled back to his ankles and drew the concealed Walther hidden in the ankle holster. With a smooth motion, he drew and fired at the Hyena. The intelligence man's head snapped back.

The Badawi Brigade soldiers paused in shock, their minds not registering the quick change of events from imminent surrender to their leader dead. Tommy took advantage of the hesitation and turned back to the front. Firing on full auto, he stitched a .45-caliber path through the guard closest to him. Weapons on both sides opened fire. Tommy could feel the rounds zip past his head as Papa fired over his shoulder.

In seconds, it was over. The Badawi men lay on the ground, dead or dying. Tommy dropped a magazine and inserted a new one before charging forward and putting safety shots into the wounded soldiers. When he turned back, he could see that Papa had the now bullet-shattered vehicle running again. Tommy turned to the sidewalk. James was still on the ground, looking up at him with wide eyes and then down at the front of his shirt.

"Shit, he's hit!" Jack shouted, running to the downed man's side.

Tommy met him at the sidewalk and together they brought him back to the Toyota. The man's shirt was soaked with blood before they could get him on the seat. James mumbled incoherently while Jack pulled back a seat cushion and dug through an aid box. He tossed bandages to Tommy as he pulled the cap off a morphine needle.

"Jack, we gotta roll, brother," Papa shouted from the front. The sounds of sirens rose in the distance.

Jack nodded his response and pushed James the rest of the way into the back seat before leaping into the front. Tommy was left in the back, pressing the thick gauze bandages against his friend's bleeding chest. James looked up at him, grinning, the morphine taking effect. He lifted his hand; the Walther pistol was still tight in his grip. "See, the holster paid off."

Tommy shook his head and took the pistol from his friend. "It sure did, James, it sure did."

Papa raced them back out of the alley and turned south, speeding through neighborhood streets until they were back in open desert. Jack pulled out the emergency personal locater beacon, set it to distress mode, and attempted to dial in the AWAC's aircraft that he knew would be in high orbit over Iraq. It was their only safety net, their only chance of evacuation if things went wrong. He set the transmitter to ping and turned on the speaker, receiving no replies. He pressed the transmit button and gave their call sign, requesting assistance from any aircraft. They were in the wind, too far from home and too far behind enemy lines for the calls to go through.

Jack made a fist and punched the dashboard until his knuckles bled. Papa reached out a hand and squeezed his team leader's shoulder. "Hold it together, man," Papa said. He looked in the rearview mirror at Tommy, who was now holding James in his lap. The wounded man's face was pale as he bled out in the back seat. Tommy shook his head and closed his eyes.

ALBAHR, SYRIA

TEN YEARS LATER

Syrian summer was harsh for those not used to it. The dry heat and the stifling winds could become unbearable. Years of living in Europe and the luxury lifestyle lessened Ziya Fayed's tolerance to this part of the world, a place he once called home. Syrian by birth, he had attachments here, but many of those were gone now. His family moved to Europe long ago, and he had no romantic aspirations for this land, nor was he eager to stay any longer than he had to.

His nose hadn't stopped bleeding from the dry winds since his arrival in the land that God forgot. He looked from the sedan window into the night, the full moon hanging low on the horizon of a cloudless pre-dawn sky. White Toyota sport utility vehicles lined a back alley while a tan Humvee, a relic of the war in Iraq, sat idle in the dark. He grinned, the moonlight reflecting off his bleached teeth. It was time.

He exited the sedan and approached the group of men from the back, not happy to be leaving the cold air of his leather-dressed Mercedes. He wore a loose, face-concealing scarf and dark leather jacket, his body dressed entirely in black. As he walked, bodyguards exited the surrounding vehicles, quickly flanking him. Fayed didn't know the bodyguards, but he was always provided with protection when he went into the field.

Fayed glared harshly at a group surrounding a fat, thick-mustached man with a scar across his forehead. Those in the scarred man's party noticed his approach and snapped to attention, parting to make room for him. He laughed under his breath, both appreciating and resenting the signs of respect he was given by the hired thugs of the Badawi Brigade.

These men were weak and uneducated. They called themselves soldiers, but they were far from it. They disgusted him—their eagerness to please, fighting for someone else's ideals, not a single free thought in their heads. Fayed didn't bother speaking with them, he knew they had no question of what they were fighting for. The scarred man saw his approach and pulled his face from a mobile phone. He waved a free hand to Fayed, smiling gleefully. He turned toward him, nodding as he abruptly ended the call.

"Good evening, Abdul," Fayed said.

Abdul Nassir smiled, revealing badly stained and chipped teeth. Lowering his phone, he leaned in close to Fayed and pointed far down the alley. The mustached man edged uncomfortably closer, the stench of tobacco causing Fayed to grimace. That he had to work with the man disgusted Fayed. He knew that Abdul considered himself an equal—and sometimes even a superior—to Fayed. As a former member of Syria's security establishment, Abdul had made a name for himself in the chaos of the civil war.

Even though technically a traitor, the man commanded respect by his reputation alone, and as long as he stayed on the right side of the government, the Syrian forces ignored him. Abdul was once a high-level agent, so high that the Americans had a code name for him. Now he was nothing more than a renegade bandit, having gone rogue from the government after the start of the civil war, switching sides for profit but still walking a fine line to keep himself off the target list of the Syrian forces.

Nassir made his money as a trafficker. Having connections and access to the border routes, he could get anything in or out of Syria. It had started with guns when they paid well, but eventually moved on to drugs and human trafficking. Establishing covers and contacts with outside parties, he was now well-armed and always well-informed. Fayed swallowed hard with revulsion and followed Abdul's arm. At the end of the street stood an ancient monastery where a lone street lamp illuminated an iron gate guarded by a solitary uniformed officer.

"But one man?" Fayed asked.

"Yes. Your intelligence was good. Tonight, we make them pay."

"Insha Allah. If it is God's will, it will be done," Fayed said.

Abdul grinned. The scar across his forehead tightened with his brow, seeming to catch the light. It flickered with moisture as sweat dripped from his slicked-back hair. He snapped his fingers. "Yes, of course," he laughed.

Men scattered and rushed back to their waiting vehicles. Abdul held the phone to his ear and spoke low commands into the receiver. He turned back to Fayed and shot him another rotten-toothed smile. "And now you will see how it is done."

The vehicle engines amongst the convoy roared to life and thundered down the alleyway. Fayed watched intently, his own excitement building as a number of men dressed in black with full chest rigs approached the distant gate from out of the shadows. Fayed enjoyed this part of every operation, watching Abdul's soldiers in action, witnessing the destruction that he himself took part in planning.

The monastery guard immediately stiffened, his posture changed to alert. He readied his rifle just as the first of several volleys of fire erupted from the approaching men. Rounds slammed into the gate guard's chest as he staggered back and fell to the ground. Gunfire echoed over the city. Fayed smiled to himself, knowing that help would not be coming tonight. The bribes had been paid, the paperwork filed. Even in a place like this, forms must be signed and stamped as fees were paid to conduct such an operation. There would be no police on duty tonight, no hired militias to protect the people inside the walls of the monastery; Fayed had used all of his connections to ensure it.

The column of vehicles lurched forward. The engine of the Humvee revved and a man in the vehicle's turret let loose a barrage of heavy weapons fire into the stone wall as the military vehicle charged forward and rammed through the gate of the ancient church. The Humvee continued into the monastery grounds, followed closely by the white sport utility vehicles.

The thundering explosion that trembled through the ancient stone structure shook her awake to find bits of dust and plaster crumbling from the ceiling, covering her bed. This city was used to war, and it wasn't the first time the fighting woke her from her sleep, but the noise was different tonight, closer and absent of the warning sirens that usually preceded the bombings. She opened her eyes, listening to the screams coming from the hallway while a staccato beat of automatic weapons fire sounded from the courtyard beyond her chamber window.

Her door burst open and a small man pressed into her modestly furnished room. Ignoring pleasantries, he rushed to the bedside and grabbed her by the wrist, trying to pull her from the bed. She recognized the man as Ishmael, one of the guards assigned by the state to guard the monastery. Normally quiet and reserved, tonight the man's eyes were filled with fright and panic.

"Sister Sarah, please come quickly!" he shouted.

Sarah pulled her arm away, lifting the bedspread to cover herself. "How dare you enter my chamber like—"

"Excuse me, Sister, there is no—" Another blast of weapons fire interrupted him. He dropped her wrist and ran to the window. For the first time, she noticed the man's rifle; he was armed. Even though in a war zone, she'd never seen a weapon inside the monastery grounds.

"Ishmael, weapons are not allowed inside the church. What's happening?"

He turned away from the window, his face pale and his eyes filled with fear. He looked at her in despair. "God forgive me, Sister."

"For what, Ishmael?" Sarah scrambled from the bed, searching for her clothing in the dark.

Ishmael stepped back from the window and ran to the door, stopping to look back at her a final time. She could read the horror on his face as his lip quivered and his voice cracked. "Forgive me, Sister; there is no time. May Allah protect you."

Ishmael slammed the chamber door shut behind him. Then she heard the lock tumble and click home.

"No!" she shouted, knowing that the doors of the monastery were all locked and unlocked with ancient skeleton keys. Sarah looked at the hook next to the door and noticed her room key was missing. Ishmael must have swiped it and locked her into the chamber room. Lights flashed from outside her window. The weapons fire and screaming grew louder.

She heard the shouting of men's voices, and the thud of their boots stomping through corridors of the building. Doors were kicked in, and women screamed as they were dragged from their chamber rooms. Bursts of weapons fire followed a terrified wailing from the sisters of the monastery. The heavy boots moved along the hallway and stopped just at the other side of her door. Her heart raced in crippling fear as the handle rattled. Sarah cowered to the farthest corner of her room and shielded her face.

A man pounded at the door, shouting instructions in a language and dialect she didn't understand. Then the lock and handle exploded with the deafening sound of rifle fire. Before she could look away, the destroyed door was kicked in and men rushed forward—filthy men, stinking of unwashed bodies and tobacco smoke. They had long beards and wore black clothing under military vests heaving with equipment. A man grabbed at her and pulled her forward. She struggled helplessly to resist and looked into the man's soulless eyes. He smiled back with a jagged grin and swung a closed fist that caught her square in the front of her teeth.

She tasted the blood and felt the pain reverberate through her body, the whiplash straining her neck and causing her muscles to go slack. More men rushed in and grabbed at her. They tore at her nightgown, and Sarah felt the cold air hit her bare flesh. The men pulled her in every direction then dragged her limp, nearly naked body through the hallways. Her mind lulled as she passed over cold stone floors, down ancient staircases, and finally into a courtyard, where she was dropped heavily to the ground. She tasted the dirt as her face hit the crushed gravel. The spinning world finally settled, her vision focusing on a tall block wall. Other women surrounded her, whimpering and crying, some trembling with fear.

The gunfire faded then halted. The women clustered together, trying to find safety in their closeness. Sarah brought a finger to her lip and quickly pulled away from the sting of her open cut. Her front teeth were loose from the man's blow. She tried to look beyond her group to survey the surroundings. They were in the outer yard of the monastery, a little-used place where vehicles were kept and the grounds were patrolled by armed guards.

Men in state uniforms lay dead on the ground all around them. Just in front of her, she saw the bodies of the monastery priests. Vehicles were riddled with bullet holes and broken glass. The buildings beyond the vehicles began to smoke as flame filled the windows. She saw men dressed in black running along the front of the buildings, tossing fire bombs through windows.

Sister Sarah heard a scream, and she turned her attention toward two men who were dragging a limp body. They tossed the man against the hood of a car. She saw that it was Ishmael. His head hung to one side as he briefly made eye contact with her. A man drew a long, rusted blade from his belt and without any word or warning, he cut a long gash through Ishmael's throat. Blood filled the exposed space and foamed as Ishmael gasped for air. The man let the body fall to the dusty ground. More men surrounded the women. One by one, they pulled the women away from the group and forced them to kneel with their heads pressed against the stone wall. A man grabbed Sarah by the hair. She yelled, pleading for him to stop, and he quickly loosened his grip.

The men on the grounds fell silent as they stopped what they were doing and looked down at her crumpled form. A man lurched forward from the dark sidelines of the chaos. She looked up at his smiling, stained teeth resting under a thick mustache. He moved slowly toward her, the other men clearing a path for him. The man knelt down and locked his eyes on hers.

"American?" he asked, his voice suddenly soft and compassionate.

Afraid to speak, Sarah held her tongue. The man stooped over her. He gently helped her rise to a sitting position and adjusted her torn clothing to cover her bare shoulders "You are American, yes?" he said in accented English, brushing the hair way from her blue eyes. "We were told all of the Americans had left."

Sarah hesitated and looked at him, tears forming at

the corners of her eyes. She wanted to reason with this man's merciful side; maybe if she answered his questions he would call off his men. She looked him in the eyes. "I am Sister Sarah Donovan," she responded in a clear voice.

The man grinned, exposing his rotten smile, then struck her hard with a closed fist.

1
_____

She watched him where he sat in a dimly lit corner of the bar. She wore leggings and a loose-fitting top with a stained apron. It was the start of her shift, and she moved slowly, wiping down old tables, cleaning the previous night's spills. He was alone, as he was every day. He wore a black ball cap so low that the brim covered his hardened brow. Piercing eyes and a strong jaw were lightly concealed by a week's old beard. He was dressed in a long-sleeve flannel shirt rolled to his elbows, exposing black-inked tattoos. His jeans were well faded along with his boots. He could easily be mistaken as a homeless vagrant. She knew different; she had known the man he used to be. She knew him when he was younger, before he'd given up on himself. Tall and handsome in another time, and not as cold as the image he tried to convey now.

The fair-haired waitress approached his table, stopping by the bar to retrieve the pint. She placed another stout near the man's hand. She shot a scowl at him as he sat slouched in the wooden chair, his tattooed forearm resting on the polished table. She let her eyes stay a bit too long, focusing on a scar that ran along his bicep. She could see that he was ignoring her. It was a game he played—he enjoyed toying with her feelings.

She scoffed at him. "The VA doesn't give you that money to sit and drink all day." She lifted an empty glass and used a towel to wipe away crushed peanut shells.

Tommy Donovan, without taking his eyes off the TV, grabbed the freshly filled pint. He took a long sip and dropped the glass back in front of him with a *thunk*.

"The government doesn't give me anything. I earned it," he scoffed back at her.

"Well, however it comes to ya, Tommy, let me at least get Billy to fix ya a plate. It's not even noon and yer' on yer' third pint." She wiped the table around him and stopped to look at him close. She scowled in disgust. "Ya look like hell."

Tommy grunted and took another pull from the glass. He adjusted his chair so that the waitress was far removed from his peripheral vision.

He turned and looked her up and down, grinning. "You never minded my drinking when I let you share my bed."

"Go screw yer'self, Tommy," she said, tossing the damp towel at him. "Yer a right pig, ya are."

He removed the wet towel from his lap and set it on the center of the pub table, laughing to himself. He smiled at the sounds of her walking away, her soft foot-steps fading into the kitchen. A door slammed behind her, and he could just pick up on the muffled echo of her voice complaining to the kitchen staff. There was a day when he'd have been interested in the girl's attention. Not anymore. Those days were gone. Tommy knew she was a good girl. In some ways, he was even still attracted to her, but he was sparing her the hardship. She didn't need to waste away on the likes of him. She wanted marriage and a family, all the normal things that he couldn't provide her. That part of him was burned up and gone; he didn't have any of that left inside of him.

He pressed back, leaning deep into the chair, watching the television—a classic replay of an old college football game. He already knew the outcome but still found himself cheering for the underdog. He took another pull from the pint, shaking his head as the quarterback fumbled a snap.

"How about that sandwich, Tommy?" bellowed a bartender's voice from behind him.

"I'm good. Sticking to a liquid diet today."

"Suit yourself."

Bells rang at the far end of the bar. A man in a priest's collar stepped out of the bright sunlight, stomping snow from his boots and clearing drops of ice onto a worn doormat. The dark mahogany door closed behind him, and the blinds clacked against the wooden door. Tommy squinted against the bright light, his pupils contracting as the old man wearing a white collar approached the far corner of the bar.

He saw the priest exchange handshakes with the bartender. Then Billy turned and pointed in Tommy's direction.

"Damn it," Tommy said, suddenly recognizing the wrinkled brow and tucked-in lip of the priest. "The last thing I needed today, another intervention," he muttered.

Tommy knew the old man. He knew him well. Father Murray had taken him and his sister in when he was just a boy. He was still innocent then. It was right after Tommy's parents were killed an auto accident. In the days after, he was passed off to a distant aunt who was more interested in his inheritance than raising him. Father Murray was close to the family and had followed their progress after the aunt had taken custody.

She was shopping for county homes and orphanages when Father Murray finally intervened. Instead of allowing the children to become wards of the state, the old priest offered them a place at his school. He ensured they received full tuition and room and board for as long as they needed it. But it wasn't a random act of kindness; most of it had already been funded through an education trust set up by Tommy's grandfather. A trust that would be vacated if the children failed to enroll in the school.

Tommy's parents always intended that he and his sister would one day attend a Catholic primary school. They insisted on a large part of the family's income be set aside for their children's future. But his parents would have never predicted their early demise in an automobile accident when he was five and his sister, Sarah, two. It changed the balance of things, or would have if Father Murray hadn't been there.

Through a negotiation with the Church, Father Murray managed to get the children into his own boarding school, and with creative financing and the less-than-eager cooperation of their aunt, the remaining funds were made to last until the children graduated. Unfortunately, that was where the Church's assistance stopped, and Tommy was left to the mercy of his last living relative—an elderly aunt who had spent through all the children's inheritance and taken multiple mortgages out against their property.

Rather than beg or sue for what rightfully belonged to him, Tommy kicked around odd jobs before eventually enlisting in the Army. With a new purpose, he gratefully left his past behind him. Some years later, Sarah—also abandoned by his aunt—went on to a convent college to become a nun.

They had tried to stay close, but their schooling—and later, their work—kept them apart and they rarely spoke, other than an occasional phone call. When Tommy was twenty-one, his aunt passed away and the last link to his sister was broken. The family home was sold, and the meager remnants of the trust divided.

She was the first to visit him in the hospital after he was wounded in action, but Tommy felt it was out of nothing more than family obligation. Whenever she tried to reach out to him, he rejected her, no longer having any wishes for a family. He just wanted to be left alone, so they lost touch over the years.

The priest nodded to the bartender and turned in the direction of Tommy. He smiled softly and stepped toward the table. He paused just short of an empty chair and looked down at the bearded man. "Look at yourself, Tommy. You've really let yourself go."

"Been hearing that a lot lately," he muttered without looking at the priest directly.

Tommy reached for his glass and took a long draw, draining the pint. He held up two fingers so that the barkeep could see them. "Join me for a drink, Padre."

It was a routine he went through every time Father

Murray came around to check up on him. He knew the old priest had a drinking problem in his younger days and had managed to get himself off the booze years ago. Tommy would always order two pints and drink them slowly, end to end, in front of the old man. Not so much to taunt him, but to make the visit as uncomfortable for Murray as it was for Tommy.

The priest smiled politely then pulled out the chair. He sat down, leaning back, and stoically crossed his arms in his lap. "I'm fine, Tommy. Nothing for me; you know I gave it up."

"Consider it more of a request than an offer," Tommy said.

He grinned and pushed away his already empty pint glass just as Billy walked to the table and thunked down two more. Tommy adjusted his chair so that he was looking directly at Father Murray then reached to the center of the table and lifted one of the glasses. "This is looking to be a short conversation." He took a sip off the caramel foam and placed the glass to his front. Tommy used a hand to slide the other glass across the table.

"So, what brings you to my office?"

Murray looked down at his folded hands and apprehensively lifted the glass, holding it just below his nose. He inhaled deeply, taking in the scent of the liquid, and then took a small sip. He paused and looked up at the ceiling. He closed his eyes and let out a long sigh. "You know, Tommy, that's the first bit a stout I've had in some time."

Hiding his surprise from Murray, Tommy asked, "Why go to the trouble of breaking your fast for me?"

"We need to talk, Tommy. It's important."

"Well, I'm listening. That sip earned you a minute or so. Say your piece, Padre, I have a lot to accomplish today," he said, waving a hand at the television.

Father Murray nodded his head in false understanding and lifted the drink again, gulping this time, readily accepting the liquid courage. Tommy noticed the frown on Father Murray's face. The always positive thinking man suddenly appeared old and broken to him. Something was wrong. He hadn't seen that look on the old man's face since the night his parents had died.

"When was the last time you spoke to yer sister?" Murray said.

"It's been a while—last Christmas maybe. Why? What's going on, Father, is she okay?"

Murray shook his head and lowered his eyes. He reached into a pocket and removed a folded sheet of paper. He carefully straightened it and slid it across the table. "We received this two days ago, by email. It was to an emergency contact address that only Sarah would know."

Tommy reached for the sheet of paper and held it up, reading slowly. He dropped the paper back on the table. "Is this for real?" Tommy asked.

"It's a ransom note. They say they want two million to get her back."

"Who—? How did—?"

"I'm sorry—Sarah was only there for a short visit to deliver medical supplies and training with the Red Crescent. This wasn't supposed to happen."

"She was where?"

"A Catholic aid center in Albahr."

Tommy hesitated, his memory flashing back to a time

and place years ago. He knew Albahr, Syria. He'd been there. Been betrayed there.

"Syria? Are you serious? Why would you send her there?"

"I'm sorry, Tommy. We were assured that it was safe; she wanted to help."

Tommy began to sweat, feeling his heartbeat steadily increasing. Suddenly agitated, he asked, "Did you go to the embassy? The State Department? What the hell are you doing about this?" He realized he was shouting and lowered his voice.

"Everything okay?" Billy called from behind the bar, and Tommy waved him off.

Father Murray nodded and took another sip from the glass before speaking. "They know, Tommy. They came to us before we received this message. They knew all about the attack before we did; they were tracking it. We were told to tell no one—not even you. They said for her safety it has to stay out of the media while they negotiate for her release. The State Department is working on making contact with the kidnappers, but so far, they've failed. Outside of this email, this is the only confirmation we have that she was even taken. We have no other proof that she survived the attack."

"No." Tommy shook his head. "They are not kidnappers. The Fed will be useless. Tell me, what is the Church doing to get her back?" Tommy said, his voice slowly rising. "You have a responsibility to do something."

Father Murray leaned across the table. Looking Tommy in the eye, he nodded solemnly. "We need your help."

"What the hell can I do?"

"I've heard your confessions, son. I know the things you did over there. You could help us, help us find the people who did this, help us secure her release. We have the money; we only need the connections."

"You don't know the half of what I've done." Tommy shook his head and looked away.

"Tommy, we only need information. You could do it for Sarah. We aren't asking for anything you aren't up to, just help us with the contacts, put us in touch with the right people. The Church can do the rest. Tommy, we need to find her before it's too late." The old priest lifted the pint glass and went to take a final sip before setting the glass back on the table. He shook his head and pushed the glass away before standing.

"Tell me who did this, everything you know about them."

Father Murray looked down at Tommy, who was still studying the printed email. "Keep the letter. Come and find me, there is someone I want you to meet," he said before turning and walking away.

2

His apartment was dark with the blinds pulled tight. He looked at them absently, not remembering the last time they'd been opened. Stepping to the sill and pulling back the shades, his suspicions were confirmed. A navy-blue sedan with tinted windows was parked across the street. The priest visit didn't go unnoticed and someone wanted to keep an eye on him. Tommy wasn't sure who, but he had his suspicions. He was a known man within different agencies and a simple cross-check against Sarah Donovan would ring some bells. He sighed a pang of annoyance and turned back toward his apartment.

The sparsely furnished place wasn't a home to him. It never had been. Even when he first moved here he considered it temporary, just a place to park until he got a job and found something better. There were no photos hung on the wall, no books on the shelves. Most of his things were still in tape-sealed boxes, the way he received them from the moving company years earlier. A badly worn leather chair was positioned in front of a television. It wasn't even his; it was in the apartment when he moved in.

He hurried to a hall closet and removed a canvas travel bag, which he took into the bedroom down the hall. After opening the duffel, he went through drawers, grabbing clothing and other items, stuffing them in. He zipped it shut and tossed it down the hall, letting it land in the living room.

From the closet, he removed a tattered and faded leather jacket. He pulled it on before moving to his nightstand and opening the top drawer. At the bottom, under his socks, was a bundled yellow satchel with a Sig 1911 pistol weighing it down. Ignoring the pistol, Tommy reached for the package and dumped the contents onto his bed. A bound stack of hundred-dollar bills, a pair of clean credit cards, and a passport fell onto the bedspread.

He snapped a rubber band holding the bundle together and placed the items into the liner pocket of his jacket. It was his get-out-of-jail kit, a reminder of the things he'd done, and a warning from Jack, his oldest friend in the Ground Division. "One day, they'll forget about the war and why we fought it. But they'll always remember the things *we* did over there, the things *we* did to win. That's when you'll have to disappear."

Tommy coldly remembered the warning. Years later, after an administration change and the debate over the methods and morality of the war, he found those words hammered home. It was all about the methods. Nobody cared about the results anymore or how many attacks were prevented. Nobody cared how evil the people were that they'd put down. The politicians had lost the stomach for the war and were now steering toward appeasement. Tommy had seen one friend after another charged for the means used to track down and kill the world's most wanted terrorists. Tommy began to fear prison would ruin his career, but it was a roadside bomb that eventually found him.

Months after being wounded, he still lay in a hospital bed, steel fragments in his neck and back. Jack visited during his final week there. "This is your out—now use it, Tommy. The world is changing. Take what you've earned and start a new life. Nobody cares about a broken soldier; they'll let you fade away. The division has connections to make sure you are medically retired from the Army with full benefits. Enjoy your pension and leave all of this behind you."

"I can still work. I know there is more I can do."

"I know that, and I know that they'd willingly give you another shot... they'll use you until there is nothing left. But Tommy, it's time to let it go."

He didn't accept it. He tried to argue with his friend, tried to convince him he still had some miles left in him. Fighting was the only thing he knew how to do. Training and going to war was the full extent of his adult life. What else could he do? It's not like there would be loads of jobs for a trained assassin in the corporate world. Tommy refused to quit. He fought his way into a special rehab program and worked at returning to active duty, but it was not meant to be. It was during Tommy's time in recovery that he learned of Jack's death in Yemen. His family was told he'd drowned helping secure a stranded vessel in the Gulf of Aden.

Tommy knew the truth, another no-name raid in a

country nobody cared about. There was no scrolling bar during the local news, no patriotic announcement in the paper. No twenty-one-gun salute at Arlington. He found out late one night via phone call from Papa, the last surviving member of his original team. Papa said he was done, he was hanging it up and returning to his family home in Syria to get away from it all. Life in the Ground Division had gotten too complicated, and it was only a matter of time before the politicians turned on them. He advised Tommy to do the same. Start a new life before he found himself all used up.

And just like that, all of them were gone, the men he called family vanished as if none of them ever existed. His closest friends nothing more than memories, and he was left alone. He was, once again, that young man who walked out of the orphanage with nothing, with nobody. It was like the last ten years of his life never occurred. Suddenly, Tommy had lost the taste for the business, and after some deep soul searching, he sent in his resignation letter to the Ground Division.

He'd thought about Jack's words often now, the warnings. They always came to the forefront of his mind at night before drifting to sleep or sitting in the old chair, watching the news—the congressional hearings, the war crimes investigations. Seeing familiar faces on trial for following orders, for doing what they had been sent to do. Senators behind microphones wanting to forget about the war and the reason they were there.

When will they come for me?

Tommy shook off the thoughts and turned to sweep the room with his eyes one last time before heading back into the hall to retrieve his bag. He removed his phone from his pocket and left a brief text message to his land-lord, telling her he was going out of town and to collect his mail. The rent would be paid automatically from his pension. He had no pets to feed, no belongings that he cared about. He dialed a phone number and pushed entry keys to a secure voice mailbox.

"I need you to clear your schedule, just like the weekend at the beach. We're going on a vacation. I need you to book a flight for D.C. leaving tonight then meet me at Logan. Sorry for the short notice."

He flipped the phone over and popped the plastic case then dropped the SIM card and memory stick down the garbage disposal, leaving the phone in the trash. He left the apartment and locked the door behind him before moving down the hallway and out to the street. He avoided eye contact with the car. Turning away from it, he heard the vehicle's engine start. Their presence didn't bother him; he would rather know they were there than suspect it without confirmation.

Winter had settled in on Boston, and even though the sun shone brightly, he could feel the chill through his jacket. Tommy took deep breaths, using the cold air to clear his thoughts. He left his car parked on the street then walked to the corner and ran across a divided one-way street, over a median, and boarded a bus headed in the opposite direction. He swiped his pass and moved down the long aisle, dropping the paid-up bus pass on an old man's lap before taking an empty seat just as the bus moved ahead. He looked out the window and saw the surveillance vehicle sitting confused in the intersection, not knowing what to do. It would only delay them. Depending on who they were, they'd probably have another team, possibly one on foot or in a second vehicle on a parallel street.

His thoughts drifted to Sarah. He remembered her as a little girl, only two when his parents passed. She looked up to him as a big brother then, not yet knowing the pain in the world. Back then, Tommy spent more time with her, enjoying her company and the bond they shared, feeling like the big brother and embracing the need to protect her. But over the years, she became an unwanted reminder of what he'd lost. Tommy resented her for it in his own childish way. He ignored her through school and avoided contact with her outside of holidays.

Sarah called him a time or two after he left the ground service, asking why he wasn't looking for work. Or why there wasn't a woman in his life. Sometimes she would stop and check in on him uninvited, or ask a friend to spend time with him, or try to arrange dates for him with women from their school days. They would talk on the phone, but it was usually a one-way conversation that ended with her lecturing him. He cared about her, but he didn't want her wasting her time on him.

After the service, Tommy had taken a self-proclaimed "time out". He protested that he needed some space to breathe, to recover. But really, he just wanted to shut everything out and reboot his life. He drank heavily, trying to drown the memories. He stopped exercising and he got lazy. Originally, he thought it would be for a month, but after he fell into a simple routine and became content with just existing, the time moved on. He had regular checks to pay his rent and to fill the refrigerator. His single trip to the VA provided him with more drugs than answers. Afraid to get hooked on the pills, he flushed them and never returned.

He took the random intervention visits from Father Murray as a challenge. He used it as an excuse to not return to the world, a stubbornness to do it in his own time. But now, this was different. Whether he respected it or resented her for it, Sarah was always there for him. Now knowing she wasn't there, he suddenly felt her absence deep in his chest, and it made him ache in a way he hadn't felt in years. It brought back the pain of losing his parents and Jack all over again. He remembered the pain of having no control to do anything; how helpless it made him feel. He wouldn't feel that way again. Tommy made an oath to himself—he would do whatever it took to be there for her. And to punish those who took her.

The brakes squealed and bled air as the bus lurched to a stop in front of the gray, limestone cathedral. Tommy pulled himself to his feet, working his way to the bus exit, carrying his bag in his left hand. He ducked his chin away from the surveillance camera that he knew was positioned above the driver. Back in the cold, he looked behind him to see he was the only one who exited the bus. The sedan was nowhere to be seen. Tommy turned and navigated the sidewalk to the ancient, stone steps and moved to the heavy, wooden doors. Finding the entrance unlocked, Tommy passed through, pausing just inside.

He stood in the warmth of the entrance and spotted Father Murray at the far end of the dimly lit nave with a tall man dressed in a tailored black suit. Tommy let the door close hard and loud behind him. The slap of the wood echoed up the chamber, causing Father Murray to look back at him. The man let a soft smile escape his face as he waved Tommy forward. But instead of waiting, the priest moved off to the left with the second man in tow. Tommy had his suspicions as to who the second man might be. He knew the Church had deep pockets and plenty of lawyers; they also had some of the world's best security people operating behind the scenes.

Tommy moved down the long aisle, watching Murray slip out of sight in the direction of where he knew the priest's private office lay. He'd spent plenty of time in the ornate room growing up, taking lectures and listening to the old priest tell stories about his parents. He shook off the thoughts and quickened his pace, moving up the steps and around the corner. Tommy found the office door open, and he stepped inside, knocking on the doorframe while he passed over the threshold.

The room was dark, draped in red felt-lined curtains and furnished with dark leather and mahogany antiques. He stopped and turned abruptly, spotting the second man, who was now holding a white porcelain teacup. The man, who was clean-shaven with close-cropped hair, had broad shoulders and thick wrists. Tommy could tell by the way the man carried himself he was military or law enforcement. He was a professional, not a hired gun or a slouch cop. He wore a fine, tailored, black suit with a blaze-red tie, so he knew the man was expensive. Tommy let his gaze stick longer than what was appropriate as he scanned and mentally conceived dozens of ways to take the man out. Tommy watched as the stranger's eyes began to show concern.

"It's okay, Tommy. Simon is here to help," Father Murray said, motioning a hand toward a worn, leather chair. "Please have a seat."

Tommy set his bag by the door and moved into the room, stopping just in front of the chair. He looked at the second man again, waiting for him to sit before taking a seat of his own. The man moved uncomfortably into a chair then Tommy dropped into his own chair and crossed his arms in front of him.

Murray straightened his robe and walked around the desk, pulling a chair close before sitting in front of the two men. "Tommy, this is Simon Arnet, from the Vatican. He is with—"

"The Swiss Guards. I know, Father. Where are they keeping Sarah?"

Simon cleared his throat and leaned close. "I'm not sure you understand what we are asking of you, Mr. Donovan. I have your records from Interpol; I understand the work you've done and your capabilities, your counter-terror background. Please understand, all we want is to ask you some questions, to use some of your contacts in the region. We won't require anything else from you."

Tommy smiled, knowing there was no way Simon had any idea the extent of his record. If anyone did, they would be trying to have him locked away, not recruited. He shook his head. "No." A vein popped out on his neck as he shook his head. "None of that will be necessary. Instead, I need you to tell me everything you know. Get me up to speed on the situation. I'll do what's necessary to get Sarah back."

Simon pursed his lips in frustration. "It's just not that simple."

The man's brow tightened, and Tommy watched as the agent's expression soured. He knew this was a person who was used to getting what he wanted. But Tommy didn't care, he didn't have time for it.

Simon took in a deep breath and continued. "These people we are dealing with... it is unclear what their motives are. They've never taken an American before. This may have been completely by accident."

"Accident? What the hell kind of accident ends in hostages being taken? You said they raided a church and took prisoners."

"Yes, prisoners, Mr. Donovan," Simon answered solemnly. "But an American girl changes everything for them and for your government. It adds to the group's danger. They may panic and—"

"Kill her." Tommy nodded. "I understand, and on the flip side, the last thing the State Department wants is another dead American firing up the public for a response. It's way easier to just deny her and go on with business as usual. I've been there. I know how this story ends."

"It's not that simple, Mr. Donovan."

Tommy grunted and cracked his knuckles. "Just tell me this: Do the State Department's 'moderate rebels' have her, or the other guys? Or is there even a difference anymore? And who the hell is following me?"

Simon shook his head and looked away, refusing to answer.

Grinning, Tommy turned his focus on Father Murray, who was pressed back in his chair, unsure of how to intervene in the conversation. "I need everything you have on the people holding her. I need dates, times, contact information, everything. I'll contact you in forty-eight hours once I get in-country," Tommy said, knowing he wouldn't get the answers and wouldn't bother to contact Murray. The request was just a delay, something to make the Vatican people spin while they queried for a solution. Tommy hardened his brow and stood, still looking directly at the old priest.

"They warned us about contacting you; they said you'd be rash." Murray leaned back in the chair, confused. His eyes went from Simon and back. "Tommy, you can't go to Syria," he muttered.

Tommy looked up at the ceiling as if searching for something. He paused before turning to his right. "Simon, is it? Listen to me. I have no arrangement with you, no contract with your people. Regardless of that, I'm going to do your job for you. It won't be discreet, and you won't want any of it sticking to that fine suit. Do you understand?"

"Now hold up, Mister Donovan—"

Tommy raised a hand, pausing the agent. "I suggest you answer Murray's questions and stay as far from this as you can."

Simon leaned forward to protest. Tommy raised his palm, stopping him again. "I have to warn you—if you stand in my way, I'll hold you responsible if we don't get Sarah back. If anything happens to her... as you said, you've seen my file."

"I have. And to be honest, you should be in prison." The agent eased back after letting the last words leave his mouth.

Tommy caught every syllable like a slow-pitched soft-ball. He grinned and said, "Let me tell you, as it stands, there is no problem between us. You should want to keep it that way. As far as me going to prison?" Tommy laughed. "That's only the shit you know about."

"Now, Mr. Donovan, be reasonable," Simon said, standing and taking a step toward him.

Tommy turned back and stretched to his full six feet, not intimidated. He turned to the door, retrieving his bag. "Forty-eight hours, Padre, I'll need details."

3

"Yes, we are doing everything we can to locate them," Fayed said into the cell phone. "I understand, Mr. Director. Yes, sir, I'll call you when I know more. Yes, of course... thank you, sir." He grinned as he disconnected the call and set the phone next to a small cup resting beside a neatly folded newspaper. Fayed enjoyed the finer things in life and had come to expect it. He looked out the window from where he sat in the tiny upscale café located in one of Paris's finer districts. The Parisian street was nearly empty; it was late morning and most people were already at the office.

This wasn't a blue-collar establishment, and tourists stayed away. Most of its patrons were respected businessmen or politicians. Expensive, its menu excluded the riffraff, and that was why Fayed frequented it. He enjoyed his standing at Interpol; his rank came with privileges. He was rarely questioned by his superiors, being thought of as one of the good ones. He was young and bright, tall, dark, and handsome. Not the profile for a terrorist bagman. They respected him and he was a jewel in his department.

He sipped at the coffee and finished the last of the croissant as he smiled at his own cleverness. He would work both sides until the payment was right, and then he would collect from them both, gaining a percent of the ransom from Abdul and a heavy promotion from his superiors at Interpol. It was a good life he had carved out for himself. If he kept things the way they were, he would soon have a high-level position with unlimited access. Unlike other wars, where his family and ancestry would bring him suspicions, in his current office, he was considered a shining example of what a Western education could bring.

"More coffee, Monsieur?"

Fayed turned to see the waiter holding a stainless-steel tray. He shook his head and waved the man away dismissively. He was alone at the sidewalk café. The winter weather was mild, but still enough to chase most of the patrons inside. His complexion was dark, but he kept himself clean shaven. If you were to question an average passerby, they would claim he was Spanish or Italian. None would suspect his Middle Eastern upbringing. He dressed in the most current fashions and blended in well among the people. He gave the full appearance of integrating into the culture, and for that he was rewarded by his superiors.

Born into a rich family, he'd been given every opportunity... traveled the world, received the best education. But the West had taken most of that from him. His family's homes and business were destroyed by war. His parents were forced away as the fighting grew worse.

Their position spared them from refugee status, yet still they were forced to relocate to Europe. His family's wealth was gone, and now Fayed was forced to stand on his own. There was no longer a business to pass down to him, and he refused to be average. He cut ties with his family, unwilling to submit to a commoner's life.

Fayed removed a twenty euro note from his pocket and dropped it to the table. He paused to push up the collar of his heavy, wool coat then sat and searched the street to ensure he wasn't being watched. He was still a policeman, and he always felt the risk of what he was doing; he had to take precautions. Fayed was not a religious zealot—he considered himself an opportunist, first and foremost. He held loyalties to no one. When he watched the regular people on the street, he felt no emotion for them. Any feelings he had were for his own wellbeing.

First-world educated in the finest European and American houses of academia, how could anyone expect him to settle for the mere salary of an Interpol inspector? Sure, with the War on Terror and the disaster they called the Arab Spring, everyone suddenly needed his unique skill set and family connections, but no one was willing to put up the salary to go with it. He was recruited right out of school, moved to the Middle East desk, and given access to even the most classified records. At first, he was a willing and motivated soldier, doing everything he could to make a difference. Gaining promotions and pay, he made a modest life for himself, but that naivety soon wore off.

As the war progressed and he learned there was no serious goal to stabilize Iraq or Afghanistan, and with turmoil spreading into Yemen and all over the region, he adjusted his own viewpoints as the public lost its stomach for the endless war. Fayed had no aspirations of becoming a middle-aged civil servant with a dwindling bank account. He didn't want a wife and three kids, living in a modest flat. He knew there was more for him, and it was there for him to take. As he moved to different regions in the Middle East, he began to collect contacts, and he watched the news with greater interest, finding where his skills could be best utilized.

As the Americans abandoned Iraq, it didn't take long for Fayed to recognize the vacuum and the opportunity. Having already made contacts, and with his freedom of movement, he found new ways to capitalize on his access. He became a weapon to anyone willing to pay him; a double agent more useful than any cell the Jihadists could muster. Although he was an atheist at heart, he was well read and knew the Quran, as well as the Bible. He could manipulate a terrorist cell leader as easily as a New York banker.

No moral obligations to hold him down, he justified his new life as a business transaction. Fayed wasn't interested in religious wars or the motivations of the industrial war machine. To Fayed, he was just buying back what was rightfully his. At first, he performed simple favors— deleting names from files, rewriting a report to make criminal activity seem legitimate, maybe approving the delivery of a package from Belgium to Baghdad, or changing the summary line of an investigation from suspicious to ordinary.

He learned there was money to be made in all corners, and Fayed found a way to get a percent of every transaction that moved across his desk. Even with the growth of the Arab Spring and spreading violence, he found ways to make order of the chaos.

Fayed had become a very rich man. But his new business partner was making things difficult for him, taking him to places he wasn't comfortable. Fayed wanted nothing more than to finish this job and end his association with the man.

Kidnappings for ransom were commonplace in the region, but this new job was complicated. Unlike the other women, the American girl—although intriguing to the cause—could easily have troubling consequences. The rest of their hostages, anonymous girls without a voice, could be quickly sold into the system. But this American girl held value, and value couldn't be ignored. The initial plan was to use her as a propaganda piece and trade her to groups that exploited such things. However, there was always an opportunity to pull quick funds from ransom, and the Church had deep pockets if they could be convinced to pay. Fayed knew he could use the commission to bankroll his lifestyle and would easily gain favor with criminal elements if he pulled off such an exploit.

To his disdain, every attempt at profiting from the girl had failed. The Americans were staying quiet and refused to pay the ransom. And her Church representatives were the worst. Rejecting offers to communicate directly with the cause, they consistently deferred them to the State Department, the many layers of contact only confusing matters. Then the American government began blocking efforts to publicize the capture or confirm the identity of the girl. Not even a sympathetic mention in media circles to spark interest and urgency. Without confirmation, she was nobody and held no propaganda value.

Fayed's foreign handlers were losing patience, and now his legitimate employers were putting pressure on him to secure the girl's release. *Such is the inner conflict of the double agent*, Fayed thought, allowing a short laugh to exit his sly grin. But as he had learned early on, with risk came profit. Still, there was a limit to his employer's good-will. They counted on him to solve these things, and the director was putting pressure on him for answers. He would have to move quickly and force Abdul's hand before things became out of control. He was in a good position and could afford a loss here, but a win would obviously be the preferred outcome.

"Monsieur?" the waiter said, catching his laugh. "Is everything okay?"

Fayed brushed the man off with a wave of his hand then stood and walked to the sidewalk. He shook his head again, contemplating the problem. He enjoyed these political chess matches just as much as the money. Their first move was always to threaten the captive's life. In response, the opposing government would make a public protest. Sometimes the family would be on the evening news with a teary-eyed mother holding a photo. This had no reaction from Fayed; it was all business to him. Of course, they could kill her if they must, but there was no profit from a dead woman, and that would also cause them to lose favor with the people—those who supported their efforts in secret. Killing her, especially a girl like this, a girl of faith, would not make them any friends.

Yes, he would have to increase his efforts, find a way. Maybe through the Church itself. There was always more to be done. The opposing government would pay—they always paid—and after the money was deposited, they would leave her with a third party. Fayed bit his lip in frustration. But why did they keep her a secret? Not a single protest from the girl's family. What sort of family abandons their daughter? Why? What was he missing? He would have to push his assistants to dig deeper. There was more to the girl that he had to find out.

Perhaps her capture was an embarrassment. Fayed thought hard, remembering. He had watched the most recent press conference. The President standing behind the podium, praising his gains in the region, proclaiming that the enemy was contained, the threats stabilized. Yes, that must be it. She was an embarrassment to the establishment. If they wanted her capture kept a secret, then he would do the opposite. Taking a deep breath of the cool Parisian air, he exhaled with a smile. If there was money to be made from this girl, he would find it.

He would leak news of the girl's capture. He would create a public scandal. That would force their hand, and they would have to pay. And if not, he would lose no sleep over her death or her loss to the slavers. After all, he would have done everything he could to help her. But in the meantime, there was no profit in death, and Fayed would have to explore every avenue before releasing her fate to the Jihadists. After all, it was nothing personal; she was just another pawn in his chess game.

4

Her hands and feet were numb from the tightness of the bindings, her wrists a pale white and fingers a swollen purple. It had been hours since the guard pulled her back from the wall and loosened them, and she knew it would be hours before they were again relaxed. It was a game that her captors played. The more she cooperated, the better they treated her. Although the comforts were minimal, it started with relaxing the wire knotted around her wrists and ankles then moved on to a heavy wool blanket then some water and a bit of stale bread.

Sarah had made it to the bread twice since her captivity but had quickly fallen back to square one, having everything taken from her and replaced with beatings. The first time was when she was confronted with the scar-faced man they called Abdul. Her refusal to answer questions about her family infuriated the man to a point that she was beaten until she'd lost consciousness. The second time was when she was reintroduced to the other women from the convent. When she saw they were being treated as poorly as she was, Sarah protested. Again, she was beaten and reduced back to being strapped to a bolt on the floor, isolated in a cell, nearly naked with her wrists wired so tight she couldn't feel her fingers.

But the worst part, even worse than the actual beatings, was the anticipation. She could hear the men working over women in adjacent cells. Though they screamed in a language Sarah didn't know, she clearly understood the pain in their cries of agony. She lay stonelike, huddled on the concrete floor waiting for them to come for her, trembling every time she heard the boots plod past her cell door, thinking her turn would be next. The cell was nothing more than a dark and musty eight-by-eight-foot square concrete tomb. The heavy stench of human waste hung in the air, and the only sounds were the whimpering of women in the neighboring cells.

Her door slammed open, and Sarah crowded back against the wall as two men entered. One stepped toward her swiftly and dropped a hood over her head then yanked her backward. She felt her shackles loosen before she was lifted under the arms and dragged down a corridor. Another door opened, and she was carried into a longer narrow room. Again, she was dropped to the floor and re-shackled. When the hood was removed, she caught a glimpse of the men leaving, and a flash of light revealed that she was back in the communal cell.

The steel door at the end of the room slammed shut with a rusty squeak. There were no windows in the cell. Cracks in the floorboards overhead allowed in the only sunlight, the small slivers being the only way to determine the time of day. There were steel anchors set directly in the concrete, evenly spaced around the perimeter of the room. Women were bound the same as she, confined to a small space with little room to move and no bed to lie on. Some with a blanket but most without. All of them constricted and uncomfortably bound, lying in their own waste.

She squinted in the low light, her head swimming from dehydration and lack of food. She tried to focus, counting the women in the room, attempting to make mental notes of each one's condition. She moved clockwise, concentrating. She got to twenty-one.

Sometimes a voice would cry out, someone she knew, faint recognition in the words. It was impossible to communicate. Raising their voices above a whisper would bring the beatings. Oftentimes, a woman would sob in her sleep and another nearby would try to comfort her. Occasionally, the door would clunk open and a man would make the rounds with rewards for behavior. Restraints would be loosened, the women offered meager belongings or scraps of food. Many times, the doors were opened and women were removed. The jailer would proudly announce that their bail had been paid and they would be returned to their families. Sarah didn't know what to believe. She only knew the women didn't return.

Her eyes opened. She wasn't sure if she'd been asleep or just in deep thought. The light through the floorboards had faded. There were heavy steps outside the door, and the metal locking mechanism squeaked against the turning of a key. The door swung in and a bright spotlight shone on their faces. The light stopped on her, and a man shouted instructions. Another rushed forward and placed a bag over her head, tying it tightly around her neck. She was unbolted from the floor and forced to her feet. Sarah was unable to stand, her muscles stiff from the hours against the concrete floor. The man grabbed her under the arm and lugged her forward. She moved her legs, trying to find a footing, trying to support herself.

She was brought into a hallway, bright light glowing through the sack over her head. She felt herself being dragged upstairs and through doorways, eventually being dropped onto the floor in another room. A door slammed shut and the lock mechanism turned. After a brief moment, she heard lighter footsteps. She felt gentle hands on her body, and the rope around her neck was loosened and the bag removed. The light was bright, forcing her eyes closed. Soothing voices warmed her.

Sarah squinted in the bright sunlight, looking into the faces of women wearing head scarves and black dresses that went to the floor. They were kneeling over her, speaking softly in words she didn't understand. There were two other captive women in the room, the attendants also removing their torn clothing and covering them with soft towels. Looking to her left, Sarah could see Carol, a blonde Canadian aid worker she had shared meals with at the convent, and Abella, a dark-haired French woman, who had arrived at the convent just days before the attack. Sarah tried to speak to the attending women standing over them, but they didn't respond. The French girl spoke to them in Arabic, and they turned toward her and replied in a hushed tone, silencing her.

Abella whispered to Sarah, but she didn't understand, not knowing French or Arabic. The woman forced a smile then mimicked the washing of her body with her hands moving up and down her arm. Sarah nodded and sat still, allowing the women to work. Sarah could see that Carol was sitting dazed beside her. With her hands now free, Sarah reached out to the girl, who flinched and pulled away. Then Carol turned and looked at her with sad blue eyes. "Where are we?" she whispered. "What's going to happen to us?"

"I don't know." Sarah took Carol's hand, which trembled in her grip.

One of the attending women silenced their whispers and stepped closer with a warm bucket of water. She moved aside Sarah's torn gown. Sarah reached out to stop the woman before spotting the bruising and scars going up and down the woman's arm. Recognizing the attendant's pained expression, Sarah drew back and allowed the woman to proceed in bathing her. The woman handed Sarah another cloth and allowed her to wash her own face and neck as she was tightly rewrapped in clean linens. When they finished with Sarah, they moved on to Carol, who was more timid and resistant. Sarah stepped in and helped in soothing her friend.

When the bathing was finished, the attendants handed the women long black gowns and showed them how to dress. The attendants then gathered all of their supplies and exited the room, leaving the captives alone in silence. Carol turned back to Sarah and again asked where they were.

"I said I don't know. I don't remember anything," Sarah said.

Abella whispered to them, but Sarah still didn't understand her French words. A sound of steps outside brought the women together. They slid against the back wall as the door handle rattled and then opened. Two armed, bearded men entered and stepped to the left and right of the door. The man with the scarred forehead then walked into the opening and looked down at them. He took another step forward and knelt, causing the women to flinch away. In his right hand was a notebook and stubbed pencil. He tossed it to the floor in front of the women.

He scowled and eyed them with contempt. "I am giving you one last opportunity to communicate with your families. To beg for your release. You will each prepare a one-page letter," he said before repeating the message to Abella in Arabic.

"What do you mean, beg for our release?" Sarah asked.

Abdul smiled at her with brown stained teeth and said, "I will give your families the first opportunity to purchase you before you go on the open market. I suggest you to be very compelling in your message; you would be surprised at what the monsters on the open market are willing to pay. You especially, a woman of a God, they would pay plenty to make an example of you."

"Why are you doing this?" Sarah asked him.

He grinned and pointed to the paper. "Write your letter." Before any more questions could be asked, the man rose to his feet and left the room with his guards following close behind.

5

L ogan was busy, as usual, and security as lax as expected. Tommy moved through the arrivals area, taking his time in front of the security cameras, looking directly into them, allowing himself to be seen. He spotted the tail as he walked to a service kiosk and reserved a flight for Turkey by way of Paris. Proceeding to a counter, he checked only a single bag. As soon as he walked away, he watched the tail move to a corner and make a phone call. He knew they would be tracking his credit cards and checking the flight manifest. Tommy sped up his pace and entered the terminal, moving calmly through the TSA gates.

He walked along the outside of the terminal, dropping into a men's room where he reversed his jacket and put on a dark ball cap. Exiting, he fell into a crowd and moved with them until he entered a bar near the center of the international terminal. It was as crowded as the ticket counter had been, and he waited patiently near a hostess stand until a high-top table for two opened up away from the entrance. He followed the hostess to the table and moved around it, pulling out a chair to face the crowd. He took a seat and ordered a lager when the waitress arrived. He set his boarding pass and tickets on the center of the table and let his jacket hang over the back of the chair.

Spotting a familiar face move past the hostess stand, he leaned back causally and nodded to a tall man as he dropped into a chair across from him. The man was of similar build and, in the right light, he could easily pass as Tommy's brother. The man was a friend, not a close one, but one he knew he could trust.

"Hello, Winston," Tommy said without taking his eyes from the crowd walking by the bar's windows.

The man placed his travel documents down and raised a hand, calling for a beer of his own. He looked at the boarding pass across from him and smiled. "I thought you retired."

"I did. I was done with all of it, but this is personal," Tommy said.

The man looked closer at the boarding passes. "I see I'm not going to Saint Thomas," Winston said with a frown.

"Like I said, this is just like the weekend at the beach."

Tommy had never been to the Islands and it was a place he always wanted to go. He liked the idea of doing nothing, sitting at a bar with a full view of the beach, sipping on drinks from a coconut while chasing bronze women. Years ago, Tommy had vacation plans and full intentions of going. He took the time off and paid the money. But as always happened in the Ground Division, at the last minute, he'd been called away on a mission.

Rather than go to the trouble of canceling and losing the money on a non-insured trip and hotel reservations, Tommy gave the tickets to his look-alike, who traveled in his place. Winston took the trip and made sure to gloat about the great time he'd had pretending to be him at the all-inclusive resort.

Tommy took the frosty glass and sipped. "I need you to pretend to be me again. It's for a week. I need you to travel both legs, use my documents. Retrieve my checked bag at the airport. Destroy the identification once you clear customs, find a discreet hotel, and hole up seven days. Leave everything in the bag in the hotel room and let the fake me disappear. Return to Europe on a train and with your own papers, hole up in Germany for a few days before flying back."

The waitress arrived with the man's glass, and he let it rest by his wrist as he examined the documents across from him, pondering a response. "You going to tell me what this is about?"

Tommy looked away and cupped his glass. "It's better if you don't know."

"Why are you trying to disappear? Are you being followed?"

Tommy pulled at his beard. "Followed, but not chased —not yet, but it's the intention."

"I see," Winston said, looking down. He looked up and locked eyes with Tommy. "You know we're friends; if you're in trouble you can come to me."

Tommy smiled and took another pull from his glass. "That's what I'm doing now. I need your help."

Winston nodded and sipped from his own beer. "Okay, I won't ask any more questions."

"You still have the regular account?" Tommy asked.

"Don't worry about the funds." The man shook his head and causally reached across the table, snatching away the travel documents. With three gulps, he finished his beer and stood. The man straightened his shoulders. "I have some expense cash left from a prior. If you called, I know it's important. Better this way—I don't need any trace between you and my accounts in case they look."

Tommy nodded and his forehead furrowed.

Winston shrugged and, before looking away, said, "Good luck to you, Tommy. Your flight will be boarding soon."

Tommy landed in Washington just after ten PM. He still wore the dark ball cap and reversed jacket, but this time, as he left the terminal, Tommy steered clear of the cameras and avoided eye contact. With his carry-on bag over his shoulder, he moved to the curbside and waved an arm, ignoring the line of waiting people. He entered a wagon and handed the driver a slip of paper. The driver, a man with dark skin and a thick accent, held it to the light then looked back at him. He looked at Tommy in the mirror, his eyes holding on his long hair and beard. "Are you sure? Do you know where this is?"

"Is there a problem?"

"No, sir—Great Falls it is."

The driver put the car into gear and entered traffic. The radio in the dash beeped and the driver looked down at the dial and then to the ticking meter. Tommy knew why the driver was questioning him. Great Falls was prone to hired cars and limos, government contractors and tech executives, not men in jeans and leather with overgrown beards. It was suspicious for him to be traveling there at this time of night.

Turning his head to the window, Tommy took in the sights of the bustling city. He caught the driver's stare again. When Tommy looked up, the man quickly turned away. He was headed to a mansion some twenty miles outside of the city in a wealthy neighborhood—a home he'd only been to once, a very long time ago, when he was a different man on a break from training shortly after joining the Ground Division. He was there for the wedding of a close friend, James O'Connell, Junior. A friend who was killed less than a year later on a mission that never officially happened, taken by a traitor's bullet in the eastern deserts of Syria.

He winced, thinking about the day his friend died and the man responsible. He was still young then and green, as yet unaware of many of the horrors of the world. Tommy wasn't able to attend his friend's funeral, and he buried himself into his work after that. But after a time, he kept the promise he'd made to a dead friend and hand delivered a letter, as instructed, to the man's father. Over a year had passed since James was killed. He'd met with his grieving parent over coffee in a downtown restaurant. A big man in life and stature, a Vietnam Veteran and a retired Air Force Colonel, Mr. O'Connell was an intimidating man. But when Tommy handed him the letter, his posture had softened, immediately knowing what it was.

James O'Connell was an important man, politically connected and a key player in the Military Industrial Complex of Washington, D.C. He was part of the inner circle that kept wars running. Conflict required a lot of equipment, and O'Connell made sure that equipment could be delivered anyplace on the globe as the founder and CEO of a top transport company with access and deep pockets. The conversation was what you'd expect of a soldier reaching out to a fallen friend's parent... staying off the murky details of how Junior perished during the first days of the 2003 invasion—the reported victim of an errant mortar shell, an unfortunate training accident. O'Connell was grateful for the visit and to hear stories about his only son.

Tommy tried to stay in the lines of a non-disclosure agreement he was bound to, even if he felt guilty lying to the man's father. The men had official cover as soldiers, and their positions in the Ground Division were so secret that James's father wasn't even aware of it. Tommy kept to his word, and kept their true identities a secret.

But there was more to it. O'Connell was a widower and alone; his son was all he had left. He read the letter and understood the frustration in his dead son's words. Frustrations over the futility of conflict and the direction the military was going; something he'd felt himself when he was a young man serving in a war a world away. It gave the two of them things to talk about, and in a short time they bonded over the loss of James.

Tommy and the colonel talked about the service and how things had changed with a new administration. How the missions they were doing were different now and the enemy less obvious. As the meeting ended, O'Connell took Tommy's hand and promised him that if he ever needed anything, he would do his best to help. Tommy knew the man was sincere and thanked the colonel for his time.

They hadn't spoken since, and he wondered if the colonel still felt the same way. Would the promise of support still stand, even with the knowledge of what he was intending to do? Maybe he would after he knew the real reason his son was dead. What he really died for, and what they really did for a living. Tommy looked out the window, watching the passing cars and felt some remorse for using the memory of a friend to try to get help from his grieving father, but he knew he couldn't do it alone and that Colonel O'Connell had the resources to help him.

The radio beeped again, a dispatcher asking for the driver's current location. Tommy scooted to the center of the bench seat and leaned forward against the glass that divided them. "What's your name?" he asked.

The driver glanced at him in the rearview mirror. He held up a name badge with too many letters for Tommy to pronounce. The driver smiled at Tommy's confusion and said, "Charlie."

"Charlie, of course." Tommy grinned back. "How much do you make in a shift, Charlie?"

The driver gave him a puzzled glance then looked down at a sign that said driver has less than $100.00 cash. "I'm not asking to rob you, Charlie. I want to know what it'll take to get you to turn off that radio and meter for the rest of the night, but tell *them* you are anywhere but here."

Charlie's hands gripped the wheel as he looked out at the highway ahead. Suspiciously, he looked back at Tommy in the mirror and said after a short pause, "Five hundred."

Tommy nodded and reached into his jacket, flipping

out folded bills. He dropped a stack through a slot in the window and let them fall to the front seat. "Here's five hundred. I'll give you another five hundred when we get back to the city. Now get on the box and tell them you're taking a fare across the state and then shut it down."

Charlie grabbed the bills and flipped through them with his thumb and forefinger before nodding and tucking them into a pocket on the front of his shirt. He picked up the radio handset and spoke quickly. "I have a destination in Maryland. The passenger is willing to pay."

A voice came over the radio. It was broken but apparent that whoever was on the dispatch end wasn't happy. Charlie reached over and clicked off the radio and the meter. He looked back at Tommy in the mirror and said, "All is good. You have me for the night, my friend."

6

J ust before midnight, the car pulled into a quiet side
street, traveling under walnut trees and alongside a
stone wall. Tommy told the driver to stop the car in
a dark space between the streetlights. He exited and
walked alongside to the driver's door. "Keep the lights off
and take a nice nap. I'll be back before the sun
comes up."

The colonel's house was walled in with a high
wrought-iron gate. Ancient, boxed, CCTV cameras were
at key points along the wall, but mostly focused on
approaches to the house. Tommy knew from his visit
during the wedding and an impromptu tour from James
that the colonel didn't have a full-time security force. The
cameras were attached to a DVR in the basement, and all
of the sensors connected to a remote support desk. He
followed the sidewalk along the wall and found the spot
he was looking for—a tall tree that was allowed to grow
too close to the fence.

Without changing his gait, he stepped into the

shadow of the tree and leapt to the top of the wall. With no sound, he was over and kneeling in the wet grass on the far side. He sat silently, listening for the wild card—a housekeeper working late or a watchdog he didn't know about. The house was bathed in low-voltage lighting. The driveway empty, yet well lit. All the home's windows were concealed in darkness but one—the colonel's study. The window was cracked and curtains swayed with a slight breeze. Tommy checked his watch again; it was nearly midnight. He'd prefer to meet the old man in his study, rather than his bedroom.

He duck-walked the short distance across the lawn, using the shadows of tall trees for concealment. Finding the perimeter of the home, he followed it to the open window. He squatted then moved to the edge and peered inside.

The study was decorated in hardwood paneling and furniture. Against a wall sat an antique service. A flat-panel TV on another wall was blaring some late-night talk show. In the near corner was a highly polished, walnut desk and behind it, in a leather chair, a snoring Colonel O'Connell. Tommy straightened his knees and stood next to the window. On the corner of the desk in an ashtray was a still-smoking cigar, a tiny trail of smoke wending toward the open window.

He placed his hands under the window's sash and felt it slide smoothly into the full open position. Looking over his shoulder one more time, he quietly pulled himself through the window, his feet touching the plush carpet as he stepped into the room. The old man in the chair hardly stirred as he crept.

Tommy walked to the front of the large desk. In the

center was an empty cereal bowl. At the edge, a half bottle of Aberfeldy and an empty glass explained the colonel's sound sleep.

He moved to the bar and retrieved a second glass then set it heavily on the desk. The colonel woke with a start and kicked his feet back, nearly falling from the chair. He scrambled forward and reached for a desk drawer until Tommy raised his hand.

"Relax, Colonel, I'm not here to hurt you," he said.

The old man dropped his arms and squinted at him. Tommy opened the bottle of Scotch and reached over the desk, filling the colonel's glass, and then his own. As Tommy's face moved through the low light of a desk lamp, the colonel's eyes suddenly lit with recognition. "Jesus, Tommy, you need a damn haircut and a shave. What the hell are you doing here?" the old man shouted, snatching the glass and taking a long drink before setting it back down and waving a hand for it to be refilled. "How long has it been? Ten years?"

"Close to that, sir."

"You nearly gave me a heart attack. Why the hell didn't you use the door like a normal person?"

Walking to an overstuffed leather chair, Tommy turned and dropped into it. "I'm sorry, sir, but I couldn't risk anyone seeing me come here."

"Are you in trouble?"

"No, sir, but I'm looking for it. And when I look, I find it."

"I see," the old man said, sipping from his glass.

"Do you?"

The old man shook his head. "Hell no, I don't. The fuck, Tommy? Explain it to me."

"I need help getting into Jordan."

The colonel paused and leaned back in his chair, studying Tommy's face as if an algebra expression was written on his forehead. "Something wrong with your passport, son?"

"Nobody can know I'm there."

"What kind of mess are you in? I have people—lawyers—I can help you." O'Connell pursed his lips and filled his glass before pushing the bottle across the table toward the younger man. "Tell me what you need."

"They've got my sister."

O'Connell's expression changed, his brow tightening. "Who does?"

"I don't know, but I have my suspicions. She was taken in the same region where James was killed."

The older man squinted and took another sip of the Scotch before exhaling. He sat quietly pondering his response. He took a long sip then slowly swallowed. "James was killed on a training exercise in northern Kuwait just before the invasion. I met his superiors at the funeral. I read the award citation. A stray mortar..." His expression dulled.

"Do you believe that?" Tommy asked.

The old man shook his head, his face changing to sadness. "No, I guess I never did." He sipped again. "But, Tommy, if that wasn't the truth, why didn't you tell me when we met?"

"To protect you." Tommy bit at his bottom lip. "We did things that people can't know about. If I told you the truth, they..." He paused, taking another sip from the glass.

"James was a soldier, he knew the risks," the colonel said, trying to relieve his guilt.

"No, he wasn't, not in the way you think. None of us were."

"Then explain it to me. I deserve to know," he said, his mouth twisting.

Tommy took in a deep breath and held out his glass for another refill. Talking about the death of a friend to the man's own father was never one of his greater talents. O'Connell leaned in with the bottle and topped off Tommy's glass. The younger man sat back in the chair, swirling the whisky before taking a long sip, allowing the burn to steel his nerves. He looked across at O'Connell and said, "Have you ever heard of the Ground Division?"

The senior man shook his head and shrugged. "James was a Ranger. He wanted to be Special Forces. I know he qualified and went to all the schools before his—"

"The Ground Division isn't military; although, sometimes we pretended to be. We maintained uniforms and rank. We sometimes deployed alongside other units. Those of us in the GD were off the books. The day we signed into the Division, our files were pulled and placed into holding someplace at Langley. When I left the Division, I was slipped back onto the Army's books then medically retired to maintain my cover. If you dug into my background, it would be full of holes and redacted lines of text. You would find my name in files and places that just wouldn't make sense."

"So, you were contractors?"

Tommy shook his head. "More like irregulars... mercenaries."

"Mercenaries? What the hell are you talking about?"

"Don't over think it. They jokingly called us the President's Shock Troops. We existed somewhere in the gray space between the Regular Army and the CIA—for when the President needs something done, something too risky for the Army, or too illegal for the CIA. Something where, if we failed, he wouldn't have to answer questions on the evening news. Something where, when men died, they could just report it as a training exercise in northern Kuwait."

The colonel's expression began to harden. He leaned closer. "Where did it happen?"

"We were never in Kuwait, the way they told it. We started in Jordan then traveled farther north into western Iraq."

"But James was killed before the invasion."

Tommy exhaled and took another sip. "That part is true. We were working with a group of Syrian Special Services named the Badawi Brigade. These guys were bad and the furthest thing from special; they were closer to thugs. They were dispatched directly from Damascus under the command of one of their intelligence agents. Our mission was to paint and escort a large convoy of transport trucks across the western border and into Syria."

"What was so special about the trucks?"

Tommy looked down at his feet and shrugged. "I don't know, they were just trucks, and the contents were all above my pay grade. When you work in the Ground Division you learn to not ask questions."

O'Connell nodded his acceptance and waved for Tommy to continue.

"We moved in two days before the bombing of

Baghdad commenced, crossing the border posed as French peace activists. We had an arranged rendezvous with the Syrian agent and his thugs in a city called Al-Qa'im. The trucks were positioned in a lot just inside of a large factory complex, all loaded heavy, some full of well-dressed civilians that they used as cover for the operation; others, closed containers. We also had our suspicions, but like I said, we weren't in the business of asking questions.

"We had one job—to mark and keep in communication with the people running the air war so nobody blew the hell out of the convoy as we crossed open desert."

"Why would we do this?"

"It was a deal made with Assad. We provided safe passage for those vehicles, and the Syrians agreed to look the other way and not bomb the hell of Israel in retaliation for the invasion of their neighbor."

"So what went wrong?"

"Nothing; it worked perfectly. We moved them all the way across the border and into Syria. All went off safe and sound with no friendly fire, but after we made the exchange and parted company..." Tommy sighed and dropped his head. "That's when it happened, the double-crossing bastards. We were scheduled to leave Syria by commercial air to Hungary the next morning, but—"

"The Badawi boys had other plans?" the colonel said, his eyes now fixed on Tommy.

"Yes, sir. Once they got their delivery and the deal was done. That's when the agent and his men decided a pocket full of Americans might hold some special monetary value. They demanded we turn over our weapons and surrender to them. They were supposed to take us to

the airport. Instead, they wanted to disarm us and"—
Tommy cracked a smile— "fucking James."

Tommy closed his eyes and let out a soft laugh before
continuing. "He always carried this small pistol in an
ankle holster, like he was James Bond. It was fast, and it
was violent. But we refused to be taken alive. We fought
hard—especially James. Sir, without him we wouldn't
have made it back. They would have taken us, and the
government would have refused to acknowledge our existence. We all knew how it would end."

"I see." O'Connell leaned back in his chair. His eyes
closed, his jaw tensed. Tommy had never seen this side of
the jovial man, and he knew a nerve had been struck.
The colonel crossed his arms over his chest. He exhaled
loudly and asked, "This man—the agent, he killed
James?"

Tommy took a deep breath and dropped his chin.
"James went down, but not before he shot the Syrian in
the face."

"And our government knew all this time? Why didn't
we go after the Badawi?"

"Like I said before, it's all off the books. In the eyes of
the homeland, there was no score to settle, we were never
there."

"What's left of this group then?"

"We lost contact with them after the withdrawal from
Iraq and the start of the Arab Spring. Most of the organization figured out there was more profit to be made
working the rebel side. They defected from the Syrian
forces and took up arms as moderates. They operate out
of a regional district known as Albahr. Most took funding
and weapons from anyone who would give it to them in

the expectation that they were revolutionaries and battling extremism."

"Are they?"

Tommy rolled his eyes at the comment. "The Badawi are opportunists. They run cells like an organized crime family. Fighting where the money is at, loyal to no one."

O'Connell nodded. "How does all this connect with your sister?"

"Only that it's the same sandbox. Killing and kidnapping is their game. I know for a fact they are active in that region. She was taken in Albahr less than a week ago. The network is deep there. I don't know exactly who it was that took Sarah, but I know they had something to do with it."

"And what if they don't have her?"

"I'm shutting them down either way. I plan to kill as many of them as I can."

O'Connell nodded and balled his hands into fists, squeezing until his knuckles were white. "What has the response been from the government about Sarah?"

"You know they won't do anything—they aren't doing anything. That's why I came to you. I need help getting into Jordan. From there I know the right people to move me north."

"And you think you can do this on your own? Tommy, you're just going to get yourself killed; you think I want that on my conscience?"

"I won't be on my own. I will need help." Tommy paused and drank from his glass. "I won't let this go unpunished. Not again. I need help moving and I need information."

"Why are you really here, Tommy?" the colonel said,

sitting up and crossing his hands on the desk. "If what you told me is true then you are more than capable of finding your way into Jordan without my help."

"If James were alive, I would have come to him; he was like my brother. I need help and I don't have anyone else."

O'Connell nodded thoughtfully and lifted the smoldering cigar. He stared at Tommy and shook his head. "What else?"

"I know what you do for a living, I know you are connected."

"This is a lot to drop on an old man. I don't even know how many laws this might be breaking."

"I understand, sir. I can disappear and you will never have to worry about this visit."

The colonel raised his hand, pausing Tommy. "Keep your seat. Now tell me, what exactly is it I can do?"

Tommy sighed in relief and continued. "I've already laid a trap. Whoever did this must have someone that knows how to reach out. Someone to barter with and make their demands. Once it's clear what I'm doing, people will be looking for me, making inquiries." Tommy steeled his expression and said, "Begging for me to stop."

The old man nodded and again waved a hand for Tommy to continue.

"Some of them will be legit–from the Church, others not so much. Those others will ask questions, they will be searching, and when they poke their heads up, I need to know who they are."

"And how will I do that?"

Tommy smiled. "Just wait. It'll get noisy fast, and people will want to know why. You have friends. Have someone open a Congressional inquiry on me, ask about the Ground Division, let the FBI look into it, get an agent assigned to the case. Then as things get interesting, demand to know more about Junior and how he died. It'll open doors and raise some eyebrows, I guarantee it."

"I can do it first thing tomorrow. And what else?"

"I need a flight out as soon as possible."

O'Connell removed a pad of paper from his desk drawer and wrote as he spoke. "Be at this address; there will be a reservation under the name Flynn. I'll get you into Jordan. I'll make some introductions, and I'll get you as much information as I can gather. But, Tommy, I'm not doing this as a friend. You now work for me. Once this is over, I want to know everything about what James was doing."

————

Colonel James O'Connell sat at his desk, silently listening to the fading steps of the man leaving his home. He waited until he heard the clunk of the front door before standing and walking across the room to a wall safe and working the keypad. Rewarded with a click, he pulled out a tanned leather binder. James moved to the desk and placed the binder to his front then opened it.

Inside were photographs of his son. Pictures from his high school graduation, his military unit, and his wedding. Under that were stacks of documents from James's school days and his military awards. Although the colonel had never let on, he was fully aware of what his son was doing all those years ago. He was no stranger to clandestine work, and was even tipped off by agents when James Junior was being recruited in the Ground Division.

If O'Connell wanted to block his son from joining, he'd had his opportunity. A single phone call would have ensured Junior stayed in his Special Forces Selection group. But he didn't do that. He was proud of his son and the choices he was making. He accepted his decisions and waited on the sidelines, watching and grinning to himself when James came home on his breaks in training to tell stories of his service. He was happy when Junior brought his fiancé home for his wedding and introduced her to his friends.

He knew his son wasn't killed in a training accident in Kuwait. Within days of James's death, his contacts had told him what they could. He was angry at having lost his only son, but as a veteran himself, he held his tongue. He would not be the one to disgrace his son's sacrifice. So the colonel continued to keep his silence. He held onto the secret even after he had learned of his son's death.

He looked back down at the binder and slid a thick stack of the paperwork aside. He lifted a clipped bundle containing heavily redacted pages of information, so much of it blacked out that it was nearly unreadable. It was the Congressional report he had demanded shortly after the visit from Tommy Donovan and the receipt of his son's final letter. The colonel was fully prepared to let it go, but from the pained expression on the young man's face, he knew there was more, and he wanted to know the truth.

Most of what he had learned about the failed mission was generic—dates and times, some vague location references. There was no smoking gun, no conspiracy, just some details of a mission deep behind enemy lines in Iraq on the eve of the 2003 invasion. But the things he'd learned tonight about the Badawi Brigade and the double cross, all of that was new. Tommy's visit had ignited an anger deep in O'Connell's chest, and now he wanted vengeance.

He put the papers back together and rewrapped the cloth band around the leather binder before pushing it away. The old man reached for his phone and contacted his head of security. The call was brief, just long enough to give detailed instructions concerning the man who would be checking into the hotel. O'Connell wanted to make sure Donovan had every resource to accomplish his mission.

7

"So, our orphan nun? She has a relative, after all."

Fayed sat at a long, black, polished table in the sixth-floor conference room of the Interpol headquarters building in Paris, surrounded by agents in his department—all heads of distinct investigations. Enzo Louis, a junior agent and little more than a research assistant, was briefing them on current investigations. When the slides focused on the attack of the church in Syria and the missing nuns, most of the men tuned out. This was not their jurisdiction, and for most part they were glad. This was not the case for Fayed, who had been searching himself for clues on the missing woman's background.

"Yes, it has recently been discovered that when she registered at the orphanage, she was checked in with a brother. One Thomas Donovan."

At the end of the table sat the director of Fayed's entire branch, a thick-chested, silver-haired man with a dark tweed jacket and leather elbow pads. He wore thick, black-rimmed glasses that hid the emotion in his eyes.

The man shook his head and tossed up a hand. "Why are we investigating this poor woman? What difference does it make if she is an orphan, or one of twelve?"

Fayed rebutted before Enzo could give a response. "Because, Mr. Director, the kidnappers may have reached out beyond the Church. Maybe this brother could help us." He smiled inside. Or perhaps this brother could go to the media for them. A plea from a relative would raise the potential value. Fayed stopped and turned his attention back to Enzo. "When did you discover this information? Why was I not alerted?"

"I am sorry, Inspector," Enzo said, walking toward him and placing a file on the table to his front. "It was not our discovery. It appears the Vatican contacted our New York field office about this man, Thomas Donovan. The discovery of the relative was theirs."

Fayed's brow raised as he pulled the folder closer. "They contacted us about a man they were already aware of? Why?"

"The brother, he has a detailed record known to us. They requested the information before breaking the news of her kidnapping to the brother," he said, beaming.

"Why the concern? Is he a criminal?" Fayed asked, the pitch of his voice rising.

"Not a criminal, but he has been party to several of our criminal investigations."

"Investigations of what sort?"

"Counter terror." The young man stepped closer to open the folder and pulled out a specific page with classified markings at the top. "He was part of an American special services branch that dealt specifically with rooting out and removing terrorists. The organization has since been deactivated. They tended to make a lack of arrests."

"No arrests?" Fayed tucked his lip.

"No, Inspector. They didn't put a priority on live apprehensions."

The director leaned in, looking at the file. "I see. How did we become privy to this knowledge? The Americans always protect their assets' identities."

Enzo smiled and flipped to another page, handing it to Fayed. The man's eyes glowed. "The bombings in Turkey. Of course. It was a joint investigation. We would have collected his name via access requests," Fayed said, looking over the page. "And where is this Thomas Donovan now?"

"We believe he may once again be in Turkey," Enzo said, his face now beaming.

Fayed pursed his lips, attempting to restrain the shock showing on his face. "Turkey? Are you sure?"

"Yes, Inspector. Once the Americans were made aware of the brother, he was quickly put under surveillance."

"Surveillance? Why?"

The young assistant shrugged. "Just normal procedure, I am sure. Being next of kin, they would want to keep an eye on him in case the kidnappers attempted contact."

Fayed nodded, accepting the explanation. He waved his hand for the man to continue.

"After this Mr. Donovan was notified of his sister's disappearance, the Vatican once again contacted us; this time more urgently. It appears that Mr. Donovan did not take the news well, and they feared he may do something rash that could endanger himself."

"But Turkey?"

"Yes, we ran a detailed search and found that he booked a flight to Istanbul, traveling through Paris. This was done within twenty-four hours of his notification."

Fayed went back to the papers and removed the page referencing the bombings. "Turkey—the border there with Syria has become rather porous with the refugee crisis. Per the record, he may have contacts there... Istanbul police, federal investigators, people that could help him."

The director nodded his head and looked to Fayed. "Inspector, what do you think he is after?"

"The Vatican may be right. He is foolishly taking matters into his own hands. And with his background, he would know that an American cannot simply travel to Syria without being noticed. He will most likely try to cross the southern border into Kurdish-held territories."

"What should we do?" Enzo asked, excitement building in his voice.

"Nothing." It was the silver-haired director. "It's not our jurisdiction. This man is free to do as he wishes, even if it does cause his own death."

Fayed nodded and feigned disappointment, pushing the pages back into the folder. He looked at Enzo. "This was good work, but I have to agree with my superior. There is nothing we can do."

He stood, taking the file and moving it into his brief-case. "If you'd pardon me, gentlemen, I have another important meeting." He quickly turned away and moved down a narrow corridor and exited onto a metal fire escape, passing several men having an afternoon smoke. He stood in a corner and retrieved a cigarette of his own as he casually searched his surroundings for open ears.

Fayed removed a phone from his breast pocket and dialed a number from memory. It rang several times before Abdul picked up. "I'll be leaving for Istanbul in the morning. I need to speak to you. You should have a party; invite our friends from Ankara."

"This is sounding very exciting. Do you have news for me?"

"Tomorrow, the usual place. I will be there at noon," he said, cutting the connection.

8

T he address took him to a small budget hotel on the south side of the capital, in an Alexandrian industrial district. The place was set back and well concealed from the road. Charlie pulled the cab close to the lobby and looked back, handing Tommy his business card. "If you ever need another nightly rental, give me a call," the man said with a smile.

Tommy nodded and handed over the remaining five hundred dollars. As he entered the hotel, he could see why O'Connell selected it. The Beltway Inn was a business traveler's hotel, a place where people would not be noticed. There were no tourists here, no families, just professionals. The lobby was small and connected to a dining room that was filled with men in work coats and business suits, sipping coffee from paper cups and looking at newspapers.

Walking toward a check-in desk, he dropped his bag and looked up at a heavyset woman with thick glasses and pulled-back brown hair. She looked Tommy up and down then asked if she could help him.

"I have a reservation for Flynn," Tommy said, avoiding eye contact.

She turned to a thick book and flipped through pages. Another bonus, this hotel wasn't plugged in. The registry was done the old-fashioned way. She stopped on a page then nodded her head before looking at a peg wall behind her and removing a key. "Yes, Mr. Flynn. Your room is ready."

Tommy reached for his wallet, but the woman stopped him, lifting a small yellow sticky note. "The room is paid up. Third floor, room 306," she said.

He gave her a knowing nod and accepted the key. The room was Spartan but perfect for his needs. He found the mini bar fully stocked and removed two shooters of Jameson, which he downed quickly before hitting the shower and finding the bed.

A knock on the door woke him from a deep sleep. He rolled to his side and saw that the clock showed ten o'clock. He lay there listening to the knocking, followed by the familiar voice of the desk clerk. "Mr. Flynn, your luggage has arrived from the airport."

Tommy squinted and rolled from the bed. He didn't have any luggage. He opened the door to find the woman holding a small garment bag with an American Airlines toe tag with the words *O'Connell Transport* stenciled on the back. He thanked her and closed the door before dropping the bag on the bed. Inside, he found a pair of black, roughed-out work boots and deep-blue work pants with a shirt and jacket to match. He removed them from the bag, laying them out flat, and found that each item was embroidered with the name *Flynn*.

At the bottom of the bag was a thick manila envelope, which contained a keycard with *O'Connell Transport* stenciled on the top and *Michael Flynn* in bold letters on the bottom. On the back was a printed address to a security gate on Andrews Field. He then found a printed itinerary and flight manifest with his name attached; the flight was leaving in just over two hours. There was also a thick, white envelope stuffed with five thousand dollars, all in twenty-dollar bills.

He dressed in the blue utility uniform, lacing the boots tight. He dumped his old clothing in a trash bin and set off for the O'Connell transport hangar at Andrews Field. It was there at a security gate that he was greeted by a small, wiry man in a dark-green flight suit— Raphael, a former officer in the Italian Airforce, now a contract pilot with OTI. The man escorted him into the back of a white sport utility vehicle, and drove him across the field to a giant hangar with the words *O'Connell Transport International* over the door. The vehicle pulled directly into the hangar where an Airbus A330 was being loaded.

The truck stopped and the man sat, still looking forward, with hands on the wheel. Without turning, he said, "You must be very important to Mr. O'Connell. He tells me that you do not exist. That I should violate the law and provide you with passage into a military installation in a foreign country. I should do things that could cost me my job and my freedom."

"I'm sure Mr. O'Connell will compensate you well for your troubles."

The man laughed and shook his head. "I just hope I can stay out of a Jordanian prison long enough to spend it." He turned and looked back over the bench seat at Tommy then pointed toward the aircraft. "We will be lifting off soon."

Tommy nodded and exited the vehicle, following the man up a walkway and to a seat near the front of the aircraft. Once he was seated and the baggage stowed, he felt the aircraft moving as it was towed onto the runway. Soon they were in the air and the man returned, dropping a boxed lunch and several bottles of water on the seat next to him.

"I don't want to know anything about you, or why you are going to Prince Hassan Airbase. You are here because my employer insisted." The man reached into a pocket on his thigh and handed Tommy a leather satchel. "Inside is a passport. It was short notice, but it'll work. There is a driver's license and a credit card with the name Michael Flynn. They are excellent forgeries but will not hold up to any serious scrutiny. I advise against using the credit card unless you want to be located." The man then removed a small black key and a business card with a printed address on the back. "This is a company apartment. Mr. O'Connell has scheduled another delivery to meet you there. You may use this apartment at your leisure as long as you remain in Jordan."

Tommy took the documents and placed them into the top of his bag. "I'll need a driver when we arrive."

"Of course, it has all been arranged. Mr. O'Connell called ahead and assigned you a guide. He is one of ours and you can trust him. We make one stop in Saudi then continue to Prince Hassan. When the flight arrives, you will stay in your seat as we move to the hangar. A man from customs may or may not board for a cursory inspection. Once customs is cleared, you will meet with your driver and be taken to the apartment. From there, Mr. Flynn, you are on your own."

The man hesitated and turned back. "Mr. Flynn, I don't know what you are planning, but you should give it time. These people are sensitive to strangers; your arrival will not go unnoticed." Receiving no response outside of a smirk from Tommy, he said, "Very well, then."

Tommy reached into his pack and removed three hotel shooters of Scotch and drank them end to end before washing it down with half a bottle of water. He still wasn't sure what he would do when he reached Jordan, but the whisky cut back on the concern. He'd been to the country a dozen times in his career and started more than one operation from Prince Hassan. This wasn't unfamiliar territory. He had friends and contacts there, but most he hadn't heard from in over two years. He checked his watch and put his seat down; O'Connell's charter jet sure beat a C17. Tommy yawned and stretched, looking forward to the much-needed rest of an overnight flight. He felt the booze take him, and he turned his head, drifting to sleep.

The jet arrived in Jordan in the middle of the day. Exiting the aircraft was like walking into a blast furnace. Even sheltered in the shade of the hangar, the Jordanian sun rolled waves of heat at him from the cement runways. His head pounded from the makings of a hangover and the want of another drink. He took a handful of aspirin and chased it with a cold bottle of water.

Just as Raphael had promised, a white SUV greeted him at the bottom of the steps. There were no goodbyes from the flight crew, and no greeting from the driver. The vehicle had black-tinted windows and, from the shape of the doors, Tommy could tell it was armored. A man in traditional Arab dress with bronze aviator glasses retrieved his bag and dropped it into the back. Tommy moved down the stairs, around the SUV, and took the seat behind the driver.

The vehicle was cool, the window tint shading the interior. Vents on the headliner blew down on him. Tommy put his head back and let the cold air clear his head. The driver entered and pulled away from the hangar, moving toward a service gate that opened well ahead of the vehicle. Tommy brushed his fingers through his thick hair. He wore dark gargoyle glasses and let his eyes survey the road.

"How far?" he asked absently.

The driver looked up from the road and back at him in the rearview mirror. "Not far."

Jordan was painted in the colors of bleach white and khaki. The bright sun reflected off everything, blinding him. The driver turned onto a wide two-lane highway and headed north. Tommy shifted in his seat and felt some-thing knock against his heels. He looked down and found a small, black, Pelican case with OTI stenciled on the top. Tommy retrieved it and caught the gaze of the driver. The man shook his head. "Leave it, the case is only for emergency. There is a Glock and extra ammunition inside."

Tommy frowned and opened the box. After loading the Glock, he dropped it on the seat beside him. The driver protested with a scowl, but Tommy waved him off and said, "A box is not a holster. If it came time to use that, we'd be dead before I had it ready."

"This vehicle has the latest armor. And Jordan is not Syria. The locals would not be pleased to find you armed if we were to be stopped."

"You're driving pal, guess you better make sure we don't get stopped."

The man nodded and reached over the seat, handing Tommy a linen scarf. "You should put this on. We will be at the house soon. The border region is dangerous with many crossing over from Syria and Iraq. There are people watching."

"What people?" Tommy asked, expertly folding the shemagh and wrapping it around his head.

The driver shrugged. "They are all here; Russians, Mossad, Iranians, CIA… take your pick. Everyone watches the border closely these days."

The SUV veered off of the highway and onto a dusty, gravel road. At the end of it was a gated community with an armed guard, and beyond that, a cluster of homes with mud block walls surrounding them.

"Mr. O'Connell pays a healthy sum for this place. You will be safe here. The community is gated, and there are roving guards around the clock."

The SUV drove down the center of the road then stopped near the last home on the right. The driver waited with the engine idling as he worked a smart phone. Then the gate rolled back and the driver pulled in, the metal barrier closing behind them. "The best security," he said, grinning.

Exiting the SUV, Tommy found the air hot and dry. The house to the front was made of stone, no windows on the first floor, and a balcony completely lined the second. The driver exited, retrieved Tommy's bag from the back, and placed it on the stoop before unlocking the front door. "If nothing else is required, I will be leaving."

Tommy turned back to look at the Glock still resting on the seat. The driver grinned with badly stained teeth. "You will find better inside, leave this one if you wish."

"I'll need transportation north tomorrow."

The driver squinted. "Yes, I was told that you intend cross the border?"

Tommy nodded. "Of course." He patted a lump at his breast pocket. "I can pay."

The Arab smiled. "You are an employee of Mr. O'Connell, same as me. The expense has already been paid. When must you travel?"

"First thing in the morning. I need to meet a friend north of the border."

"And you are sure this friend will be there? The regions north of here are in disarray. May a suggest Damascus? I think you would better enjoy your stay there."

Tommy shrugged. "This isn't a vacation. And yeah, if my friend is still alive, he'll be there."

The man nodded his head again and returned to the driver's door. He stepped back and handed Tommy a business card. "If you need something call this number and ask for Ali. Otherwise, I will be here at five AM. I can take you across the border—but I must warn you, Syria is not a friendly place."

For the first time since arriving, Tommy smiled. "I'm counting on it."

The Arab shook his head and returned to the SUV. Tommy crossed his arms as he watched the vehicle leave and the automated gate close behind it. A pair of jets raced by low overhead, flying to the north, reminding him of the war zone that was close by. He walked the perimeter of the building, finding that the wall completely surrounded it. Inside, it was far cooler. There was no air conditioning, but the building was constructed in a way that encouraged air circulation.

He stepped into a large, open room with a fireplace on the back wall and a corner kitchen to his right. The refrigerator was stocked with water and local produce, nothing to get excited about. He rummaged through cabinets looking for booze but came up dry, literally. There was a modest dining room with seating for two in the center of the space. He left the kitchen and dining areas and climbed a staircase to his left. The top floor was an open studio with a pair of beds and a modern European-style bathroom across from him.

Tommy passed into the room and dropped his bag beside the bed. An armoire was on the back wall, which he found to be locked. Remembering the key he was given, he slipped it into the keyhole and felt it click true. Inside was a pair of M4 rifles, an MP5 and several spare magazines along with another sealed Pelican case stenciled with OTI. "I don't think James told me everything about his dad's business," he said to himself as he removed one rifle and loaded it, leaving the cabinet door open. Then he took the case and placed it on the bed. Upon opening it, he found a satellite phone and another Glock with three magazines. This would help him sleep, but he would need more than weapons to find Sarah. And for that, he would require help from an old friend.

9

Ankara can be a beautiful city in the winter, Fayed thought as he sat in an open-air café overlooking Kugul Park near the city center. He was comfortable here; he blended in. He had a nice flat that was bought and paid for, and associates who ensured his around-the-clock security. He could walk freely here and, on occasion, find a woman to spend the evening with. Turkey was wealthy compared to other Arab Nations. They had one of the largest armies in Europe, and their streets were well guarded. The United States even housed a large air force base in the center of the country.

The primary problem in Turkey was extremism, and it was everywhere. It was in the men on the street and in the dark parts of the city, where most people refused to go. There was a rift between the military and the government when it came to the politics of terrorism. The president was an ideologue, who tended to associate with the extremists, while the military commanders realized the threat that radical Islam could have on the nation.

There were no secrets about the border clashes with Kurdish rebels and the mixed motives about the war with ISIS. While the military did what it could to battle the extremists, the president seemed to take their side and only do the bare minimum of what was necessary. He saw the Americans, who were constantly pushing the government to be harder on ISIS, as a nuisance. To him, the real threat was in keeping the Kurdish resistance weak. In his eyes, every day the Kurds and extremists battled on the front lines was a good day for Turkey.

Given these factors, the military was forced to sit back and watch as the two groups destroyed themselves. Why get involved in a war that was already beneficial to its population? To date, their involvement was more about containment; to be more passive than do anything that would turn the tide one way or the other. It was no surprise to Fayed that an American familiar with the regional chaos would pick Turkey to make his border crossing. There were little to no efforts made to keep people from funneling into Syria to join the extremists.

Watching a couple pass by, he caught the movement of a man in a pressed, white shirt sitting alone at a corner table. The man wasn't eating and only had a glass of ice water front of him. When Fayed looked in the man's direction, the stranger quickly looked away. Fayed smiled to himself, sipped his tea, and picked at a roll of walnut baklava. Without looking back, he knew he was being watched from at least two directions. He grinned, knowing they were friendly. If not, his own security would have informed him by now. He held up a hand and called a waiter, ordering a second tea and another plate. Just as the waiter turned, he saw two men in black suits enter through a side gate, directly behind them was Abdul and a third guard.

The man moved through the space and sat without speaking. His guards spread out, standing by walls and along the entrance. When the waiter arrived, Abdul pushed away the tea, ordering a plate of figs and bottle of Raki with two glasses. "We are in Turkey, we will drink like the Turks," he said with a grin. When the waiter moved away, Abdul looked to Fayed and said, "You have information for me?"

Fayed nodded and reached inside his jacket, removing three folded pages. He slid them across the table to Abdul. "The American nun has a brother."

"A brother?"

The Syrian shrugged and held up a finger, seeing the waiter return with the tray of Raki, a pitcher of water, and two glasses. He remained quiet as his drink was made. He then lifted it in a mock salute and drank thirstily with his eyes closed. "To understand this land, you must drink Raki. With Raki, all becomes clear."

Fayed ignored the comment and, once the waiter was gone, continued. "The brother may be of concern to us."

"How so?" Fayed asked. "We all have brothers or sisters of some sort. Is the brother wealthy?"

"No, but not many of us have brothers like this one. He may be of some importance."

Abdul grimaced and took a fig into his mouth, chewing slowly. "Explain."

"He is a counter terror expert."

"As are you. That's why you are compensated handsomely," Abdul rebutted. "I hope this is not the reason you have brought me here, my young friend."

Fayed clenched his fist and relaxed it. He reached for his own glass, sipped at the clear liquid, and let it burn in his mouth. "He is in Istanbul."

This got Abdul's attention. He looked across the table at the inspector. "Istanbul? You're sure?"

Fayed shook his head. "Unfortunately, no, I am not at all sure. He flew in two days ago from Boston then vanished. The people who alerted us say he may be after his sister."

"And what are you doing about it?"

"I had hoped to have him intercepted here. I checked the airport, and we questioned the taxi drivers. We traced him to a hotel by the water. The room was paid up for two weeks with his own credit card, but the maid said the bed has not been slept in. The man has vanished."

Abdul nodded. "This is curious, but still, he is only one man."

"We don't know that. He may be connected."

"How so?"

Fayed indicated the folded papers. "He did work in Iraq and Syria before the withdrawal. He may have contacts."

"That war was a long time ago." The Syrian smiled brightly. "Things have changed since the Americans left. We own the streets now, and we have their backing." Abdul took another sip of his drink, letting the liquid swish in his mouth before swallowing. "Still, I understand your concerns, but the girl is under lock and key along with the two other Western women. We will be rid of them all soon enough, and we have you to make sure there are no connections to us."

"And how do you plan to be rid of them? Have you received word of ransom from their families?"

"Ransom? Ha! That is your job, Fayed. I do my thing and you do yours."

Fayed looked at him with a concerned expression, which caused Abdul to release a mocking laugh. "Relax, I don't plan to kill them—not yet. I have a high-dollar bid for the Canadian woman. And I am very close to sealing a deal for the French one. She speaks our language and will go over well on the markets. They will make great wives to our allies," Abdul said, stuffing another fig into his mouth.

Fayed shook his head, frowning. "Moves like that will only make us a bigger target. You should stick to the trades and stop meddling in these things."

"You worry too much, Fayed; you've grown soft. Get me a ransom for them before they are sold and this will all be over. Until then, I will move my operations away from the border regions and closer to Albahr. At least until you can get this matter sorted."

Sighing, Fayed looked down at his hands. "Albahr is where his sister was taken. Is it wise to stay in the place? This man is most likely to visit."

Laughing, the Syrian rose to his feet. "If he comes to Albahr, he is dead."

10

_____

It was dark and cold in the room, the floor hard and uncovered. The ceiling, covered with chipped paint, had a crack down the center. Hours had passed since they had seen a guard or the women who brought them food. The French woman was gone. No explanation was given; in the middle of the night, the room opened and she was taken away. Sarah and Carol were moved to a new room; this one with a single bed and a chair, no windows—another cell with a steel door. Carol was asleep as Sarah sat in the chair beside the back wall.

She looked up as she heard the screech of the iron lock. The guards again entered first, but this time the man who followed was different. There was no scar; he was fat and bald, his face leathered and covered with a black beard. The men stepped slowly into the room, examining it. Carol was awake. She rolled to her feet on the far side of the bed, cowering. Sarah pressed back in the chair, staying quiet. The man looked at them and pursed his lips. "Relax, I'm not here to harm you," he said. "You need to ready yourselves; you will be leaving tonight."

Carol hesitated and looked up at him. "Where are we going?"

The man's smile faded. "You are going home," he said, looking at her before turning to Sarah. "You, on the other hand, we are finding difficult—nobody wants to claim you."

Sarah leaned forward and looked at the man intently. "Where did you take Abella?"

"The Frenchie?" Jamal hissed. "She is fine. She is waiting to be returned to her home, the same as with this one. If you would be more cooperative I could help you as well."

He took a step toward Sarah, causing her to flinch. He smiled again then straightened his lip. "My name is Jamal. You shouldn't be afraid of me. I am one of the only ones here to help you. To help gain your release from this place." The bald man looked at his wristwatch then nodded to the guards. "You will be leaving soon." The man turned and left the room with the lock clicking.

Carol stood and walked toward her. "Is it true? Do you think I'm going home?"

Sarah got up and moved closer. "You can't trust them, Carol. Don't let your guard down."

Nodding her head, Carol took a step back to the bed and sat with her hands together. "This means we are being separated."

"Yes."

"What did he mean when he said nobody would claim you?"

Sarah shrugged and sat beside her on the bed. "I am an orphan."

"You have no family?" she asked.

Sarah's expression warmed. "I have a brother, and I have the Church. I have faith in the Church to free me, and if that fails– my brother will come for me."

"Your brother?" Carol asked.

Sarah nodded. She knew more about her brother than she let on. When he was wounded and in the hospital, she was the one who sat twenty-four-hour vigil by his side. She was the one who prayed over him, squeezing his hand, listening to the nightmares and the words her brother screamed when he was still delirious from the drugs. She knew he was far from ordinary, she knew he was a warrior to his core. "Tommy isn't a patient man. He acts as if we aren't close, but I know he would die to help me. He won't sit by if he knows I'm here." She looked into her friend's eyes. "Tommy isn't like us. He doesn't follow our rules, he doesn't wait for things to happen."

Carol look at her, confused. "Is he a criminal?"

Smiling, Sarah shook her head. "Maybe to some. Tommy has done things in his past—things that the rest of us would consider far outside the lines of a civilized society. Things to protect us from people like this, the people that nobody else wants to think about. Tommy has never talked to me about it, but I'm his sister; I know. I also know he's a good man, but a good man capable of some very dark actions, and I'm sure that if he knows about me, he will do them again."

11

He wore a burnt-orange, button-down collar shirt with a black jacket and well-worn black, denim pants. Tommy was standing at the gate before he heard the approaching SUV and saw the bright headlights reflecting off the wall. The gate opened and Ali jumped back in his seat, startled to see him standing in the center of the driveway. Tommy grinned and moved around to the passenger side and dropped into the front seat.

"It's not customary for a client to ride in the front," Ali said, placing the vehicle in reverse. "It will look suspicious."

"Are you armed?" Tommy asked.

"Of course, and you?"

Ignoring the question, Tommy handed Ali a crumpled postcard with a return address circled on it. "Take me here."

Ali looked at the card and flipped it, staring at a 1980s photograph of a street scene and a fancy café. "It is not far, but it no longer looks like this. I could recommend something better," Ali said, guiding the vehicle north and onto a two-lane highway.

"I'm not going for the food."

"Ahh, so this friend of yours, you will meet him there."

Tommy sighed and shot Ali a hard stare. "You ask a lot of questions."

"Only so I may better assist you. I have been well compensated to make sure you have a safe journey."

Shaking his head, Tommy held back a laugh. "Just get me to the café."

Ali nodded and said, "The border checkpoint is just ahead. I've made arrangements; we will have no problem crossing. This is a less frequented border crossing. It is out of the way, but will be less intensive than the main crossing points."

"Why is it less frequented?" Tommy asked, his curiosity piqued.

Ali glanced at him before focusing back to the front. "Because of the danger. The further from the big cities, the less stability."

Tommy squinted and kept his eyes fixed on the shoulder of the road. The sun was rising, and his glasses did little to block out the hot, white light. Looking ahead, he could make out the shapes of the shifting sand and buildings on the horizon. It had been years since he'd traveled almost this same route. Then, he had been headed for Iraq, but things felt oddly familiar to him.

"Tell me, Ali, what sort of assistance can you provide?" Tommy asked.

"I can come up with most things if given the proper notice. Mr. O'Connell is very resourceful."

Ali slowed as he approached a line of queued-up vehicles in the distance. Tommy could see the checkpoint and vehicles being processed for the crossing. Ali was correct in calling it *less frequented*. Unlike most crossings Tommy was used to, with several lanes of paved road and backed-up commercial trucks and vehicles, there was just a single dirt road and smaller cars and busses to indicate local traffic. Instead of sophisticated barrier systems, there was a low concrete wall with Jordanian police vehicles.

"It's not too late to turn back," Ali said, keeping both hands on the wheel. "There is a turnaround just ahead. This is what the contractors call the airlock; only one vehicle at a time is allowed in. Once it is cleared on the Syrian side, the next will enter."

"What am I getting into?" Tommy asked. "I mean beyond the border."

Ali laughed. "Leaving Jordan will not be a problem, but once we cross, many things can happen. There are several groups trying to carve out their own place right now. Every terrorist group you can think of. You also have the well-meaning rebel groups, and of course the Russians, the Kurds, the Iranians, even some of your American opportunists—everyone has a stake right now. A pale face like yours won't be safe anywhere.

"The guards on this side will allow us to pass, of course. They don't care too much who leaves, especially when the proper payments have been made. The Syrians on the other side... well, it depends on who controls the crossing today."

"*Who*?" Donovan asked, instinctively placing the Glock under the seat.

"Yes, the territory has been shifting. Government one day, rebels the next."

"And today?"

"We're about to find out," Ali said, dipping his chin toward a uniformed Jordanian man who waved them forward. The Jordanian soldier hardly looked at them as he held the gate. Spinning his index finger, he rolled them onto a dusty, single-lane road. "Like I said, the payment has already been processed."

"They know you here?" Tommy asked.

"Not me, but the company. We make several trips a week through this crossing, delivering supplies to relief organizations across the border."

At the end of the road was another barrier where three men milled about. They wore a ragged mix of military uniforms and civilian clothing with no insignia to identify anyone as being in charge. Each man was armed with an AK-47. Ali maintained his speed, only stopping at the last second before hitting the makeshift barrier. "Stay calm, my friend. I have done this many times," Ali said, watching as Tommy removed the Glock from under the seat and placed it between his knees.

Tommy slowly analyzed the surroundings, spotting a bullet-pockmarked building with an olive-drab Range Rover parked out front. Two of the bearded men were leaning against the fender of the military vehicle, one wearing a red-and-white checkered scarf and carrying a rifle at the ready. The others were lax in their postures. The third rebel approached with his rifle hanging from the sling. He wore scratched sunglasses and a dark-green scarf around his neck. Tommy thought the man walked in a way to impersonate a Hollywood cowboy. His swagger was spot-on.

The man smiled, curling back his lips as he inspected the front of the white SUV. He lifted the glasses and squinted to see behind it, looking to the distant Jordanian checkpoint. Ali kept his hands on the wheel and looked straight ahead. "He will ask for a fee to cross. This is what the friendly rebels do. They board busses and take anything of value; they steal cargo from relief convoys, and for travelers like us they will demand a fee. I'll offer cash, but if it isn't enough he will ask for the vehicle."

"Ask?"

Ali nodded. "That will be where it starts, and then we will barter until we come to an agreement. Because of your pale skin, it will cost us a bit more. This is how things are negotiated here."

Tommy grimaced, having heard the tune before from hard men in different places. The message was clear, and it usually didn't end well. He'd already been on alert from the time he'd entered the vehicle, but now his senses kicked into high gear as he opened his knees and let his right hand find the Glock. He lifted it inconspicuously, hiding it between his thigh and the door. There was a time when things like this wouldn't have bothered him. But he wasn't on any payroll now, and his tolerance for fuckery had dissipated.

"What's the rating on this vehicle's armor?" Tommy asked casually.

Ali turned his head toward him in alarm as the rebel stepped to the driver's window and tapped the back of a steel rod against the glass. The man's body language wasn't threatening; he was still playing the intimidating cowboy role. He appeared as disinterested as a tollbooth operator. Ali lowered the window but kept his eyes on the men posted by the Range Rover. Ali lifted a hand with several folded bills tucked between his fingers. The man looked down at the money and grinned. He leaned closer and pressed his head into the window. "And where is the rest?" he asked in Arabic.

Before Ali could respond, Tommy swung open the passenger side door. He extended his arm and fired two rounds into the upper chest of the man with the red scarf. He then pivoted; a second rebel had turned away, trying to decide if he should run or fight. Tommy ended the man's indecision with three rounds, two of them hitting the fighter's back. When he turned toward the SUV, he watched Ali take two shots into the remaining rebel, the cowboy's rifle still hanging from the sling, his fist squeezing the folded currency. All three were now dead or bleeding out on the dusty road.

"This is not how we do things," Ali shouted, opening the driver's door and stepping into the street. "There is a process here!" Tommy ignored him as he walked to the rebels' Range Rover. He dragged the men's bodies and leaned each one against a tire. He walked back to the SUV and looked past Ali to the Jordanian side of the border, where a police vehicle lit a flashing blue light on the roof.

"How will they respond?" Tommy asked.

Ali shook his head in frustration. "It will take them some time before they come over to investigate. Either way, this isn't their jurisdiction; there is little they can do here."

Tommy grabbed the dead rebel who lay next to the

driver side door and dragged him to the Range Rover to join the others. He then removed a can of petrol strapped to the back hatch and poured the contents into the vehicle. He looked back to see Ali still standing stunned beside the SUV.

Tommy moved to the barrier and kicked aside a plank blocking their route then threw a match into the Range Rover, engulfing it in flames. As he entered the SUV, Tommy said, "Let's go, we still have a long day ahead of us."

Ali slid into the driver's seat and pounded the gas pedal. The vehicle rushed down the road, leaving a trail of dust behind them. When Tommy looked in the side-view mirror, he could no longer see the distant Jordanian checkpoint. There was only a dark cloud of roiling black smoke to show they'd been there.

Ali clenched his teeth, and white knuckles gripped the wheel. "We needed that route open to return. They will know who we are. They know we were the last to cross before the fight. I made phone calls to the guards to expedite our crossing; they know who I am."

Tommy dropped the magazine from the Glock and replaced it with a full one. "Who cares? We took out some bandits on the road. We did the people here a favor, and you know as well as I do, the Jordanians won't give a shit either. Like you said, they have no jurisdiction on this side of the border. Continue to pay them and they will let you through; they won't expose themselves for some dead terrorists."

Ali grunted, keeping his eyes straight ahead. "There are rules here. We do things to remain unnoticed. Someone will notice this."

Tommy grinned and returned the Glock to the seat between his knees and looked ahead as they entered onto another highway filled with trucks and small sedans. "Going unnoticed was never my plan. How much farther?"

"Not far. This address is in the next city. The area is under Russian protection, and we may see more road-blocks. I suggest you treat them differently if we do," Ali said, again looking at the postcard given to him. "How do you know this place? It's a small café not frequented by foreigners."

"It's not your concern. You can drop me close, and I'll walk the rest of the way. I don't want to implicate you any further."

Ali grunted. "Mr. Donovan, I can tell that you have an anger within you, but I still feel obligated to tell you that this city is ravaged by extremist groups. This is not a safe place."

"This isn't my first rodeo. Drop me a block from the café and find your way home."

"And what should I tell Mr. O'Connell?"

"Tell him I will be in touch soon. I have your card. If I need anything, I'll call," Tommy said, focusing on the terrain ahead.

Unlike Tommy's previous trips to Syria, with its bustling cities and markets full of honking cars, this time he found the roads bare, with little traffic. The city street, lined with shabby shops painted with Arabic graffiti, was nearly empty in the early morning sunlight. Many of the buildings were crumbling, showing obvious signs of war. There were open windows with blowing curtains, but not many people to show their faces. They drove past an apartment complex that was completely in rubble. Next to it, a lone boy guided a line of skinny sheep down the shoulder of the dusty road, keeping his eyes fixed ahead, avoiding the white SUV.

Ali slowed their approach and turned onto a narrow side street, which was almost like a sub-world of its own. Finally, there was some life in Albahr. Tommy could see a shopkeeper placing small tables and chairs in front of the café. He adjusted the shemagh on his neck and holstered the pistol under his left armpit. He pulled his wallet to offer Ali money, who again waved it off, saying, "I'll watch and make sure you reach the destination."

"That won't be necessary." Tommy gripped the door handle and exited onto the hot street, immediately hit by the scent of body odor and stagnant water.

Without looking, he knew the residents of this street had fixed their eyes on the tall stranger, a white man where white men didn't belong. He wasn't concerned. He knew that with the civil war or not, foreigners still traveled here. Not counting the aid workers, there were plenty of Russians, Germans, and others.

Albahr was a city at war, but a city spared from the worst of the fighting. He watched as women in heavy gowns walked the street, holding baskets of produce. A young boy kicked a ball as an old man followed close behind, leading a donkey cart. Tommy stepped closer to the café and paused, fumbling through his pockets as if looking for a cigarette. He twisted to check his back trail before proceeding toward the small, open-air café at the end of the street. He spotted a trio ahead, loitering in front of a closed shop on the left side of the street. The men leaned against the partially open, roll-top, steel door, eyeing him suspiciously. Their posture changed as Tommy feigned finding a slip of paper. He studied the blank scrap and looked left and right as if he were lost.

From the corner of his eye, he watched the men nod to each other. A tall man stood in the center, wearing a black shirt with an olive vest. But what stood out was the red-and-white checkered scarf wrapped loosely around the man's neck—the same as the man wore at the Syrian border crossing.

"Every gang has its colors," Tommy thought, feigning his confusion as he watched the man step into the street with the other two falling in behind him. Tommy pretended to not see them and turned to his right, heading into a narrow alley. Walking ahead, he could smell the stench of urine and garbage, but the space was vacant of people. He stopped and turned back just as the trio stepped into the alley to join him.

The tall man approached him quickly, speaking in broken English. "Why you here? What you want?"

Tommy held his hands to his front and put his palms up, letting the man step closer. The two sidekicks seemed embolden by their leader and held close to his sides. Tommy shook his head with a dulled expression, and this time took a strategically placed back step, drawing the trio into the exact position he wanted them.

Scanning the attackers, he only saw one weapon—a long-bladed knife in the tall man's belt. The other two pumped their fists and grinned at him, eager for an easy victim. Tommy knew where this inquiry was going; the men were looking for a simple score, an American they could take and sell off to a rival group. Or to make one of their famous propaganda videos.

Now inside of Tommy's striking range, the tall man planted his feet and drew the knife. It had a long, curved blade, the cutting edge chipped and rusty. Tommy let his hands shake, seeing the blade.

"You a reporter, yes? Who, CNN?" the man said, causing the others to laugh. "You come with us," he ordered, pointing the knife at Tommy. "You come, I take you home." He held the knife in a butcher's grip in his right hand, with the blade pointed up. It fit into Tommy's plan precisely, as he wouldn't have to turn the man's wrist to do his work.

"Ya zabludilsa. Ne podskajete dorogu?" Tommy said, asking for directions in Russian.

The tall man's expression quickly changed. He paused and drew his lower lip between his teeth, now thinking Tommy was Russian. The kidnapper's mind flashed from having an easy score, to something else, something dangerous. Hurting a Russian soldier would be an instant death sentence. The Russians were known to destroy entire neighborhoods in retaliation for a single soldier's death. The scarfed man plastered a smile on his face, getting an idea, and Tommy already knew what it was. Returning a lost Russian soldier to his post would gain him favor with the local commanders, maybe even access.

The two henchmen stepped closer as the tall man's knife hand slacked and his expression softened. Tommy, now taking full advantage of the confusion, stepped in hard across the man's body. He grabbed the knife hand and guided it up into the leader's throat. Missing the bone, the blade cut cleanly through the left side of the man's neck. The tall man released the blade and gripped his carotid artery, which was already spurting blood across the red-and-white scarf.

Without missing a movement, Tommy released the wrist, gripped the handle of the knife, and drew it back. Ducking and turning away, he twisted and lunged the blade into the chest of the henchman to his right. Two men were now down in the street bleeding. Only one man remained, and he was standing against the alley wall by the tall man, who was now on his knees with both hands clutching his throat.

The remaining man put up his arms and babbled surrender. Seeing the man had no fight left in him, Tommy took a striking step forward and punched him in the sternum, bending him over. Tommy grabbed the back of the man's jacket and whispered in his ear in Arabic. "Women were taken in this city. Stolen from a church. I want them released or I will kill every single one of you. Tell this to the man in charge."

Without waiting for a response, Tommy shoved the man down into the pile of his bleeding comrades. He stood and straightened his shirt, shaking his head at the drops of blood now staining his shirt sleeve. Rolling his shoulders, he left the alley and turned back onto the bright street as if nothing had happened.

He felt no remorse or guilt for killing a pair of street thugs. Tommy knew what this part of Syria was all about, the center of a nation destroyed by civil war. Albahr was considered a safe haven to some. Mostly to those on the outer edges of extremist bubbles. Groups that one day could appear loyalist and the next take up arms and fight alongside the extremists. There were also Russians in town, not regular forces but contractors, and that complicated matters. Officially there as a quasi-peacekeeping force, they worked to provide law and order where none really existed.

With so many players and rifts in the area, it lent to great hardships for the local populations just trying to survive. What looked like safety and security provided by the Russian-backed security forces was really like living in Nazi-occupied France. People were always closely watched, and any mistake could be reason to have you swept away and arrested in the middle of the night. Criminal elements controlled all the businesses, and if your family members were kidnapped, you had little choice but to pay the ransom or never see them again. There was no room for neutrality; you had to take sides or be considered the enemy. Tommy had sent a message that someone new was in town, and he had chosen a side.

He walked slowly down the sidewalk, passing closed shops, and stopped in front of the café. A frail man in traditional Arab garments looked Tommy up and down as he moved past the entrance and took a seat at an open table. He sat with his back to the wall and looking down the street the way he'd come. The old man approached and spoke to him softly in a concerned tone. He waved an open hand and muttered words that Tommy knew meant that he wasn't welcome there. Tommy ignored the warning and smiled, placing several folded bills on the table. He looked back down the road, in the direction of the SUV, and watched as Ali made a three-point turn and vanished in a cloud of dust. Only then did he acknowledge the man and order a plate of bread and tea.

The man shot him a worried expression, not so much a look of concern for Tommy, but with eyes that betrayed the old man's fear. He looked at Tommy again and shook his head before returning to the inside of the café. Soon after, a bearded man dressed in dark-blue garments walked to the table and sat heavily across from Tommy, carelessly dropping a plate of wood-fired pita bread and filling the already placed cups with tea. "What the hell are you doing here, Tommy?" the man asked.

Tommy held back the smile, warmed at seeing his old friend. His face was tanned, thick crow's feet had formed at the corners of his eyes, and his beard had grown gray, but he was the same man Tommy remembered. Strong and confident, he looked ready to wrestle a bear if the moment presented itself. The man broke off a bit of the bread and washed it down with the tea.

"It's good to see you, Papa," Tommy said. "I never pictured you working a kitchen."

Elias Beda shook his head and scowled. "Don't call me that; I'm no one's Papa anymore." The man looked up and down the street with concern. "We need to go inside. You have no idea how dangerous this is." The man stood and returned to the café without looking back. Tommy grabbed a handful of the bread and followed Elias inside, hearing his friend say, "Just your blue eyes alone put a bounty on you with the local Jihadist."

"So the travel brochure about the peace-loving people of Albahr was misleading?"

"Fuck you, Tommy. Come on, we can't meet here."

He was led through an empty dining room filled with the scent of a wood fire and roasting meat. Elias moved into a narrow hallway before climbing stairs to a small bedroom. Elias waited for Tommy to enter and closed the door behind them; he then went to the window and looked left and right before ducking back inside and closing the curtains. "Where is the rest of your team?"

"I'm alone," Tommy said, stepping to the center of the bedroom, searching for a chair. Not finding any other furniture but a small hutch, he sat at the foot of the bed. With as much confidence as Tommy had, being back in the presence of his mentor again, he suddenly felt like a young soldier looking for guidance. "I need your help, Papa."

"Alone?" Papa shook his head and turned to face him. "What the hell is wrong with you?"

"I told you, I need your help."

"You stupid bastard. You shouldn't have come."

Elias rubbed his forehead with the back of his hand, wiping away sweat. He frowned and looked at Tommy. "Don't you see what is going on? There is a war here. How can I help you? Tell them I am out of the service, I'm retired."

"You're not listening. I'm not working for anyone, and I'm not leaving."

Elias paced through the room and stopped near the wall, leaning back against it. He looked down at Tommy's stone expression. "Why are you here?"

Tommy let his eyes drop to the floor. "You're the only one I could come to for help." He paused and looked up into the eyes of his old friend. "They have my sister."

His jaw dropped. "Who has her?"

"I don't know. She was taken from the Christian church in Albahr nearly a week ago. I have nothing else to go on; nobody is talking, and our government isn't lifting a finger to help."

"You're telling the truth, aren't you?" Elias said,

moving away from the wall. "You really came alone. Have you lost your damned mind? Do you know how dangerous this is?"

"I don't have anyone else. You and Sarah are the only family I have left. Everyone else is gone."

The older man moved to the bed and sat beside him. "Who has her?"

"I told you I don't know. The group made a ransom demand to the Church then went quiet. I thought that maybe—"

"I don't know what you think I can do for you, Tommy. I told you I'm retired; I'm out of it." Elias sighed and turned back to the window, watching the breeze sway the curtains. He hesitated before dropping his head and exhaling loudly. "I know it doesn't seem like much, but this place—and my father—are all I've got. I've been walking a fine line to keep us above ground."

Tommy stared down his old friend and slowly shook his head side to side, calling his bluff. "I've known you too long, Papa. I know why you came here and it wasn't to fry bread. I know you came here to fight, or you would have already taken your father and left."

Elias clenched his fists and pumped a frustrated arm. He closed his eyes tight then slowly opened them. "Tell me something; promise me that you aren't here to feed the fire in your stomach, you aren't here just to get yourself killed. I was there after James died. I watched you snap, and I saw how long it took to get you back. Tell me this isn't you trying to bring yourself back to some dark place."

"Papa, I told you they have my sister and nobody else is going to help."

"Then give me something to work with."

"I told you what I know—she was taken north of here. I don't have all of the details, but it was a planned attack, and whoever was responsible had the connections to pass communications to the Church and the State Department without making noise."

"Why was she here? Is she with the company? And don't lie to me."

Tommy shook his head. "No, Sarah was doing aid work, delivering medical supplies, when they were attacked. All of the women were taken away to be sold, I imagine. They asked for a ransom, but nobody is acknowledging her existence, and whoever has her isn't publicizing it."

Elias pressed knuckles against his lips. He shook his head and tried to conceal his knowing expression. "Albahr is a bad place, officially under government control, with security guaranteed by the Russians. But it's on the fringe of several rebel groups. Some of them more familiar than others."

"Red-and-white scarves?" Tommy asked.

"Yeah, one of the worst. I try to keep them off my street, but they always find their way back. They are the lowest of the low, and they are connected."

"When you say connected, do you mean the former Special Services, the Badawi? The thugs we met in Iraq? I heard they are operating here. I know that high-stakes kidnapping used to be their game."

"The Badawi we knew is history—it isn't a thing anymore, not the way it used to be. They broke up and scattered like rats all over this region. You can still find pieces here and there, but the group has been dissolved.

What's left is something worse." Elias paused and looked away.

"You know more. Tell me about the church attack, your eyes betray you."

Elias sighed again and dipped his chin. "I never was good at poker. I know about the attack you mentioned, the one against the church. There have been several in recent weeks, all in the same area, all about the same time. Many women have been taken."

"Then you know who is responsible?" Tommy asked.

Elias shook his head, pondering a response. "Who-ever did this made a hell of a storm. A lot of people went missing. I know some local families paid the ransom and a few women were released, mostly those in political positions. The ones who didn't, or the families that couldn't afford it... rumors are the women went into the underground market."

"If there is a market, there has to be a way to get inside."

The older man stood and walked back to the window. "There is a way, but it will take some time, and it could get very messy."

"I don't mind messy," Tommy said. "Just get me a thread hold, any loose end that I can grab onto."

"I've seen this look in your eyes before, Tommy. You are a time bomb waiting to explode. You should step back and let the government handle this."

Tommy's face hardened. "I can't do nothing. I'd rather die than sit by while this happens to her."

"This isn't you, Tommy. You're a professional; you don't go out and do things like this. Jack didn't train you to be a renegade, to go off the reservation without a plan."

"Jack is dead. I'm nobody now. Besides, you don't know shit about me, Elias. I'm not the same man anymore." Tommy clenched his teeth and looked away. "All my friends are gone—" He stopped and let his head hang, his eyes focusing on the floor. "Even in this shit hole, you've got it better than me. I don't have anyone— no family. The only time I see my friends is in my dreams, and I spend my days alone, drinking. I drink until I pass out so I don't dream about them at night."

Elias shook his head. "Fuck you, Tommy. It can't be that bad."

"I'm gone, I'm all used up. But not Sarah. She's a good person, and if I can give up what's left of me to help her, then I'll do it."

Elias frowned and moved toward the wall, pulling out an old wooden stool. He sat heavily then looked across at his friend. "I can help you—I will help you—but I'm not looking to get myself or any of my friends or family killed. I'm not signing on to be part of your suicide mission. If we do this, then we do it right."

Tommy pursed his lips and nodded.

"No fucking around, Tommy. You've got to let me do my thing, and I'll make this work. I'll reach out and find out what I can." He stopped and looked at Tommy again, shaking his head.

"Clean yourself up and get some rest. I'll wake you when it's time to move."

12

"And you're certain it was him?"

Fayed held the phone receiver in his hand, already nervous about transmitting such important information over an open phone line. He now grew angry, having to explain himself to someone he considered of lesser intellect. He was taking too many risks, and who knew how many people could be listening? "The man's description matches who we are looking for. How many blue-eyed men cross at remote stations then kill the guards on the other side?" he said with sarcasm oozing from every word.

Not entirely alone, he stood on the street corner under a lamppost, looking out over the wet cobblestone. He spoke in hushed Arabic and was cautious to make sure no eavesdroppers were within range of his voice. Couples passed by, walking hand in hand, taking in what they considered romantic venues. This was a popular street, connecting many different attractions favored by tourists. He'd chosen the spot intentionally, in case his phone was triangulated. If it was, it would be better to be picked up in an area with heavy phone traffic. The city was always subject to surveillance, and even with taking the added precaution of disposable phones, open-air communications was a risk.

"So the attacker was white. How do we know this is our man? You said he was in Turkey. How the hell did he get to Jordan?"

"Obviously, we were misinformed," Fayed said with a sigh. "And it's not only that, our informants say that after he killed the guards, he burned the bodies and the evidence then continued on into Syria. Why would he take time to cover his tracks? Also, there were no attempts made to stop him. He entered the country untouched and on no flight manifest. Someone bribed the Jordanians and allowed him to pass into Syria without inspection."

"What are you saying?" Abdul asked.

"He is not working alone. This is no rogue operator; he has to have been assisted by the government. This has to be part of a larger operation."

Abdul grunted, "Nonsense, you know how they work these days. If there was an operation, you would know. I pay you to tell me these things in advance. Not days later. Now go back to your people and get me the information I need to have this man removed." The line went dead as Abdul slammed the receiver.

Fayed closed the burner phone and dropped it into a trashcan as he walked past. The Paris streets were dark and he was in a well-off part of the city. Tourists walked sidewalks and peddlers tried to sell them knock-off purses and watches. He scowled and turned the corner as he headed back to his apartment. Abdul was right, of course. He was paid to predict these situations. He was normally a confident man, but when he got word that the brother was spotted on the Syrian border, something awoke a fear deep inside him.

Maybe he'd played the game too long, enjoyed it all just a little too much. He pondered the situation. If this man had so easily moved without Fayed noticing, then what else could he do? No, it was impossible; the brother didn't know anything. It probably wasn't even him; just another ruse like the trip to Turkey, something from the American CIA, used to smoke them out. Of course it was a trick. He stopped momentarily, feeling a shiver in the cold air. It was his paranoia. He'd always been careful, but for some reason this operation was going all wrong. He looked ahead into the shadows to where his building was lit brightly from the front doors.

Fayed turned into the lobby of his building, nodding to the doorman as he entered the elevator. He was an expert in his field, and he could not allow them to play him. He would take another look at Donovan's Interpol record and cross-check it against the Forces's records. If there was something suspicious, it would alert him. He could use his special access and request additional records from French military intelligence, but that would have risks of its own. Accessing the files would notify the agencies that he'd looked at them. But he was, after all, working the case, and the sibling of a kidnap victim was relevant information.

Moving into the apartment, he found that the walk

had calmed his nerves. He sat beside the laptop in his study, pouring himself a glass of cognac as he entered the security codes, remotely connecting him into the intelligence directorate's secure mainframe. He entered the subject's known names and serial numbers then cross-referenced them with databases he had access to. The first two files that appeared in the table were the ones he was already familiar with from the Interpol background screening. The third file was something new. It wasn't about Donovan in and of itself, but of an Interpol and international courts investigation into the assassination of a terror suspect in Damascus, dated from 2009.

Donovan's name appeared in the report several times, but his counter-terror unit had been cleared in the operation. Fayed highlighted other names listed and added them to the search query. When he ran the search again, the screen was filled with files, each one related to the assassination or disappearance of suspected terrorists over the last decade. Watching the files scroll by caused his blood to run cold.

Names and dates all over the Middle East and stretching into Eastern Europe. Assassinations, kidnappings, and hostage rescues. This man, Donovan, was somehow remotely connected to all of it. Fayed shook his head and scrolled through the list. "No, there has to be something else. This is real life, not fiction; the real world doesn't function like this."

Only three files specifically listed the name Donovan in the details. Fayed clicked a link and opened a file from Iraq dated after the invasion. In it was listed the names of several top terror suspects who had been transferred to a secure custody in Qatar. The report said all six men were killed while under twenty-four-hour guard in a secure hotel. The released terrorists had essentially been living under house arrest under the supervision of the Qatar government. According to the report, early one morning all six of the men were found dead in their hotel rooms. No trace of an assassin. Fayed continued to scroll down and froze. The American who traveled to Qatar to write the report confirming the men's deaths was T. Donovan.

He shook his head and grinned. "So the same man that killed them investigated their death."

Fayed closed all the open files and entered into a NATO transportation database, looking through personnel lists and travel documents from many different airbases. Hitting on several Thomas Donovan's, opening and closing many, he felt tightness in his chest. T. Donovan frequently traveled in and out of NATO bases. Many times as an Army staff sergeant, sometimes a Marine, even a Navy Chief. Other times he was listed as a Department of Defense employee, or an aid to high-level State Department officials.

"Who the hell are you?" Fayed said, his pulse racing.

He clicked the only file with an image attached. A photo opened of a young, eighteen-year-old Thomas Donovan, dressed in an Army uniform, standing rigid and looking straight ahead. The photo was for an identification card taken over a decade ago. Fayed clenched his jaw and printed the only picture he had of the man he suspected was hunting them.

The man was still young, probably still active. He wouldn't be retired. He would have reach and contacts. Probably part of a special unit, one specifically equipped to go after men like Abdul Nassir. He thought back to the list of dead terrorists, and Fayed clenched his fists. What had they stumbled upon with the American girl? He would have to contact Abdul right away. She needed to be dealt with before the American dealt with them.

13

It was still dark, hours before dawn, when they traveled in the cool morning air. The rusted Daewoo drove down the street, pulling alongside a brown lot once known as a soccer field. There were several stone monuments and other statues reduced to rubble lining a walkway. Tommy pointed at them and Elias shrugged. "Rebel fighters knocked them down when they came through about a year ago." Elias parked the car next to a bullet-pocked Kia sedan on flat tires. He reached into his shirt pocket and dialed a number on his mobile phone. Listening intently, he waited for the speaker to stop before saying "okay," and then disconnected the battery and placed both pieces under the seat.

"You worried about someone tracking the phone?" Tommy said.

"Just a habit. Even just being part of a friendly militia there are risks. The Americans, and even the Russians, love to use their drones to target cell phones. I don't want them tracking us or trying to capture the signal to listen in," Elias answered. He paused and pointed to a two-story building at the back of the lot and a smaller stucco building across the corner from it. Then he guided his finger down an opposite walkway that led away from the stucco building, to a crumbling amphitheater where people probably gathered for plays or shows years ago. "The drop will happen somewhere in here. They couldn't be certain and the location changes from time to time."

"*The drop*? Who did you call?"

"You were right, I didn't come back home to fry bread. I have a friend that works the airport; he owed me a favor. He knows everything that moves in or out of Albahr."

"So, you aren't retired?"

Elias swallowed and said, "I'm plenty retired, but it takes connections when you are running an effective neighborhood watch."

"Neighborhood watch, aye." Tommy looked at him. "I noticed the difference when we turned onto your little street. Is that you?"

"The police here are shit; every block has to take responsibility for its own security. But even that only goes so far. We can keep the thugs out, but we'd be screwed against real opposition. So, the key is stopping it before it gets to us," Elias explained.

"So you stay connected and trade favors."

"When it benefits my people."

Tommy nodded thoughtfully. "And this friend, he knows where the missing women are?"

"No, but he knows the path the money takes."

"Money?" Tommy blinked, letting his eyes adjust to the darkness.

"It's always about the money. Money, women, and guns. Every war is the same."

"What about religion?" Tommy asked.

Elias laughed, shaking his head. "If wars were really fought over religion, we'd have found peace a thousand years ago. War is about power, and power of the few. And to control power, you control the money, drugs, and guns. Go back into history as far as you want, it's always the same. Always will be."

Tommy sighed and looked out of the side window. "If you say so, brother. So tell me about the money then."

"Just so happens our friend says the man you want arrived a little over an hour ago."

"*Our* friend?" Tommy assessed skeptically.

"Kohen."

"The Israeli?" Tommy said, surprised. "I thought he was dead. Why is the Dagger in Syria?" Tommy knew the man only by reputation, having never met the Israeli assassin face-to-face. The man earned his nickname by leaving a dagger near the resting place of his victims, usually impaled in their chests. He was a man who killed to send a message, as killing without a message was considered too simple.

"He's Mossad; this is where the action is."

"Why the hell is he helping us?"

Elias grinned, his face expression brightening. "Because I have been helping him. Things have gotten shady in my neighborhood, and Kohen helps me keep the rats away. Lately there have been a lot of rats that need dealt with. And the more rats we kill in Syria, the less there are to cross into Israel."

"And you told him about me?"

"No, you stupid shit. You *told* him when you sat your ass in front of my café in broad daylight. Of course, his people saw you—and of course, he wanted to know why. He also knows about the mess you made at the border. And yes, we all know about your little dance in the alley. You killed people on my street and thought that would go unnoticed? Why would you do that?"

"The mess at the border? That was hardly a mess," Tommy said, brushing off the statement. "And ridding the world of two fuckwads in an alley, that was to put the locals on notice that the rules are about to change here."

"Who do you think you are?" Elias pursed his lips. He shook off the question, not wanting an answer. "It doesn't matter; the Dagger says he owes you for the Damascus job. He'll help us, but even his help has its limits."

Tommy nodded his head, remembering the 2009 mission that killed one of the men responsible for the embassy attack in Spain a year earlier. A killing that Mossad conveniently took credit for to keep Interpol off of the backs of the Ground Division. "What does the Dagger have to say about this? Who is this man we need to talk to?"

"He says the foreign money man will be moving through here in the next six hours. The rebel groups have lots of cash, but it's all in electronic format. With the banks and networks destroyed, it's getting harder for them to come up with hard currency. That's where the money men come in. One will make a dead drop, hiding a bag of cash. Later another man will come to take the money. We pick up either one, and he should give us the information that will lead us to the missing girls."

"Why do I feel like I'm running an errand for the

Mossad? What the hell does this have to do with getting Sarah back? If he knows where the organization is based, why can't Kohen just tell us?"

"The money men don't know the details of the organization because people like us tend to follow them. It's a level of security."

"Then we should wait for the pickup and follow that back to the organization."

"No, you said you are after the women. Koehn says the man making the drop has a reputation. You said you wanted a lead; well, here is your lead."

"What sort of reputation?"

"He has a fetish and an interest in meeting the new captives. Kohen says this courier is a real disgusting creature."

"Doesn't Kohen know where the girls are? Why can't he just tell us who we're looking for?"

Elias scratched at his beard. "I'm sure he knows everything, but this is already more than he should be relaying to a couple retired guys working off the clock."

Tommy pulled the Glock from his shoulder holster and pulled back the slide, verifying he'd chambered a round. Elias reached into a canvas bag on the floor and opened it, revealing a pair of black HK MK23 handguns with matching suppressors. He pulled one out and handed it to Tommy while taking the other for himself. He then handed him a small earpiece with a connected two-way radio.

Tommy smiled, putting the Glock back into the shoulder holster and palming the .45-caliber handgun. "At least you held on to your toys," Tommy joked. "I thought you might be all washed up."

"Washed up my ass," Elias grinned. "I'm the one that got you here, now what's the plan?"

Tommy let his eyes scan the surroundings and switched back into command mode, his nerve endings tingling with energy. "You head over to that pavilion area and get comfortable. I'm going to park myself on one of those benches down there by the statues. I think if I play bum, I'll blend in."

Elias nodded and left the car. Tommy waited for him to vanish out of sight before exiting on his side and moving into the shadows of a large tree as he watched Elias slowly walk down a rough, stone path. He observed him cut through the unkempt weeds and move parallel to the amphitheater and finally drop to a sitting position against a stone wall near the small building structure. Tommy stood silently observing his surroundings for a few minutes longer.

The park was very quiet. The light had just begun to break the horizon. He could see other people, presumably homeless, most sitting or sleeping in the shadows. They stayed well hidden, but Tommy's trained eye could pick out the man-made shapes or unusual movements on the ground. When he was comfortable that they hadn't been followed and were not being observed, he made his way across the field to an empty bench.

Tommy lay down so his view intersected with that of Elias, and also so he could see over and beyond his partner's blind sides. He called on the internal radio and made sure his friend had a visual on his position as well. Then he settled in. He had brought along an old, battered blanket that he wrapped himself in before he curled onto the bench. The temperature was cool, but he knew it

would warm rapidly as the sun rose. He didn't find it difficult to stay in the position, but he found it difficult to stay
awake while at the same time pretending to be asleep.

He thought about Kohen and the mission in Damascus. It seemed like a lifetime ago now. After six months of
tracking the cell responsible for the embassy bombing
that killed three Marine guards, two State Department
employees, and an Israeli dignitary, the Ground Division
had finally located and identified the terrorist known as
Chasm in Syria.

At the time, Tommy was behind the scope of a preci-
sion rifle when a black Mercedes pulled up in front of the
Damascus Central Courthouse. The news had just
crossed the wire that Chasm had turned himself in to the
local authorities, knowing that Mossad and others were
hot on his trail. Tommy watched as the target and two
others exited the vehicle. He positively identified the
target but was given the abort order. He asked for clarifi-
cation and was ordered to shut it down. Tommy knew
that the Dagger's team was still moving into position, and
this would be the last opportunity to eliminate the target
before he was taken into protective custody.

He violated his orders and took the shot. He and the
rest of his team went quiet, vanishing into hiding as was
the original plan. Days later, the Dagger took responsibility for the assassination and followed it up with a large
car bomb placed in front of Chasm's terror cell headquarters in Raqqa. The message had been sent, and without
evidence of a crime, the Ground Division was able to
return to the United States.

Now things were different; the enemy didn't know
they were hunting them. The wires were still clear, so

they still had the advantage of surprise. Soon another message would be sent, and the hunted would go back into their dens.

He had been lying in his position all morning and into the afternoon. The heat was on him now. He occupied his time by watching pedestrians move through the park. His cover of playing a bum had worked well. Most people who walked by him intentionally avoided him or pretended that he wasn't there. It's easy to disappear when nobody wants to see you.

Tommy came out of his thoughts when he saw a small man walking across the lawn. He was moving fast toward the small building structure, constantly looking behind him. The young man wasn't dressed the same as the other pedestrians in the park. He was wearing Western clothing—a striped, short-sleeved polo shirt, and tan cargo pants. He appeared to be in his best "business casual" travel clothes and carried a rather large backpack over his shoulders. Tommy watched as the man continued toward the restrooms and passed just meters in front of Elias.

"Possible target," Tommy whispered into the radio.

"On him," Elias responded. "When he enters the structure, I'll follow him."

"I'll cover you from outside. Careful, he may just be a lost tourist that needs to take a shit. Maintain cover as long as possible."

Tommy watched the man move toward the door to the building then suddenly stop. He turned and hunched over to tie his shoe. As he worked, he looked behind him and turned to check his back trail. He stood by the door for several minutes, presumably checking to see if he was being tailed. Interesting spy craft, but on this mission, all it did was confirm that this was the man Tommy was looking for.

The suspect slowly turned and walked to the door. Nervous, he stopped again and looked back before pushing the door and disappearing inside. Tommy shifted his focus to Elias and watched him move to his feet, casually walk to the door, and pass inside. Quickly, Tommy was also up and fast stepping to the building. He posted himself on the wall just outside and in the shadow of a tree.

"It's him. Go, go, go," Elias commanded over the radio.

Tommy ran for the door and burst inside, where he saw Elias tangled up with the man. His friend was behind him. He had hooked the suspect's left side in a tight half-nelson. Elias was gripping the man's right elbow joint tightly and twisting his forearm down and away from his body. Tommy looked to the man's right hand and saw a long, curved knife.

The man was struggling, but Elias had him easily outweighed and outmatched. The man's twisted and outstretched right arm gripped the knife tightly, refusing to let go of it. Tommy stepped forward, planted his left foot then gave the man a stiff punch to the gut with his right hand. The man let out a dry gasp as his weight sagged. Suddenly his head dropped forward, his right hand opened, and he dropped the knife.

Elias let the man's limp body fall to the floor before dragging him against the wall. He pulled his arms up over his head and tightly zip-tied him to the plumbing of an old sink. Tommy stepped to the door and secured it shut with a rubber wedge he kept in his gear. Elias had moved back to the knife, examining it on the ground without touching it.

"I caught the dude red-handed. He was facing that sink, trying to place his bag behind that wooden panel. When he saw me, he pulled the blade so I jumped on him."

Tommy approached the man on the ground. He was young and clean-shaven. Looked to be Pakistani, possibly Afghani, but it was hard to tell. The man's arms were stretched over his head, his wrists looped around the plumbing of the sink. Tommy looked at him closely and could tell he was conscious but feigning sleep. He walked closer and stood on the man's ankle, slowly applying pressure.

The man let out an exaggerated yelp. "Stop, stop," the man yelled.

"Good, you're awake. And you speak English," Tommy said.

"Why do you attack me? Why did you do this to me?"

"No time for games. We already know what you were up to, now tell me about the money." He started slowly, hoping to gain more about the organization, paving the way for information on the location of the women.

The man again lowered his head and sat quietly.

"Fine, if it's going to be like that, we can do things that way also," Tommy said as he took a step toward the man and tightened the flex cuffs.

The man yelped again before laughing hysterically. "It does not matter what you do to me. Arrest me, take me to your prison in Cuba. The fact that you do not know what this is all about tells me how ignorant you all are. You will be dead before the sun sets."

"Possibly, but I am willing to give you an option on whether or not you join us," Tommy said.

"I don't matter, I am only a part of all of this," the man said, still laughing. "I am nobody."

Tommy looked over at Elias, who had been standing back, covering the door. Elias was shaking his head. Tommy opened his hand, gesturing for Elias to give him the backpack. Elias handed it over and Tommy unzipped it, finding bundles of cash inside—bricks of American dollars and Swiss francs. He pulled one out and held it in his hand. "There is a lot of cash here."

The man looked away, ignoring the statement.

Tommy looked to Elias and shrugged his shoulders. The man was still tied to the floor. His body was sagging, but he looked at Tommy defiantly. Tommy shot the man a quick wink before turning his back and walking toward a far wall of the structure. The floor was covered with rubble and the space stank of urine.

He turned back. "No more time for bullshit. I'm going to be straight with you. Your people have something I want. A woman. We know you are in the business of taking women. I've heard you are the type of monster to visit these woman against their will. Now all I ask is for you to tell me where they are." He pulled his MK23 pistol from the holster on his hip. The man looked up and smiled, still defiant.

Tommy returned the man's smile and stomped down on the prisoner's exposed ankle, causing him to cry out.

He stepped closer and held the pistol close to the man's face, silencing his screams. "I normally don't operate this way. But since we are on a tight schedule and just happen to answer to no one, I'm going to make an exception for you. You seem to have all the answers so I'm sure you won't mind me taking shortcuts," Tommy said as he pulled a suppressor from his pocket and threaded it onto the barrel of his sidearm.

Tommy pulled back the slide and showed the man the chambered round.

"Now, my friend and I are in a bit of a time crunch, and unfortunately I couldn't give a shit less what happens to a rapist scumbag like you. This place where the women are being held, I want to know where it is. We can do this one of two ways. You can tell me. In that case, we will leave you here unmolested. I'm sure someone will come along to free you eventually."

"You fool, you can't do anything to me! Nothing you do to me will save you. You are already dead!" the man yelled, now a thick Pakistani accent shining through.

"Or," Tommy continued, ignoring the man's protest. "I can ask you a series of questions, where you will be punished for wrong answers or not cooperating."

"You already lost," the man said, laughing hysterically.

"Slowly now, where are the women being held?"

"Nobody cares about those whores. I will tell you nothing," the man spat back. "I could buy a dozen whores with my shoe. Now you tell me—what is this really about?"

"Okay... you are about to feel a slight discomfort," Tommy said as he placed the end of the suppressor against the man's left ankle and pulled the trigger.

Even with the suppressor, the .45 pistol's discharge was loud and made Tommy's ears ring in the confined space. Tommy had looked away just before he pulled the trigger to protect his eyes. When he looked back, the man was kicking his feet. The destroyed ankle flopped grotesquely at an odd angle as the man kicked and screamed.

Elias gave Tommy a shocked look, unaware that he would actually fire. Elias moved toward the man and pinned his head against the wall and stuck a strip of duct tape over his lips, silencing the screams. The man moaned through the tape but stopped kicking his legs.

"Okay, now that you know how this game works, let's try again. That's one point for me and zero for you," Tommy said. "Where are the women being held?"

Elias peeled the tape from the man's mouth. Between whimpers, he told Tommy that he didn't know about any women, claiming he was just a college student from a University in Egypt who makes extra cash delivering backpacks to this building two times a month.

Tommy squatted down and patted the man on his head. "You suck at this game. You're too old and stupid for college, my friend. That was another wrong answer, and a rather large lie." Tommy placed the barrel over the man's left knee. "We already know that you have information on where the women are being kept. Your cell sold you out. They told us what a monster you are, how you treat women. They told us how to find you because you disgust even them. They told us you would come here to make the drop. Do you think we are here by accident?"

"Impossible!"

Elias reapplied the tape, and Tommy pulled the trigger, punching a hole through the man's kneecap. The prisoner's back stiffened and he strained his arms against the ties. He tried to kick his leg, but it wouldn't cooperate.

He was shaking his head side to side, moaning through the tape. Beads of sweat formed and ran down the side of his face.

"I seriously do not have time for this. Tell us where they are!" Tommy yelled. "Where do you go to feed your fetish?"

The man looked up at Tommy and shook his head violently. Without saying a word, Tommy aimed the pistol at the man's lower leg, fired, and destroyed his tibia. The man again flexed and screamed in pain through the tape. He rocked his head side to side before blacking out from a mix of shock and pain.

Elias looked at Tommy. "What the hell are you doing? This isn't what we talked about."

"Just get him up before we lose him to blood loss," Tommy answered sternly.

Elias grabbed a small glass vile of smelling salts from his kit. He broke the bottle and waved it under the man's nose. "Wakey, wakey, sleepy head," Elias said as he gently slapped the man on the cheek.

The man's head jerked back as he swung it to the side drunkenly. He moved his head up and gave Tommy a shocked look. His face was still filled with pain and agony.

Tommy knelt down directly in front of the man, using his gloved hand to make the man look him in the eyes. "This is where you were hoping it was all a bad dream. I'm sorry, but I am your worst nightmare."

The man whimpered, pulling his head back, mumbling incoherently through the tape.

"So, this is where we are at," Tommy said. "We already know you came from the airport. Your cell ratted you out;

they told us you would be here. They made a deal with us. If we get rid of you, we get to keep the money. Now you have no reason to protect them," Tommy bluffed. "All we want to know is where the women are."

"I cannot tell you anything. I do not know. There are so many places they could be."

"The women from the church in Albahr. All we want to know is where the women are kept. Then we will leave you all alone to disappear and go about your evil ways."

Elias shook his head in frustration. "Let's go, this guy is useless. We've already wasted too much time."

Tommy raised the pistol, and the man reared back, shaking his head. "Why do you care so much about these whores?" The man dropped his head and spouted off an address. "That is all I know. I was told there will be new ones there, brand new. Now that is all, leave me."

Tommy looked up at Elias, who nodded. "I know the place; it is in a bad region on the far side of the city."

Tommy gripped the heavy pistol in his hand and pressed it against the man's forehead. "One more question ... who is running the Badawi Brigade? Tell me who is at the top!"

The man let out a sobbing laugh. "Just let me go or take me away to your Guantanamo Bay. I know you will not kill me; you Americans have no resolve. You are the good guys, you always play by the rules."

"You got the wrong people, I'm no good guy," Tommy said, pulling the trigger.

14

Jamal stood on the steps of a cement block building. Night was falling over the city. In the distance, he could hear the reports of gunfire and the rumble of explosions from the outer limits. There were always smaller battles being waged between the rebels and loyalists. If things carried on too long, the Russians would call in close-support sorties from their aircraft.

Jamal tried to keep out of those things. He was a business man, after all. He stepped into the street and looked to the left, spotting his two men standing watch in the back of a white technical—a large pickup truck with a mounted machine gun in the back. One man was resting, sitting on a side rail of the truck while the other leaned over the machine gun that overlooked the roadblock. The heavy machine gun gave them courage, and that was enough for Jamal.

The government troops rarely came by here. This old warehouse was outside of the patrolled safe zones, but still close enough to take advantage of the military presence. Jamal paid his bribes and those in charge willingly looked the other way while he existed, and that allowed Jamal the freedom to run his brothel any way he wanted, without being under their watchful eye. His guards here were good and he paid them well, but it was also known that this place was under the protection of the Badawi Brigade. The threat of reprisals from the Brigade is really what kept most people away.

His men were complacent and spoiled, knowing that the real fighting was still miles away to the north and nobody would dare mess with the property of the Badawi. And even those who had the courage to mess with Jamal, had the Russian military to contend with. The Russians didn't play favorites and they policed the neighboring sectors with deadly efficiency. This worked for groups that were disciplined enough to color inside the lines, and the Badawi brigade was certainly one of them.

Jamal's building was at the top of a T-shaped intersection in the old city center. Although once a prized industrial area, most people rarely ventured here now, the block just outside of the military patrolled sector. There were no homes in this district and what industry remained was now bombed out beyond recognition. Undesirable for most, but it made prime real estate for Jamal. The trading of flesh was unpopular with the state, and having the space to do it in the shadows was important. It put him in the white space on the page, a place where the governing institutions could easily deny his existence while remaining cooperative in what he was doing.

An old military bunker made of concrete and sandbags was at the bottom leg of the intersection directly in front of the building. Straining, he could see one of his armed men standing under the dim streetlight slowly walking the length of a chain-link fence. To his right was the only open road allowing access to the property, and the only avenue allowing vehicle traffic in or out of this small compound.

Checking his watch again, Jamal looked at the phone in his hand, eager for any news of reinforcements from Abdul or permission to relocate to a more secure location inside the cities security, for the night at least. He had less than eight soldiers here this evening with others being sent to reinforce the larger building in the city. Jamal was told that eight was plenty, but with word of the recent killing of his courier, he had requested more. Rumors were already circulating amongst the guards at the compound over the news of the dead money man. His body was found at the site of the money drop, all the currency missing.

He looked at his watch again, impatiently waiting for the minutes to pass until midnight. Jamal didn't consider himself a bad man; he just performed a task like everyone else in the country these days. He was a business man providing a service, an auctioneer of sorts, a flesh peddler to be exact. If it was true that a hit team was on the ground in Syria searching for the missing women from Albahr, then he needed to have them moved to the city, and the sooner the better. Too many people, including the money man, knew of this compound in the industrial district of the city—a place converted to a prison for those valuable enough to be ransomed or traded on the open markets. And if the money man was tortured, he surely would have talked about this spot. Everyone knew women were traded here.

Earlier in the day, he sent word by ground to Abdul, requesting permission to move the women to a new location. That was hours ago, and he was starting to wonder if Abdul had received the message at all. He considered trying again, calling by phone, but use of mobile phones was highly restricted for fear that they would be targeted by American drones. Even though unlikely, it had happened in the past, and mobile phones were frowned upon.

He was ordered to keep the phone off and to only turn it on at the top of every hour. Jamal paced nervously and looked left again to the technical. This time he froze, the blood draining from his face. The men on watch were gone. Snapping forward, he could see that the streetlight over the bunker to his front was now out, no sign of the roving guard near the gate watch. He turned and ran into the building, barring the door behind him, shouting the alarm as he reached into his pockets, searching for his phone. Even though he shouted, he heard no response from his men inside.

He heard a thump in the next room and the lights went out. He held the phone in front of him, his thumb pressing the power button desperately, starting the boot sequence, watching the silly Samsung logo, the glow of the display lighting his face. Rapid firing from an AK47 in the back of the building caused him to flinch in time with the metallic *thwack*, *thwack* of suppressed gunfire. They were here and he knew he had nowhere to run. A woman screamed, and Jamal pressed back against the wall, hiding in a corner. He tried to dial for help, but his hands shook violently and his sweaty fingers slipped on the touch screen.

Jamal wasn't armed; he never carried a gun. He held his breath and tried to plan an escape. Maybe he could run. He considered unbarring the door, going outside, maybe disappearing into the night. The plodding of heavy boots to his front forced his hands into balled fists over the phone. He looked up and swore that he saw the green glow of a demon's face moments before he lost consciousness.

———

The room was dark, void of any light. Tommy stood in the corner, night vision goggles pulled over his eyes. In his hands was an odd-shaped syringe. In the center of the room, hands strapped to a table, was the man the women said was in charge of the brothel—the one they said treated them like merchandise. Tommy had found enough evidence in the building to know they were telling the truth. The building was a disgusting house of horrors. Women gathered together like cattle and only released from their stagnant holding cells long enough to work their shifts in the upstairs rooms. That wouldn't happen anymore; Tommy made sure of it. The place was out of business and the building burned.

The man was awake now, his head shifting side to side, startling at any noise or movement. Tommy had yet to speak to him. They had tied the prisoner there while he was still knocked out. He wanted to kill him right off, but the man had information. Information he wanted. Tommy used the time to inject the man with a tracking microchip into the fat at the base of his neck. The sharp pain brought the man back to consciousness. Now Tommy watched Jamal's eyes glow back through the night vision goggles. He observed the man's terror at finding himself restrained and in total darkness. Tommy walked across the room, making no effort to silence his footsteps. The man called out. Tommy ignored him. He opened a door at the back and stepped into a darkened hallway, where he climbed plank steps before removing the goggles and exiting into a lit room.

A red carpet covered with overstuffed cushions blanketed the floor, the windows covered with heavy drapes. A plank table held the stacked bundles of cash from the money man. Elias entered from a side door and handed Tommy a plate of roasted meat and vegetables. He wasn't hungry, but he knew food was fuel.

"You need to eat, and to sleep," Elias said. "You've been going nonstop since you arrived."

Tommy tossed the empty syringe to a table and exchanged it for the plate. He moved slowly to the far end of the room and dropped to his rear, leaning against an overstuffed yellow pillow with decorative fringes. He yawned and took a mouthful of the meat, grabbing at it with his fingers. Still chewing, he said, "The tracker is in place. You sure it'll work?"

"It'll work. It's passive; it only needs to be close to an active cell phone tower and it'll ping a location. The battery should last for a hundred hours, give or take. It's not the fancy stuff the agency uses, but a pet tracker will get the job done." Elias opened a smart phone. He grinned then turned the display, showing Tommy the red dot overlaid on a satellite map.

"Good, and what about the women? Are they safe?"

"Kohen is taking care of it. He notified a security official on the payroll. They'll have questions, but the women will be freed," Elias said, sitting at the table and moving aside a bundle of the money so he could sit over his own plate.

"Any information on Sarah?"

Elias shook his head. "She was separated from the others shortly after they were taken. The women don't know where they were taken." Elias tossed Tommy a bottle of water. "What are we going to do with him?" he said, signaling his head toward the locked door.

"I'll talk to him. I didn't come here for the women. I came here for Sarah."

"And you think the man in the cellar knows where she is?"

Tommy shook his head. He set the half-empty plate beside him and stretched out his legs. "No, I don't think so. If he did, they would have already moved her. But he'll know of some place hard, something too big to hide. A location we can hit them at. I knew this would take time. Every step is just another rung on the ladder. I'll take them all if I have to. I'll continue to hurt them until they expose themselves or give her up."

"We'll hurt them together. I'm in this with you," Elias said, his face turning hard.

"I know, brother." Tommy's eyes searched the safe house. The room was decorated as if a family lived there, but there was nobody in the place with them. "What is this place, anyway? Who does it belong to?"

Elias frowned. "This was my family's home. Well, it was until I was forced to send them away," he said, looking back down at his plate. "When I retired, I moved back here. I had a romantic idea that things would be the same as they were when I was a boy. That I'd take over my father's café. Start a family. I knew war was coming, but I've lived nothing but war my entire adult life, and this is my home too. I have a right to live here if I choose.

"I don't know what you think of me, Tommy, but I haven't just been hiding, sitting aside while my home has been destroyed around me. I still have a warrior's spirit and the mentality of a lion. I did what I could, Tommy. When the other men fled, I stayed, I organized people to stand with me. I sent my wife and daughter away, but my father and I—we stayed. We've done what we could."

Tommy smiled and nodded. "I know you did. I never doubted you. When I heard you'd returned to Syria, I knew the reason why. I knew you wouldn't stand by and let this happen to your home."

"And now you're here. This is my home, my city. What will you do here, what do you think you will accomplish?" Elias asked. "Don't encourage my people then vanish."

"I want Sarah back, and I will keep killing them until I find her. When they pop up, I'll knock them down. Every one of them will feel pain."

"And what if she is already gone."

Tommy dropped his head and closed his eyes. Elias could see that the man had already considered this question. "Finding Sarah is the only way to stop the killing. I find her, or they kill me. It's the only way for this to end. I have no issue with killing them until my end of days."

"I see. So, what do we do next? How do we stop the killing?"

Tommy pushed the plate away as he settled back into one of the large cushions. "How much money is there?"

Elias looked at the bundles of cash. "Hundred thousand American, another hundred thousand in Swiss francs."

Tommy squinted. "We need a secure place in Albahr, something not connected to you, a place to operate from."

"Easily done. I know a spot."

"We need weapons."

"This is a war zone, Tommy; my militia has everything we need. Armor and rifles won't be a problem. But this isn't the CIA, and certainly not the Ground Division. The stuff will be chewed up and old."

Tommy nodded his approval. "Just get me a bullet launcher and I can do the rest."

"Anything else?"

"I want to build a bomb."

Elias smiled. "Of course you do. How big a bomb will you be needing?"

"One that will get their attention."

"So naturally, a really big bomb then. You want fries with that?" the older man said, shaking his head.

Tommy yawned. "No, but this militia you keep talking about, would any of them be looking to enhance their personal savings with Swiss francs?"

"If you are looking to raise an army, I think I can round us up a few shooters," Elias said with a smirk. "But they aren't mercenaries, just shop owners, mechanics, family men like me."

Tommy pursed his lips. "Like you?"

"Hey, l fry bread for a living, remember."

Tommy laughed. "Well, if they are willing to fight, split up the francs between them and put them in orbit around the city. Tell them to raise hell with the Badawi Brigade where they can, but for the most part stay quiet until we call. I want to start making it hard for these guys to live here. And Papa, make sure none of this points back to you or your family."

Elias made mental notes then looked back at the locked door. "And the jailer?"

"This one is different. I'd like to walk in that room right now and kill the bastard for what he's done, but I need him. We have to let him cook for a while. I'll talk to him when he's ready. I have a strong feeling he will point us in the direction of the next strike."

15

Fayed slammed his hands on the desk. He reached for the paper and read the teletyped message again, hoping he had somehow missed some fine detail. He clenched his fists and balled up the paper, tossing it to the wastebasket, then stood, straightening his jacket. Normally his director would call him for an update, but not today. Today the man was waiting for him to personally debrief the situation to him and his staff—in the main conference room of all places, a spot where Fayed would be front and center before all of them.

It was a mistake. The women were becoming a vulnerability. They held little value in the larger scheme of things. As to why Abdul insisted on holding them, he didn't know. Leverage only had use when it came with a benefit. Now these women were making them the hunted in a place they should be in control. Fayed looked down at his disposable mobile and scrolled through his missed calls. Several were from numbers he recognized as Abdul. He shook his head, clenching his teeth. It frustrated him to no limits that the fool refused to use burner phones he'd provided to him.

Fayed gave him a list of rotating numbers and disposable phones to make their conversations impossible to track. Instead, Abdul held the same two to three phones, reusing them again and again. The fool had a greater fear that someone would plant a bomb in one of his mobile devices and blow his head off, the way the Israelis had done to Yahaya Ayyash in 1996. Spies had managed to plant RDX explosives in the terrorist's phone and monitored his calls day and night until the one time Yahaya picked up; a press of a button, and Yahaya's head was gone. Now, because of that, Abdul refused to rotate phones, ignoring the greater risk of his calls being traced all because of something he'd read about in a spy novel. The man's stubbornness was causing him more problems than he was worth.

Fayed was again damaged, his reputation once again at stake. Now he was in the uncomfortable position of explaining how fifteen hostages were located and recovered alive from a compound in Syria, how all of this was done by local police and without his office having any knowledge of it. His office and the local police were supposed to be working together. Why was Ziya Fayed, the head of Middle East Affairs and a direct liaison to the Syrian and Jordanian Police, left out of the loop on a successful rescue raid? Why? Did they question his loyalty? Fayed shook his head. Of course not. It is because local security forces had nothing to do with it. This was the result of the Americans operating under their noses.

His phone buzzed and he lifted it, seeing the caller ID was a number that Abdul frequently used. His director was not the only one wanting to know what happened. All of his careful planning and organization was being brought down by a single fool, one arrogant man who could not be reasoned with. For the life of him, Fayed could not figure out how. Moving down the hall, he pushed into the conference room. Instead of meeting with his director and his staff alone, he saw that they were joined by another man dressed in a black suit with a red tie. Watching Fayed enter, the men shifted in their seats and stood.

Before Fayed could react, his director turned. "Agent Fayed, this is Simon Arnet with Vatican Security. You may remember he reached out to us for assistance in the church kidnapping case," the director said, then waved a hand for the men to re-take their seats. The director pointed to Fayed as he continued speaking. "Inspector Fayed is our top resource in the region. I have asked him here to help bring us all up to speed on the quickly developing situation coming out of Syria."

Simon cleared his throat and looked across the table at Fayed. "First, we are very grateful for the release of the Sisters, but—"

"Sarah Donovan, of course. The American is still missing," the director said, finishing the man's sentence. "We are still looking into that; the women are now under police protection and we will have an agent of our own there as soon as he can make the flight from Tripoli."

"Excuse me if this is a breach of protocol, but how were the women found? You said it was a local police raid, a rescue of sorts. I was under the impression that they were not very effective in the region."

At this, the director turned and looked at Fayed to

respond. Fayed swallowed dryly and said, "They are not traditional police. After the rise of the civil war, most of their duties were turned over to government security forces, as many of the police officers were moved into handling conflicts on the front lines."

Simon looked down at a spiral notebook then back up at Fayed. "So these security forces, they were able to locate and free the sisters. What was your role in all of this then? Were you given advanced notice of the raid?"

The director turned to Fayed and nodded for him to continue. Fayed pursed his lip, upset at having to divulge so much information to a relative stranger. There was no point in lying; the statements would be made readily available to the press within hours, and he had to find a way to turn things around. "Early reports of a police raid have been misleading. The freed women—at least in preliminary interviews—have stated that it was two men. Two men with faces covered—"

"Only two men?" the director said, turning to look at Fayed with surprise. "Are you sure? The initial assessment said there were eight dead hostiles and fifteen hostages rescued. This is an awfully large accomplishment for two men."

Fayed shook off the question. "I understand, sir. The women could be mistaken. The attackers' faces were covered with black hoods and night vision devices. It's possible they saw multiple men at different times—that could explain a discrepancy in numbers. Also, you must consider they are in shock. It is possible that a local militia group did the initial fighting, and these two were the ones to make contact with the women."

Simon nodded in agreement. "That does seem

reasonable. But still, it is rather fascinating that a group would take on such an endeavor and then leave empty-handed. Why would two men—or a local militia—go to the trouble then vanish? Are they possibly a special weapons team? Is this something more organized than we are willing to consider?"

Fayed clenched his jaw. "There is more; they didn't leave empty-handed. A man was taken prisoner. The women saw him bound, gagged, and taken away by the same men who freed them. The women were left alone for some time before the police arrived."

Simon's head perked up and his eyes tightened. "Who was this man they took?"

"The women identified him as their jailer."

"Ahh," the director said, his head nodding as if he'd stumbled onto the correct answer of a pub trivia question. "So, it's possible they were not after the women at all. Perhaps this was a rivalry amongst groups, the jailer was the target all along, and we have just reaped the benefits. That would explain why the women were left unattended."

Fayed pursed his lips with a sudden thought of a way out. A way to save face on his perceived intelligence failure. He rubbed his chin and smiled, turning to the director. He would play to his superior's vanity. "Yes, sir, I think you are correct. This appears to be exactly what is in motion here. A territorial dispute among rival factions, the jailer was the true target, the women nothing more than collateral."

The director grinned. "Then we have to take advantage of this, Fayed. I want you to travel there immediately. You must gather everything you can about these people and this location. Do whatever you need to resolve the disposition of Sarah Donovan and the other Western women."

"But, sir, Albahr is a war zone. It's hardly safe for an investigation. Perhaps I could interview the women once they are taken out of the region."

The director shook his head. "No, Fayed, this is your case; you should be the one to solve it. Go find Sarah Donovan." He smiled and looked up at Fayed. "Bring her home to us."

"How? There is no structure. We have no legal authority there. I feel it's best to stay away."

"Nonsense," the director said. "I'll contact our friends at the UN. We already have some teams on the ground; they'll make sure you have a full police escort. You'll be treated like royalty all the way."

Sighing and feeling defeated, Fayed bit his lower lip and folded his hands in front of him. He shook off his superior's offer. Bringing others into the fold would complicate his dealings with Abdul. Fayed raised his hand in surrender. "No, you're right. This is my area of expertise. I'll make the contacts and I'll make the trip. I apologize for doubting your recommendation, Mister Director."

The old man smiled wide. "Yes, of course, you are the expert when it comes to the conflict zone. Make your arrangements and travel at once. Do us proud."

16

J amal was fastened to a hardwood chair—his ankles taped to the chair legs, his arms forced out in front of him and zip-tied to grommets in the table's surface. After several hours of being confined in darkness, a single light hanging over the table was illuminated, brightening the space. He felt pain behind his ear where he'd been struck during the attack. His neck was stiff, and his voice was hoarse from thirst and the screaming he'd done through the night. He blinked his eyes rapidly, trying to focus.

Tommy Donovan and Elias entered the room, Elias wearing a face-concealing black mask, Tommy dressed in a dark shirt. They didn't speak. Tommy walked to a corner of the room and removed a second chair then dragged it across the floor, allowing the old wood to scrape and scratch over the rough stone surface. Elias walked around and stood directly behind the prisoner as Tommy slid the chair across from Jamal then sat down.

Flexing, he folded and placed his arms on the table and stared at Jamal sitting across from his, still not speaking.

Jamal's head twitched nervously. Sweat beaded on his forehead as he tried to swallow through the dryness in his throat. He turned his head to try to see behind him before looking back to his front. "What do you want?" he asked in Arabic.

Tommy grimaced and asked in English if the man was thirsty. Jamal nodded eagerly, and Elias stepped forward. He draped a towel over the man's head and yanked it back, dumping the contents of a water bottle over the prisoner's face. Jamal struggled, choking and gagging as he fought the restraints and the drowning sensation.

Just before the man succumbed, Elias snapped the towel away and took a step back, holding a position just behind the prisoner. Tommy sat as stoic as he'd been before, waiting for Jamal to recover from his spasms. When the man looked back to the front, he was gasping for air, drool pouring from his mouth. The prisoner lifted his head and looked at Tommy with pleading eyes. Slowly, he focused on the man across from him, his lower lip quivering.

"The women we rescued told me your name is Jamal. They called you the Jailer. They told us the things you did to them. The things you allowed to be done to them. Do you know why you are here, Jamal?" Tommy asked. "Do you admit to the things you have done?"

Jamal shook his head. "It's not me. I've done nothing. Abdul is the one you want."

"I see," Tommy said. "Tell me about Abdul, this man whose name you readily speak."

The man's eyes widened. "Abdul Nassir, what is there to tell?"

Elias stepped forward and slapped the man's head with his open palm. "The Hyena?" he asked. "He's dead."

Jamal turned away, shaking off the slap and surprised by the men's reaction to Abdul's name, and having heard the Hyena moniker before, the prisoner's head dropped, knowing he had already made a grave mistake. He'd said too much without even considering the consequences. "I don't know that name *Hyena*. Only the name Abdul Nassir. That is who I answer to. I was holding the women for Abdul. I only know Abdul Nassir."

"This Abdul, tell me about him. What does he look like?" Tommy asked, leaning in.

"He's nobody. He's old and bald, he's fat, he wears a scar on his head."

"A scar from a bullet?" Tommy asked.

Jamal shook his head. "I don't know. I was told that Abdul was wounded during the Iraqi war in a battle against the infidels. Badly wounded, but he survived, killing all of the enemy soldiers."

Tommy clenched his fist and glanced over Jamal's shoulders at Elias, who signaled for him to move on. "The women, where did they come from?" Tommy asked.

Jamal looked away and shook his head.

Tommy scowled. "Are you thirsty?" he asked.

"No, no, no," the man shouted, leaning forward as Elias pulled the towel over his face and yanked him back. Another bottle was drained and the man began sobbing. His head hung heavily while he coughed and hacked onto his lap. When he looked back up, snot ran from his nose.

"Jamal, I need you to stop thinking that I don't know the answers to these questions." Tommy paused to allow Jamal to stop hacking. "I am only asking you for confirmation and to see if you are being honest with me. Now I don't have a lot of time." Tommy paused again and placed his .45 on the table. Jamal's eyes became fixed on it. "I met an associate of yours recently. He was not cooperative." Tommy stopped again, taking in a deep breath and exhaling loudly. "Now, let us try again. The women, where did they come from?"

"From the church in the city center. Everyone knows this."

Tommy pulled a notebook from his thigh pocket and placed it on the table, flipping through pages for show as the prisoner watched him nervously. Pretending to check his notes against the things Jamal was telling him. Tommy feigned looking over an entry then nodded and removed a pen from his shirt pocket and jotted several lines into the notebook. Then he looked back at Jamal. "We removed fifteen women from your facility. Where are the others?"

Jamal's jaw clenched. He opened his mouth to speak, but before he could, Tommy interrupted him. "Think very carefully, Jamal. Where are the western women?"

"Not all of them were brought to me. Abdul held onto the three others, the Western women. They are more valuable as ransom. Only the ones to be sold on the market or used locally are sent to me."

"Like cattle, aye, Jamal?" Tommy said, taking the .45 back into his hand and squeezing the pistol grip tightly until his knuckles were white.

"It's just the way it is. I don't make those decisions. The Western women are negotiated for."

Tommy nodded his head as if he understood the comment and smiled. "Very nice, Jamal, you are learning." Tommy paused and wrote another set of notes then looked up. "Now, I need you to think hard before answering. Where did he send the other women?"

Jamal froze. Tommy saw the look of terror on the man's face, but he couldn't tell if it was because he didn't know, or if he was afraid to give up the information. The man clenched his eyes shut and stuttered a response. "I don't know for sure."

"Are you thirsty, Jamal?"

This time the man didn't scream; he clenched his face and tried to hold his breath. Elias draped the towel and yanked back his head violently, waiting for the man to stop holding his breath and gasp for oxygen before draining the bottle. Jamal propelled forward, choking and coughing the water from his lungs. He begged through the restraints for mercy.

"Why are you fighting me on this, Jamal? I know you are a coward. Why else would you have been left to tend to caged women? Why are you not a soldier with the others? Because you are a coward, Jamal. You stay back and kick at the cages of mothers while others fight. Just tell me what I want to know and I'll leave you."

The restrained man began to sob again, his head hanging forward, no more strength left to hold it up. Tommy looked across at the defeated man. He was pitiful, yet Tommy felt no mercy for him. "I'm going to ask you a final question. You will decide how I respond to the answer."

Jamal pried his head up from his chest and locked eyes with his captor.

"Where is Abdul?"

The prisoner flinched, looking away. "He can be in many places; he travels... he moves often."

Tommy nodded in mock approval. "Where does the money go?"

Jamal clenched his eyes shut and hung his head. He sighed. "Duma Street, across from the Al Kishwa Hotel. All the money goes there."

Tommy grinned and stood from his chair. He turned toward the door. Elias tossed the towel on the table and both men left the room together. They switched the lights off and the room again fell in darkness. The sobs of Jamal sounded behind them as Tommy climbed the stairs and entered back into the parlor.

"I need you to reach out to Kohen, find out if Abdul is the Hyena."

Elias nodded. "And Jamal?"

Tommy looked at the floor. "I'd like to kill him but you know we can't do that. What do you know about the area he mentioned, Al Kishwa Hotel?"

"It makes sense. It's in the secure district, busy. Lots of government forces, Russian convoys, checkpoints, roadblocks. It's a loyalist area; a good place for them to hide if they want to avoid trouble."

"I see." Tommy dipped his chin and closed his eyes to think. "Did you have any luck recruiting?"

"That was an easy job. There are many here looking to fight for the right cause."

"Good." Tommy paused thinking. He rubbed his chin then continued. "Find a few men you can trust. Have them move Jamal outside the city and prepare to cut him loose. Ensure that he is blindfolded and cannot identify them—"

"And let the tracking chip do its work," Elias interrupted. "Then we follow the rat back to the nest. You forget, Tommy, I'm the one who trained you."

Tommy smiled. "Yes, it's good to have you with me. Is the safe house ready?"

"My father opened it and delivered the weapons and explosives this morning. We can move at any time. It is a high-walled home, near the city center."

Tommy walked to a corner of the room and unzipped a small bag. Inside was a satellite phone, the same one given to him by O'Connell's men. "I have to make a call, then we'll leave."

Almost six thousand miles away a telephone rang in the middle of the night. James O'Connell rolled to his side, looking at the number on the satellite phone beside him. He'd been expecting the call. Reaching with his arm, he knocked over the alarm clock before removing the phone from its charging cradle. He let it rest in his palm for several seconds before pulling himself to a seated position then put the phone to his ear. "Yes."

"It's started," Tommy said.

Tommy heard the listener on the other side of the line exhale then take in a deep breath. "So that was you on the news. They said something about women being freed from a terrorist compound. Was your sister with them?"

"No, but I'm still looking."

"Tommy, you were right," O'Connell said barely

above a whisper. "Soon after you left someone started pinging the databases searching your name and your past. Just like you said, they opened an inquiry. I have a friend at the FBI. He's low level but... son, you were spot on. People have been looking into you and your past, but it goes deeper than that. Somehow—and I have the highest confidence in my staff—but somehow they traced you through Jordan."

"Who?" Tommy said. "I need to know who is looking and how it was leaked."

"I can't be certain. Not yet. I talked with a few friends and opened another investigation into Junior's death and I asked about the Ground Division. People are getting nervous."

"I understand."

"They aren't happy you're there. Whoever you're after has contacts, and he's using them. The one you're looking for, he's connected to DC somehow. His rise to power, it wasn't an accident. None of it was; he was backed."

"And the last thing these special benefactors want is to see that one of their chosen beneficiaries is responsible for sacking a church and kidnapping nuns. Well, I don't care."

"Tommy, I won't be able to protect you."

"I'm not asking for protection, just the names. Can you find out who is looking into my past?" Tommy said.

The old man paused. Tommy could hear his breathing on the other end of the phone. "It won't be easy," O'Connell answered.

Tommy let the phone rest in his hand as he looked at his watch then across the empty room. "Did they get to you? Are you okay?"

"Don't worry about me; I'm still in the clear. I've backed way off, but my man is still listening."

"I need you to do more digging, find out how they tracked me. I want to know who and how. If you can be discreet, contact Simon Arnet at the Vatican. He may know; they have more insight than they admit to. Drop the name Abdul Nassir and see what pings back." Tommy paused again. "Colonel, be careful. I'll call when I know more," he said, disconnecting the line and powering off the phone.

17

The black Mercedes rolled up to the security checkpoint. Ziya Fayed did not like having guns pointed in his face. Especially when they were guns in the hands of Syrian security forces, men known to switch sides at a moment's notice. They were at a checkpoint just outside of the international airport. The city center was well guarded these days, and as wary as Fayed was of the security forces, it was where the women were being processed before their release.

The vehicle was armored with bulletproof glass and doors, the wheels equipped with run-flat tires. Without looking, he knew there would be another security vehicle behind him, and a police escort vehicle to his front. Why he was being stopped for inspection while under armed escort was beyond him. Probably just another jurisdiction dispute in a city under siege. There were always problems between the military, charged with the defense of Albahr, and the local law enforcement, which was more concerned with day-to-day security.

A soldier in an olive-green uniform walked to the passenger window and looked inside, inspecting the interior. "Papers," he said without making eye contact.

Fayed handed over his passport booklet and Interpol access badge. The soldier took the documents and eyed them closely before holding them to Fayed's face for closer inspection and comparison. He grinned and handed the papers back before waving to the men at the barrier. "Sorry for the delay, Inspector."

Retrieving his papers, Fayed rolled up the window. The driver pulled through the barrier, passing a Russian Army BTR-82A armored vehicle, the large eight-by-eight-wheeled armored beast that stood watch over the checkpoint. Two Russian soldiers hardly looked up at them as they passed. The inspector cursed his luck, not happy being sent back to this place. The driver accelerated and made the turn onto Duma Street, weaving through traffic before rolling to a stop in front of the Al Kishwa Hotel.

Fayed turned to the driver and handed off a folded bill. "Keep the car close, I don't intend on staying long. I will be leaving as soon as possible," he said, exiting the vehicle. A man in a black cap had already retrieved his bag from the trunk and was guiding Fayed toward the entrance. The inspector fought the urge to turn around and look at the building behind him. He knew Abdul's men would be out front, noting his arrival and reporting it back to their boss.

Fayed kept a suite permanently reserved at the hotel, a security measure that he demanded. Some would say it made more sense to rotate rooms and hotels to make his travel plans less predictable. But Fayed preferred to use the same room and have his people sweep it just hours ahead of his arrival.

His phone rang and he stopped near the entrance, fishing it from his pocket. He shielded the screen from the bright sunlight and saw Abdul's number. He looked back up and could see the porter moving ahead down the hallway, directly to his usual room located on the first floor. Fayed gritted his teeth and answered the phone.

"You've arrived. I thought I told you to call me as soon as you were in country."

Frustrated, Fayed moved away from the hotel entrance and stood along the building's tall exterior walls. His eyes scanned the structure across the street. Men in dark clothing moved in and out of double doors, most of them openly carrying weapons. "I've just arrived at the hotel. Why the impatience?"

"Circumstances have changed."

"Yes, I am quite aware."

"Are you? I've lost another property and more men, and there are whispers on the streets that Americans may be involved. I need to know who is doing this. Is it Mossad? CIA? Has someone sent a hit team after me?"

Fayed sighed and shook his head as he turned back toward the entrance, where doormen were unloading a white suburban, transferring luggage to a cart. "I have a meeting with the local police chief. I will be fully briefed on the current situation—once I know more, I will report it all back to you. You need to relax."

"Very well, I want a full briefing at dinner then. I will be traveling in from Damascus within the hour. I will have the location sent to your driver," Abdul answered.

"That's impossible, we can't be seen in this city

together with everything that has happened. Besides which, I plan to depart Albahr right after the meeting. It'll have to be another time."

Fayed heard a sadistic laugh on the other end of the phone before the voice came back cold. "You will not go anywhere until we've spoke face to face. I want guarantees that you have this under control. I don't want to lose another property, not one more man. Do you understand me?"

The investigator exhaled and squeezed the phone, his face angry. "Fine, dinner, then I must take my leave—"

The air suddenly became a white-hot inferno, a bright flash of white and red. Fayed was lifted off the sidewalk and tossed against the hotel's exterior like a rag doll. Time seemed to slow but Fayed never lost consciousness. His head was alive with sounds, a loud ringing and the screams of everyone around him. He rolled to his side and could see that the Suburban was still to his front. The porter crouched behind it, the luggage cart tipped on its side. Doormen were running left and right, pulling people into the hotel lobby.

Then he heard the gunfire. The distinctive report of AK47 rifles. Still on his side, Fayed drew his pistol. Across the street, he watched gunmen storm out of the double doors with red-and-white checkered scarves covering their faces. As soon as the men emerged they were cut down, ambushed by hidden men. He forced himself to a knee, scanning, and saw two men in dark vests and black masks. They had rifles to their shoulders, rapid-firing into Abdul's building. He squeezed his service pistol, contemplating what to do, when a heavy machine gun opened fire from his right.

Ducking down, Fayed turned and saw a Russian armored vehicle approaching, the gunner firing blind into the street, taking out everything, providing supporting fire to the men in red scarves. He felt a tug at his jacket and stared into the face of a porter trying to drag him into the lobby. Fayed stared at the man with wide eyes then turned to follow him inside.

18

M en moved aside as a silver Volvo cargo van wove its way through alleyways, navigating the back streets toward Duma Street. In the back, Tommy sat on the floor with his knees pulled up to his chest. He wore a vest with two incendiary grenades clipped to the front, just above his abdomen, and a Russian suppressed 9A-91 carbine assault rifle in a holster under his armpit. Elias sat across from him.

"You were right about the route; this city's perimeter has more holes than a golf course," Tommy said, pulling his grime- and stain-covered canvas coat shut and fastening the bottom snap. "Where'd you get this filthy jacket? It smells like a donkey crawled up another donkey's ass and then died in it."

"Hey brother, you said you wanted a foul jacket; now that is one foul jacket." Elias laughed, watching his friend close the final snap, then his face turned serious. "I could go with you. My men are more than capable of running the diversion."

Tommy shook his head. "No, I need you out front directing the attack. Besides, I do better on my own. That way I know everything in front of my barrel is a target."

The van drove around a curved street then stopped before backing into another alleyway, this one shaded from the sun. The driver glanced back and nodded. Elias acknowledged the man then crawled across the floor and opened the sliding door before looking back at Tommy.

"Is everything in place?" Tommy whispered.

Elias frowned and tightened his brow. They'd already discussed the plan in every detail, but being professionals, it never hurt to hear it out loud one last time. "My men are waiting on the opposite side of the block. The car bomb is already in place near the intersection. It will be loud, but my man assures me the blast will be manually remote-triggered and directed up to minimize casualties. Then my teams will direct fire from two sides of the building, pulling all the guards to the front."

Tommy nodded. "Once the attack starts, who will they call for help?"

Shaking his head, Elias looked to the other man in the van. "Most likely they won't call anyone. The bomb will bring in all the attention and support they need. For sure local security forces, but eventually the Russians."

"Okay," Tommy said. "And the rest of the building?"

"There will be two guards outside the back door, with another inside. Those guards may move inside or stay in position. Once inside, there is a large entryway with a stairwell on the right. Follow it directly to the top; avoid the other floors. The money room and offices are at the top at the end of a hallway. Get in and get out," Elias said.

Listening to Papa reciting back the full plan, as they'd

done countless times before, gave Tommy a comfortable feeling of déjà vu—they were back on mission and ready to do some serious damage. Elias caught his moment of reverie and snapped him back. "Tommy, we will stay for no more than five minutes then disappear. When the security forces arrive, we will have to pull back. You have to be moving by then. We have no back up, no quick reaction force, and no plan B. If we make a mistake, we're dead. Are you sure this is worth it?"

"If we want to hurt them—this is where we do it." Tommy looked at the van and said, "You have to get rid of this. We can't leave them anything to trace back to you and your people."

"It's taken care of. We'll torch this one and egress will be by foot. I hope you've memorized the route. My people will dump their weapons in the sewer and vanish into the crowds. I'll have a second van meet you at Monument Park to guide you to the hide."

Tommy stretched out his hand and took his friend's. "Good luck, brother."

Elias looked at his wristwatch and pressed a button, starting a countdown timer. "The fuse is lit—five minutes, my friend, then we have to go," he said, leaving the van to join two other armed men already in the alley.

Tommy turned and dropped his boots onto the gravel surface. The hot air smelled of sewage and burning rubber. He looked down at his own watch and stepped off. Walking hunched over, he moved along the building and turned a corner, following the building's wall to the back. His hair was pulled down over his eyes, and a matted scarf hung sloppily around his neck. He focused on the ground, walking ahead with an exaggerated limp.

He spotted the far-off doorway and veered toward it. He felt the tingle in his body, the adrenaline loading his system, same as with every strike. He was ready. His targets became objects. No longer human beings, they were just things that needed to be moved so he could meet his objective.

As Elias had predicted, there were two shaggy, black-bearded guards with red scarves around their necks. The men stood near the back entrance, both armed with rusty Kalashnikovs dangling loose. They weren't professionals, probably local militia or recent volunteers assigned to the demeaning task of door guard. It didn't matter to Tommy; they would fall just the same. The bearded man nearest Tommy looked up and watched him approach. The man grinned and tapped the guard beside him. Both seemed amused at the sight of a disabled person struggling to walk.

Tommy paused and put a hand on the stucco wall, feigning to catch his breath and balance. He heard one of the guards call out at him, shouting obscenities, ordering him to turn around and go away. One thing Tommy hated as much as terrorists was bullies. Hearing the man's shouted obscenities and watching his exaggerated hand gestures gave Tommy an internal smile. This would be a two-fer for humanity.

Keeping up the hobo act, he took another staggering step forward. The second man laughed with amusement as the first stepped away from the stoop. Holding his rifle in one hand, he continued his shouts, occasionally looking back to his partner, both men laughing as he moved toward Tommy. The man let his rifle hang from a sling as he shouted, kicking gravel in Tommy's direction.

He spat on the ground and cursed him. Tommy flinched away, letting the bits of gravel hit his pants as he continued his path forward, seemingly unaware of the danger.

The man gripped the rifle and raised it to strike Tommy with the buttstock just as a large explosion ripped through the air and reverberated the ground. Windows in the upper floors of the building shattered from the shockwave, bits of glass and debris raining down. The threatening guard's eyes went wide. He dropped the rifle and held a hand over his head, looking at the billowing cloud forming in the sky. Tommy, fully prepared for the moment pulled a knife sheathed at the small of his back. With a practiced lunging step forward, he caught the guard under his jaw and rammed the blade home, allowing it to pierce through the top of his victim's skull.

He tossed the man aside and flung open his jacket, bringing up the carbine assault rifle. Two controlled bursts, and the remaining guard fell with hits to the upper chest and face. Tommy didn't wait for confirmation of the kill. He snatched his knife back from the first tango's head and moved to the door. He grabbed at the steel lock mechanism and pushed, surprised to find it unlocked. He stepped inside and saw a man crouched in the entry, looking toward the front of the building where Elias's militia team was now filling the street with a deadly barrage of crossfire. A single suppressed round to the back of the lone man's head knocked him to the ground, the body rolling forward unnoticed.

Leaving the entryway, he moved toward the stairwell to his right. He heard footsteps racing down, and he ducked to the side, making himself small with the 9A-91 at the ready then tucking into a corner as two men rushed out. They hardly had time to identify the dead man on the ground before Tommy had them zeroed and was stitching rounds into the sides of their bodies. The men fell with a thud in the entrance, and Tommy stepped over them into the dusty stairwell. The surface of the poured-concrete steps was dry and brittle. Every window in the stairwell was shattered allowing unfiltered bright light, dust and smoke from the blast to pour in. The hollow space echoed sounds of shouting and the occasional breaking of glass from above. He paused long enough to determine the area clear before walking up, leading the way with the carbine sweeping a path as he moved.

Gunfire increased from the street, and he heard the thumps of a heavy weapon; the police or Russian military had arrived on scene. Elias would be forced to pull back. Tommy turned, lowered his caution, and began to take the stairs two at a time, racing for the top floor. The distinctive smaller explosions from fragmentation grenades cracked in the distance. Tommy ran past closed doors and moved to the top step. A wooden barrier hung partially open. He pushed it in and heard the zip of a bullet fly by his head. Wood splintered from the doorframe and Tommy dove to the ground, firing at the flash of movement to his front. The 9A-91 carbine assault rifle held a 20-round box magazine, and Tommy bled through half of them, firing blind into the hallway.

He felt a stinging pain in his side and a tug at his clothing. Landing hard, he rolled through the fall and came up to his knees, placing more shots into the already crumpling figure to his front. He stepped to his feet and placed a gloved hand to his side. He brought it up, seeing the crimson traces of blood against the tanned leather. Tommy shook it off then continued on. He kicked in the first door to find an empty room filled with stacked boxes. He moved past and continued to clear the spaces until he reached a large room at the back of the hallway. The door was hanging open, the previous gunfight having damaged a hinge. The thump of a 12.7mm machine gun outside reminded Tommy that he was out of time.

Tommy rushed the door. Inside was a cowering man; a handgun lay on a tabletop beside him. The man backed away, his arms up, pleading. Tommy shot him twice in the chest. Hearing a whimper, Tommy spun to the back of the room. On the ground, chained to the floor, was a blonde-haired woman. She cowered and looked away, crying. In English, she begged him not to hurt her. Tommy stepped forward, looking over his shoulder to verify the rest of the room was clear. His heart raced as he reached down and brushed the woman's hair away. It wasn't Sarah.

The gunshots outside turned to screams and sirens. He was out of time; if he was going to get the woman out of here, he wouldn't be able to search the room for information. He had to go. Tommy pulled his knife and pried the rusted hasp from the floor, freeing the woman. He pulled her to her feet and looked her in the eye. "Can you walk?" he asked.

She looked back at him with a blank gaze. She nodded her head and gripped his arm tightly. Pulling away, he moved back to the door and closed it then turned to a large, open window covered with a white sheet. He ripped the sheet down and could see the roof of the neighboring building only a short drop below them. He pushed the woman ahead of him, and not taking time to ask her, he grabbed her wrist and lowered her down to the opposing roof.

Tommy stopped and turned back toward the dead man. Sweeping the room a final time, he found random paperwork on the desk. Behind it were two steel safes. He wanted to look inside for anything that could lead him to the other women, but knowing his time was up, he popped both incendiary grenades and rolled them to the back, setting the room ablaze. If he couldn't have whatever was important enough for the Badawi to lock in a safe, then Tommy would destroy it. He turned back then dropped to the adjoining roof alongside the woman.

The narrow rooftop was packed with antennas, satellite dishes and clotheslines. He dragged the woman behind him, snatching a black garment from a line as he moved along and pulled her into cover around a corner. Tommy could see that she was close to full shock, her face pale white with her pupil's wide. He needed to get her someplace fast while she was still on her feet. He pulled the garment over the woman's head and straightened it to ensure she could see him. Mindful of the pain in his side, Tommy eased into a sitting position and, for the first time, opened his jacket to check his wound. The bullet had cut through the fat on the side of his abdomen, blood was leaking from both ends.

"You're hurt," he heard the woman gasp.

Tommy nodded, then removed his crumpled scarf and tucked the ends into the bullet hole, wincing from the pain. He took a deep breath and looked back at the woman. "It's fine. I was wanting to get rid of the love handles anyway."

He forced himself back to his feet and continued leading the woman away. They followed a walkway onto another rooftop and then to a fire escape, taking them down into a crowded street. Police cars raced past with sirens wailing. Crowds of people pushed by, trying to move away from the chaos. Tommy closed his stained jacket back up. Keeping the woman close by his side, he merged them into the procession of people. He spotted policemen running on the opposite side of the street with rifles up. A Russian armored vehicle convoy rushed past them. Tommy quickly found that traveling with the woman was a benefit. All of the police were searching for attackers, single armed men, not a couple moving together within a crowd of civilians.

At the end of the street, Tommy pulled away from the main road and moved them toward a green park. Monuments lined the sidewalk and people stood along the curb, still watching the chaos of events in the distance. He heard men say there was an attack against the hotel and that neighboring buildings were on fire. Tommy ignored them and kept moving toward a stand of Turkish pine trees before dropping to a bench and letting the woman sit beside him on his injured side. He leaned back into the bench, exhausted from the gunfight, the pain in his side clouding his thoughts. He looked at her and asked her name.

"I'm Carol," she stuttered, then looked at his tattered and stained clothing, "Who are you?" she asked.

He ignored her question and grimaced away the pain. "Do you know Sarah Donovan?" Tommy said between labored breaths, keeping his eyes steeled on the distant mob, watching it slowly fade as the sirens wailed.

"Of course. I know Sarah. I was with her when we were taken."

Tommy turned to look at her. "Sarah is my sister."

Looking Tommy in the eyes, she said, "Yes, Sarah spoke about you."

"Do you know where she is?"

"No, we were separated. But Sarah said you would come for her."

"She did?" he asked, his expression softening.

Her head nodded. "She knew you would, that if nothing else you would come." The woman looked around. "She said nothing would stop you—that you'd die trying."

Tommy winced and swallowed hard, dropping his head at the words, in the knowledge that his sister hadn't lost faith in him. He took another deep breath and, with a grunt of pain, returned to his feet. "Come on, I have to get you somewhere safe."

He watched armed men moving through the park. A pair dressed in black with yellow insignia broke off from the group and turned toward them. Tommy looked away, leaning toward Carol, watching the men in his peripheral vision. The two were on the hunt, slowly moving through the anxious crowd, examining faces as they passed. One of them looked up and locked on Tommy's position.

"Stand straight up, they're on to us," he whispered to Carol, turning her so that her back faced the approaching men, shielding his movements. Tommy shifted his position and stood directly to her front and readied the suppressed MK23.

Carol looked down at the weapon then back to him with wide eyes. "Who are they?"

"Special police, paramilitary types; definitely no friends of ours."

"What are you going to do?" she whispered.

"I'm going to kill them."

Tommy kept his eyes in the distance while watching the two men approach from the corner of his vision. Carol began to tremble. Tommy gripped the pistol in his right hand and put his left hand on her shoulder, gently squeezing it.

"It's fine, close your eyes," Tommy whispered, keeping his own eyes engaged on the approaching men. They were now within fifty feet and closing fast, focused and moving directly toward them. Both policemen carried holstered weapons, hands resting on the grips.

When they closed to within twenty feet, the men stopped. The one to the left pointed at Tommy and began to speak while the other drew his pistol. Before the words could leave the first man's mouth, Tommy pushed Carol aside as he brought up his weapon. He fired four shots and paused. The first man was on his back, and the one on the right had bloody hands clasped around his neck. Tommy focused and fired a kill shot into the wounded man's face then turned, pulling Carol behind him.

Even with the suppressed rounds, the bodies on the ground drew attention. Women near the street began to scream, and the crowd was again in a panicked motion. Tommy heard a shout from behind him and spotted a blue Toyota van on a narrow access road. A man was leaned over the hood of the van while another waved toward him frantically. Papa's pickup crew had arrived.

Tommy turned and beelined directly toward them. He felt the air move by his head and heard the zip of a near miss.

Instinctively crouching, he saw a group of policemen firing at him from the main road. Looking ahead, he could see the man by the van returning fire with the AK47. Tommy, not wanting to be caught in a deadly cross-fire, gripped Carol tightly by the wrist and led her into the cover of trees while still moving toward the van. The gunfire intensified and was joined by wailing police sirens. The man by the van door began tossing canister grenades that popped and spilled dirty yellow smoke.

Taking the signal, Tommy turned to Carol and looked her in the eyes. "Run to the van, I'll cover you."

She returned his stare with glassy eyes but nodded. Tommy didn't wait to see if she was running. He brought up the 9A-91 and held the weapon at his shoulder, firing fast bursts into the officers. Blowing through a full magazine, he let it drop to the ground, reloaded, then fired again until the yellow smoke was engulfing him, screening his escape. He walked backwards, firing two more bursts before turning and running the rest of the way to the van with his head down. When he reached the vehicle, it was already moving. Carol was huddled in the back and Tommy dropped in beside her, hearing the door slam shut behind him.

Tires squelched on the pavement as the van raced away, moving down the access road and turning a corner before dropping into an alley, where another small car fell in behind them. Tommy rose to his knees, readying the 9A-91 to fire on it when one of the men shook him off. "He is with us, my friend," he said.

The van turned right onto a main street then left again into a tight alley, where it screeched to a stop. The car, a rust-red Fiat, pulled alongside, and the van door was again pulled open for Tommy and Carol to switch vehicles. In the back of the Fiat, Tommy quickly checked his weapons. Carol was sitting crunched over, her head pressed into Tommy's side with her hands gripping his left forearm in a death grip. He let the weapon rest on the seat beside him then put a hand to the side of her head and looked down at her.

"Are you oaky? Are you hit?"

She shook her head and pulled away, looking up at him. Her face was dirty and streaked from tears. Tommy tried to smile to reassure her, but instead pursed his lips, knowing it wouldn't do any good. "You're going to be okay. These are friends, and they'll get us somewhere safe." A muscle in her jaw twitched and she dipped her chin, acknowledging his words. She moved his left arm out of the way and curled up, taking shelter by his side. Tommy swallowed hard, flinching away, but then put his arm on the scared woman's back and allowed her to rest. "You're going to be okay," he said again, looking straight ahead as the small car left the congestion of the city and headed toward the safe house.

19

The situation was changing rapidly. Sarah was bound and gagged, dragged from the room where she'd been kept, and then forced into the trunk of a large sedan. The car stopped several times in different locations, moving so frequently she lost track of the amount of time she'd been in the trunk. She heard crunching gravel under the wheels of the car and saw the glow of the tail lights. The car came to a stop. Doors slammed and feet approached the rear of the vehicle.

When the trunk lid popped open, she rolled to her back, trying to focus on the figures above her. It was dark and the heavy clouds blocked out the moon. Men stood over her, looking down and speaking in Arabic. A bright light shone in her eyes, causing her to look away. Hands reached into the trunk, roughly grabbing and dragging her out, letting her drop to the ground with a thud.

She heard a voice in English; this one she recognized, but unlike the last time she had heard the man, Jamal, his voice was cold and hard. "We are taking you inside. If you ever wish to leave this place alive, you will do exactly as we say," he said, walking behind her as two larger men dragged her toward a stone building, her toes scraping against the gravel. "I don't care if you live or die. If it was my decision, I would bury you in the desert."

Sarah didn't speak. Her throat was dry, and she found words impossible to form. They pulled her through the building, passing through a large room filled with sleeping men, then down a long corridor and eventually tossed her against a wall, where an old woman with a silver head scarf hissed and grabbed her by the hair. The woman forced Sarah into a crouch and pushed her into a small room, where she smacked her body until she crumpled to the floor in a corner. She grabbed her wrists and bound them together with a plastic zip tie. Sarah looked up and could see that another woman was lying on the floor across from her.

The old woman shouted at Sarah in Arabic and kicked a waste bucket closer to her. The guards laughed as the woman yelled insults. Jamal smiled, shooing the woman away, then entered the doorway. Sarah slid away from him tighter into the corner, pulling her knees into her chest. Searching the room, other than the waste bucket, she found only a tattered blanket. She squinted, trying to focus on the second woman who was lying motionless on the floor.

"Water," she begged.

Jamal, still standing in the doorway, flinched at the words then looked down at her, disgusted. He tossed her a half bottle of water. "I should do with you as your people did with me," he said and spat at her feet.

Sarah took the bottle with her bound hands and

drank, coughing as she finished. "I don't know what you're talking about."

"Then you need to think hard. You need to tell me who is looking for you so we can end this."

Sarah looked down at her dark, blistered, dirt-covered feet then back up at Jamal. "What more can I do? I've already told you everything. Please just let me go."

The man smiled and shook his head.

Sarah looked at the other woman and suddenly recognized her as Abella. "What have you done to her?"

Jamal ignored the question and placed a black hood over the French girl's head. He then looked to Sarah, and using his left arm, he pinned her head against the wall then dropped a second hood over her head and cinched it tightly around her neck. "There is nothing left for you to worry about; your fate will be decided soon."

20

F ayed hadn't yet unpacked his bag. He left his room and waited in the lobby, watching the fire in the building across the street be extinguished. He intended to return to France as soon as he could catch a flight. He'd had enough and wasn't waiting around to be killed. Fayed moved out of the lobby doors and onto the sidewalk, stopping beside a uniformed officer. Speaking to his back, Fayed asked, "How bad is it?"

The officer turned and looked back at him. He shrugged. "So, I suppose our meeting is canceled then?" the policeman asked.

Fayed suddenly recognized the chief of police. He was scheduled to meet with him about the rescued women in a couple of hours. His curiosity turned to fear as he put the timing of the meeting and the explosion together. Was he being targeted, or was it a coincidence the building was hit as he arrived at the hotel? "Tell me, what happened here?"

"There was a car bomb, followed by an ambush on the residence across the street, but the attackers botched the placement. The blast wave was vicious, but fortunately most was directed away from the crowds on the street. Someone also set fire to the top floor. The rest of the building will be okay; the concrete construction prevented the fire from spreading."

Fayed focused on the building across the street and could see covered bodies on the ground in front of the doors. He counted at least six. "Are you certain that building was the target?"

The policeman glared at Fayed and rolled his eyes, not speaking. He looked at the inspector's dirty and dust-ridden clothing, the dark stains under the man's eyes. He laughed. "You had an up-close and personal view. You should be telling me what happened."

Fayed shook off the comment. "Did you catch the terrorists?" he said.

The man leaned in close, locked eyes with Fayed, and grinned. "Is that who you want to say did this? Is that what you are telling me that you saw? You saw terrorists? Then where are all the civilian casualties? Where are the dead bodies? Look around you, man, you know what they were after. Do you know what that place is over there? Do you know what they do there?"

Fayed shook his head, shocked at the officer's response. "No—what is it, an apartment building?" he lied.

The officer frowned. "No, not at all. And for the record, I have no intentions of getting my people involved in this. Consider the afternoon meeting canceled. I have already ordered the rescued women be evacuated to Damascus. If you wish to reschedule our discussion, you can contact me through the provincial office."

"Wait, before they get involved in what?"

The officer shook his head and scowled. "Another turf war, right? I am plenty aware of what goes on here. You don't have to poke fun, no reason to laugh at me and my people. I know that I have little to no control in this city.

"The women—fine, someone wants to throw me a gift and release them to me. Fine, I say; I will take the credit. I will keep them safe. But I know that it isn't about the women; it's just another move to weaken the opposition. An opportunity for more bloodshed."

"And who is the opposition? Who exactly are you speaking of?"

"Really?" the man said, grimacing at Fayed. "You dare play stupid with me on my own streets? You insult me as buildings burn in my own city. You play your games; play both sides, my friend, but do not insult me." The police chief turned to rejoin his men near a police car with a flashing blue light.

Fayed, feeling exposed and alarmed, reached for his phone, searching for the driver's number. "I need to leave the city," he said as soon as the call was picked up.

"I don't care if the routes are blocked, find a way."

The phone vibrated in his hand as a second call came through. Fayed gritted his teeth and switched to Abdul.

"What in the hell do I pay you for?" the angry voice demanded.

"This is not my fight; you are on your own."

The line filled with laughter. "My people are on the

way to the hotel. Stay in your room until they collect you."

"Where are we going?"

"Stop. You're not in charge here. If you want to keep your head, then return to your room. And wait for them."

21

Security vehicles raced over the dusty streets outside. The room was dark, only a small gas lamp in the corner to light the space. The windows were open and a slight breeze swayed the curtain. The safe house was nothing more than a two-bedroom home in a modest part of the city. High clay walls surrounded the perimeter and sides of the house. A large entryway was open, the gate long ago fallen away from decay and disrepair. The opening provided a wide view of the front street.

Tommy lay on his back, atop a wooden bench. His forehead beaded with sweat as an older man sutured his side. The man applied one last loop and knotted the final stitch before snipping the end. He dressed the wound with antiseptic and gauze then returned his things to a black leather bag, ignoring Tommy. He walked across the room and spoke in hushed tones to Elias then placed two bottles of pills on the table before leaving.

"You trust him?" Tommy asked, his head still swimming with the effects of the morphine.

"As much as I can trust any veterinarian, I guess."

Tommy laughed. "You hired a vet to work on me? Are the drugs at least made for people?"

Elias shrugged, lifting the bottle of pain killers and antibiotics, tossing both to Tommy. "Wasn't much of an alternative; people are lying low after that little war you started out there. Mohamed is the only guy I know that was willing to go out after dark." Elias grunted. "You didn't manage to grab anything of value from the building, did you? Or were you too busy blasting through the place like a bull in a china shop?"

Tommy shrugged, looking at the bottles and swallowing a pair of the pills dry. "There was nothing there, and not a lot of time to snoop. I spotted a pair of locked iron boxes. I tossed the thermites and bolted," Tommy said, grunting as he turned himself into a seated position. "If there was anything of value in that room, it's burnt to a crisp now."

"So just the girl?"

Tommy nodded. "Yeah, took the girl and a left a big load of hate behind."

Elias put a finger to his lips and pulled away from the window as the roar of a vehicle convoy moved past. Bright spotlights briefly lit the room with a halogen glow. The rumble of the engines faded and the convoy moved on. Elias pulled back the curtain and looked out before saying, "Russian presence patrols. We really poked the bear today."

"What relationship do they have with Badawi?"

"None that I know of. The Russians are here for themselves. What remains of that group functions in the security of their shadow. This is a known Russian sector, so nobody messes with it—we'll be safe here. The Americans won't drop bombs here, and most of the anti-government forces keep their distance out of fear of massive retaliations."

Tommy fetched a drinking glass from the table and took a sip of water. "Damn, you have any booze in this shithole?"

Shaking his head, Elias walked away from the window and opened a cupboard, retrieving a dark bottle. Tommy dumped the rest of his glass and Elias refilled it with Arak, a clear alcohol. Tommy took a quick gulp then urged for the glass to be refilled. After taking a deep breath, he said, "What will the Russian reaction look like?"

Elias smiled. "That bomb in front to the International Hotel was like taking a shit on the Russian Commander's front porch. They try to give the impression of stability in this sector. When a battle erupts in front of a hotel filled with dignitaries and visitors, it takes away that mirage. They will increase patrols, possibly make raids and arrests in the known hotspots around the city. Fortunately most of those places aren't any friends of mine."

"What about the church attack? That didn't hurt their feelings?"

"The paperwork was filed, brother."

"What the hell does that mean?" Tommy said.

"It means the Badawi took the appropriate measures to pay off the security forces. That's how things work here. You toss some coin in the right direction, and the authorities will look the other way."

"That's messed up," Tommy grunted.

"Yeah, well, talk on the street is that may be changing.

The Badawi interest in the human trafficking arena is causing a stink with the Russians—especially when it gives them a black eye." Elias nodded. "Look, we're living in a very fragile state of give and take here, man. All of these players living in the same house of cards. It takes a bit of mutual cooperation to hold it all together. Someone like you comes along and starts kicking walls down, it causes problems."

"What, is this like 1930s Chicago? Are we in a Mafia turf war?" Tommy tightened his brow and stared thoughtfully at the open window. "Maybe we can use that."

"Use it how?"

"We can get the other players to put pressure on Badawi to release Sarah and to get them out of the kidnapping business. I need to let them know what's going on. Make them aware of what I'm doing here, and why."

"And how the hell do you figure on doing that without getting yourself killed? You're already a target without giving up your identity."

Shaking off the comment, Tommy asked, "How's the girl?"

"She's resting. I already placed a call to Kohen. I have to warn you; his generosity is wearing thin. He wants to meet with you. He'll be here tonight."

Tommy grinned and adjusted his position to take pressure off his side. "Good, we can use him too. What did you find out about her?"

"Her name is Carolyn Beaufort. She is a Canadian aid worker. Carolyn was posted at the same church where Sarah was taken. A few days ago, all of the Western women were separated from the others—there were three of them in total. Carolyn was sent to the building on Duma Street. They told her she was going home, but that wasn't the case."

Tommy raised his eyebrows. "Then what was?"

"She was to be sold off, forced into a marriage with some big shot that likes to collect Western women as trophies," Elias said, frowning. "Sounds like we got there just in time."

"Does she know anything about the others? Where they were being held? Anything?"

"Not really." Elias shook his head. "A day earlier, she and Sarah were separated. They told Carol she was going home, and that nobody was coming for Sarah. She is still out there, but..."

"But what?" Tommy said, looking up.

"Jamal wasn't telling us everything. He had met with them on different occasions. Carol says she saw him at least twice. You were right about him; he's a scared rat. We followed him about a kilometer from where we dropped him. He made a phone call and was quickly picked up in a white station wagon. We followed it back to a compound just south of here. It sits on the city's edge, near a canal."

"An outpost?"

"Most likely. Lots of fellas in tracksuits, armed with AKs."

"You still watching them? Sarah could be there."

Elias grinned. "Yeah, could be. The place is heavily guarded. And these guys are pissed. Lots of traffic in and out. You kicked off something big when you set fire to that hornet's nest. I think that's what's got Kohen spooked. He has people working in this city, and now you've got every player in town on a manhunt."

"Chaos is good for business."

"Then business must be great because the city has been turned upside down since we hit Duma Street."

"Screw 'em. Take what little cash we have left, give it to your people and tell them to raise hell. I want it to look like a full turf war has been launched before we make our next move."

Elias grinned. "I've missed you, old friend."

"There is something else," Tommy said fishing the 'O'Connell Transport International' business card from his pocket. He looked at the card and turned it over, showing the scratched in writing on the back to Elias. "His name is Ali, if anything happens contact him, tell him you were with me and they'll help you."

Elias nodded and took the card reading the back before placing it in his breast pocket.

There was a low tap at the door. Tommy reached down and lifted his pistol as Elias did the same. The older man slowly moved to a side window that over-looked the entrance. He dropped his guard, unbolting and opening the door to a short man dressed in Arab garb: dark pants, a white cotton shirt, black vest, and a thick scarf around his neck. He had a round face partially concealed with a long gray beard. His skin was tanned and leathered from the sun. He stepped inside and his eyes scanned the room then stopped on Tommy. He looked back at Elias and said, "Is this the one causing all the trouble?"

Tommy squinted. "You're Kohen? I thought you'd be taller."

Kohen let out a gruff laugh and removed his jacket and the Shemagh from his neck. "I thought you'd be younger," the man said, stepping closer. "You've become a popular person these days."

"Not as much as you'd think. The women here won't even look at me."

The silver-haired man laughed and shook his head. He reached into his vest and withdrew a folded flyer. He straightened the paper and dropped it on Tommy's lap. "Oh, I would disagree."

The single-page document was printed on cream-colored paper. Across the top were several faction symbols. In the center of the page and enlarged, was a photo of Tommy. The photo was at least ten years old. His face was thinner and clean shaven, his hair short and close cropped. Below the photo in block letters was printed *Thomas Donovan*. Below that, Arabic writing filled the bottom of the page. Tommy read the document, his expression unchanging. "I can speak the gibberish, but I'm not able to read it. What does it say?"

Kohen grinned. "It names you an enemy of the people and offers a one-million Syrian pounds reward."

Handing the document to Elias, Tommy shrugged. "Million? What's that, like six bucks American?"

"It's about five thousand dollars," Elias answered.

Tommy's jaw dropped in mock surprise. "I feel insulted." He pointed to the flyer. "That's a government photo, and not from a passport. That was on my old military ID. How would they be able to get that?"

"Very good, Mr. Donovan. My agents asked the same question and are already looking. It would have to be someone friendly with your intelligence services. We did preliminary digging in open sources, and my people were unable to find that photo. As a matter of fact, we found no photos of you. Your personal records are buried deep, only accessed through secure channels."

"Part of the job, I guess." Tommy reached for a loose-fitting T-shirt and pulled it on, grunting as he lowered his arms, and looked up at Kohen. "But there is something else that is bothering me. How do they even know who I am? Only a handful of people know I entered the country. Even less know me by name. So who is feeding Badawi my information? How do they know it's me?"

The Israeli nodded and reached into his shirt, removing a small leather pouch. Inside were three pages folded together. "I can see you still have your wit and ability to ask the good questions. Anyone can kill, but to be an asset to me, you have to be a thinker. It is apparent that someone is helping them with intelligence."

Taking another long sip of the drink and finally feeling the pain in his body grow numb, Tommy asked, "What did you find out about the Hyena?"

"Ah yes," Kohen said, "We've confirmed the man you named as Abdul Nassir is the one you call *the Hyena*. We've tracked him for over a year now, based on interests of our own. He moves frequently, stays out of Albahr most of the year, only stopping in occasionally then quickly leaving."

"How the hell is he alive? I saw the bastard take a shot to the face," Tommy said.

"That question is irrelevant. What's important is that he is alive, and we do believe he is the one responsible for holding your sister. He is very good with his movements. My men are experts, and he has managed to vanish from their surveillance for weeks at a time on several occasions. But there is one means that he has failed to elude."

"And that is?" Tommy asked.

"Electronic surveillance. He frequently uses mobile devices. We've digitally paired his voice to several mobile numbers. We know his voice signature and can trace him through multiple databases. The interesting thing is that a high frequency of his calls originates from or are to a subject in Paris. The numbers change, but the voice on the other end remains the same.

"And more interesting, he made two phone calls earlier today. Both to a location in the Al Kishwa Hotel. One call immediately before your attack. And again another phone call immediately after. Someone appears to be keeping tabs on you, or there is a very strange coincidence."

"Do we know who he is calling?"

Kohen frowned. "Not yet, but we're still working on it. The second contact switches his number frequently and has only been traced through his association with Nassir. Even though Nassir sticks to known numbers, his phone is often powered off and he keeps his conversations short, so nearly impossible to locate. But there is another problem."

Tommy thought then said, "Let me ask you, Kohen, could we distribute some bounty flyers of our own? How about we drop our own reward for the Hyena. Make it an actual million dollars."

Kohen nodded thoughtfully. "It wouldn't have many takers; his people are loyal, and even if someone wanted the reward, the money would be useless here. The assassin would be dead before he could spend it." Kohen bit at his lower lip and scratched at his beard, picking up on the real effect the flyers would have. "But this may work to send a message. An arrogant one, but an effective message, nonetheless. Do you have a million dollars to offer?"

"No, but I have no intention of paying it out either. I want to put Nassir on notice, get him angry and draw him out. Also, if he thinks there is a price on his head, if he feels he is being hunted, legitimate or not, I think it will pull him closer to his home in Albahr, where he thinks he is safe."

The Israeli held his chin in his hands, looking down at the slate floor, then nodded slowly. He pulled a small notebook from his sleeve and scribbled onto the tattered pages. "I can make that happen quickly, but the flyer isn't the only reason I came here."

"The girl?"

"Yes, you'll have to hold her. The city isn't safe to try to move her, and won't be for several days."

Tommy sighed with irritation. "I'm planning to make things a hell of a lot worse."

"I thought you might be," Kohen said with resignation. "Would it be a wasted effort for me to ask you to hold off on what you have planned? Maybe to allow me to gather intelligence for you?"

Tommy shook his head. "No can do."

"In that case, maybe we can provide you assistance, help you end all of this sooner rather than later."

"And what would you want in return?" Tommy asked.

"I would like a heads up on your next move. It's embarrassing for a man like me to be surprised by a hotel bombing in the middle of his district. I'm not asking for permission, but a warning would be nice."

"Anything else?"

Kohen squinted and stroked his beard. "We want Nassir."

Tommy grimaced and studied Kohen's face. "You're serious. Why would you want the Hyena?"

Kohen nodded. "To us, he is just Abdul Nassir, the Butcher. He has a high value. Your sister is the reason you're here. I can help you find her location, I can provide the backup to secure her release, if you agree to work with us."

Tommy looked across the space to Elias, who was sitting at the kitchen table. The man shrugged a response. Donovan's head hung down while he bit at his lower lip. "We know of an outpost near a canal. Is she there?"

"We know of this place; it is the center of Nassir's operations."

"Is Sarah there?"

"It is likely. I'll need some time to confirm it. Give me a couple of days to move assets into place."

Tommy shook his head and grunted, rising to his feet. "You have hours, not days. I'll hit the compound in the darkest part of the morning. If you want to join in, have your people here, ready to go."

22

F ayed held a cigarette in his left hand, the phone to his ear with the other. He paced the room and pulled back the curtain, watching the flashing lights and vehicle convoys racing past. He nodded and spoke into the phone. "Yes, sir, I'm fine. Absolutely fine."

He shook his head and turned back, hearing a knock at the door behind him. "Mr. Director, I am okay. The blast was directed away from the hotel, the police quickly locked down the area, and everything is under control. Yes, sir, I will be returning to France as soon as possible."

He clicked the receiver, ending the call, and turned toward the door as it opened. Two men, clean-shaven and wearing tan canvas jackets and black slacks, entered the room. The two could have been twins, with very little to distinguish a difference between them outside of their height. Fayed recognized them immediately as part of Abdul's personal security guards. They were professionals, not Syrian or Arab. He knew they were Chechens, as Abdul liked to hire Muslim mercenaries from that region

—men who would be loyal to the dollar with no sympathies for local conflicts. Even though Fayed had seen the two before, he only knew them by their names and reputation for violence. The Basayez brothers, Aslan and Doku, were wanted in several countries. They were expensive and successful at accomplishing their tasks. Aslan, the eldest and larger of the two, stepped forward and pointed to Fayed.

"Mr. Nassir asked us to escort you to his location. Come now."

Fayed took a step back, still clutching the phone in his hand. "I'm sorry, but that is impossible; I have been recalled to France. I must depart immediately."

The big man shook his head, his hard jaw hiding any emotion. He casually opened his jacket, showing the grip of a concealed submachine gun. "Mr. Nassir demands it."

Fayed reached to grab his small travel bag, but the Chechen spoke again. "Leave it, you won't need anything. Our people will gather your belongings and have them moved."

"So, I won't be returning?" Fayed said, the tenor of his voice rising. Fayed knew that if Abdul had sent the Chechens then he must be in serious danger. If not, he would have sent the routine drivers, or regular body guards. He sent Chechens when he wanted something done, and he had made it personal.

"Come," the man said, stepping aside. Fayed flexed his arms, straightening his body and walked between them, striding quickly as he made his way through the lobby and past the porter, onto the night street. He tried to hide his fear of what was ahead of him. A convoy of black Range Rovers were parked in front of the hotel. A door on the center vehicle opened and Fayed was rushed inside. He sat back in the cool leather interior. The tall Chechen moved in beside him as the other moved to the front passenger seat.

Abdul had money and resources, and when it came to vehicles he spared no expense. The vehicles were top-of-the-line. They were armored and bulletproof, the windows tinted so dark it was impossible to see in from the outside, but clear as glass from within. The tires were heavy and designed to run even when flat. The Range Rovers pulled into traffic, racing away from the city center, following a canal eastward. They stopped at a Russian military checkpoint then to a badly potholed intersection that ran parallel to a canal. Fayed turned in his seat, examining the unfamiliar terrain; he'd rarely left the city. "Where are we?" he asked no one.

The bodyguard beside him grunted. "We are going to the villa that once belonged to an important man. It overlooks a village lost in the early fighting with the extremists."

"Once belonged?" Fayed asked. "Where is this man now?"

"Yes—this man left at the start of the conflict, when the war was just outside his home's gates. Nassir rents from him now." The man laughed. "He finds the price very reasonable."

Fayed nodded. "I see," he said, knowing the real owner was probably dead. They turned onto a street, passing through the ruins of a small village with destroyed military vehicles on both sides of the road. A battle had taken place here, a battle ignored as Fayed could clearly see the remains of a Syrian soldier sitting in the passenger seat of a transport truck. The convoy moved out of the village and onto a winding gravel path that traveled up the hill. He watched as large wooden gates were opened, allowing the convoy to enter the walled compound. Through the gate they followed an olive-tree-lined road to the top of the hill. "And Abdul is here?"

The vehicles stopped alongside a lit cobblestone walkway. The man turned in his seat just as Fayed's door was opened. "Yes, he is waiting for you."

As Fayed exited the vehicle, his eyes surveyed the property. Unlike other homes in the area that had faded due to a lack of maintenance, this one was well landscaped, with fountains and shrubbery. There was also a large number of guards armed with rifles and submachine guns, walking in roving teams. Fayed had never seen this place or known of its existence, and now that concerned him. He was always careful to not get too close. You have to be worried when you pierce to the center of a known criminal's life. To know things that they would kill to keep quiet. He was afraid now that this oasis in Abdul's life may be one of them.

They walked the winding path, which opened into a yard made of fine grasses and a stone patio illuminated by gas lamps. At the end of the patio was a short, stone wall with a view of Albahr expanding out from it. At the face of the wall stood Abdul. He was looking out over the city. The bodyguards moved Fayed closer then stepped away, ushering him forward. Abdul turned, hearing the footsteps behind him.

"Ah, the great Interpol inspector, my eyes and ears to the world against me."

Fayed shied away from the words, knowing of his recent failures. "Abdul, why did you send for me?"

The man didn't speak. Instead, he began walking the path toward the front of the large, stone villa. Fayed fell in beside him, walking slowly. Finally, Abdul said, "I've changed my mind about the women."

"In what way?" Fayed asked.

"You were right about them. I should have listened to you; they are bad for business. I should have stayed well clear of it. Let's get past these complications and turn a corner. I feel it's time to take a new direction, to go on the offensive." Abdul pulled the wanted poster from his pocket and handed it to the young investigator.

Fayed studied it, recognizing the photo of Tommy Donovan he'd sent to Abdul days ago. "I have to caution you—"

"You would be wise to hold your tongue," Abdul spat, his eyes cold. "My decision has been made."

Fayed paused and nodded. He was still somewhat confused, not sure what Abdul's plan was. He took a deep breath. "I see, but a wanted poster may not be enough to solve our problem. It may not be enough to end the attacks."

Abdul stopped on the path and turned toward the inspector. "You have failed to give me good information, Fayed. Of course this won't end the attacks; we are beyond that now. Your methods have failed, and I have found a more expedient approach."

Fayed swallowed hard, misunderstanding Abdul's words. "This is not what I do, I can't help you track this man down here, not in this city. I've helped you plenty in recent years, but fighting a war on the ground, I cannot help you with."

Abdul reached out and cupped Fayed's cheek, silencing him. "Yes, I understand. I don't need you for fighting."

"Then why am I here? What do you need me to do?"

"Walk with me." Abdul grinned, continuing on the stone path leading back to the front of the house. "A vehicle will arrive soon; take it to the outpost across the canal. The two remaining women are being held there. I want you to kill them."

Fayed's jaw dropped. He wasn't sure what to say, and he could see by Abdul's expression that he was serious—and also testing him. If he answered incorrectly he would die here on this stone path. Instead of speaking, Fayed dipped his chin. From behind Abdul he watched two men approach with Jamal, the jailer. The Jailer held a leather pouch and a suppressed pistol. Abdul stepped aside and put a hand on the Jailer's shoulder.

"Now, this is a loyal soldier, Fayed. You should watch Jamal and follow his lead."

Fayed stared at the bald man absently as he was passed the leather pouch. He opened it, finding a crucifix, a pair of wallets with local currency, and two passports—one American, the other French.

"What is this?" Fayed asked.

"These were the things taken from the women's rooms. When you are done, leave them with the bodies so they may be identified," Abdul said, giving instructions as if they were a recipe to baking a cake.

Fayed stared into the satchel. "This is your solution?" he asked.

"With the women dead, what will there be for them to fight for?" Abdul replied.

Lights shone on the path as a pair of vehicles stopped and men exited the lead and tail Range Rovers. Jamal grinned and handed Fayed the suppressed pistol.

"What is about to happen?" Fayed asked.

The Jailer laughed, looking to Abdul with a sadistic grin before turning back to smile, showing his stained teeth to Fayed. Abdul put a hand on Fayed's shoulder. "You will enter the vehicle and Jamal will take you to the women."

Fayed clenched his teeth, swallowing his fear, his hands shaking as he gripped the pistol. "There must be a better way," he said in a low voice.

Not flinching, Abdul grinned. "As I said, that is something you must do. Once this issue with the women is resolved, we will decide how to deal with the brother." Abdul waved a hand toward the vehicle. "Now you must leave."

"And where will you be?" Fayed asked, gripping the pistol, his eyes fixed on it.

"I will join you at the outpost shortly, but first I must see how to deal with this nuisance in my city. The mayor is not happy with us." Abdul turned away. He walked back toward the villa, leaving Fayed alone with Jamal on the cobblestone path looking at the Range Rover.

23

W ith no moon, the sky was coal black and the canal smelled like a monkey's ass in a hot zoo. The small boat drifted along the current-free water, sliding along the bank covered in high grass. Tommy was dressed in black with Ivan body armor covering his chest and night vision goggles pulled down over his eyes. The goggles were stolen from Iraqi troops and then purchased in the black market by Elias's people. They were old and not what he was used to but Tommy was thankful to have them. Elias was in the bow of the boat, lying on his stomach, guiding them to the shoreline.

The two men slid from the small boat in unison and dropped, without a sound, into the cool water of the canal. Elias shoved the boat toward the center of the channel, allowing the breeze to carry it away. Tommy fell to his belly, feeling the pain in his side from the still tender wound, stitched up only hours earlier. He pushed the pain aside and directed it to the enemy to his front. He crawled up the bank then took a position in the high, reed grass at the top. Elias moved farther to the right and covered his flank.

The outpost in front of them was poorly lit, he could hear a generator humming from the other side of the building. There were many approaches with almost no cover. It was an oddly conceived position with several avenues of attack. The building was once a cultural center, a large structure with an open gallery in the front, hallways and small offices in the back. Kohen had provided the intel on the layout, and as Tommy surveyed the structures, he could see that Kohen's briefing lined up true with what he was seeing. It was a nice spot for a library or museum but horrible for a fort.

The outpost was located on a point of land where the canal made a wide U, giving the men inside the false sense of being protected by the waters covering them on three sides. Tommy had already counted at least ten guards at the front of the outpost, most positioned in and around lazily constructed fighting positions and offset barriers. The main approach was fortified with a low, crumbling, ancient wall. There was an open gate where a road entered the outpost and formed a large circle drive-way. The drive itself was lined with several vehicles sporting mounted machine guns. More men patrolled along the road in pairs, and other guards stood static to the front of a small guardhouse placed halfway between the gate and the main structure.

He let his eyes scan the guard posts and immediately noticed the lack of binoculars and night vision devices. These men were comfortable here, they considered themselves the top of the pyramid. And for the most part they were right, with any opposing forces being tied up with the Russians and Syrian security forces. Tonight, though they would be tested.

Tommy flinched with the static pop in his earpiece. *"Vehicles on the move from the south approach."*

Kohen had men of his own positioned on the approach roads to the outpost, identifying vehicles on the east and southern approaches. Elias had local fighters in a ravine, a hundred meters away, all of them ready to move in when he gave the word to attack. Although working together, the teams had separate motivations. Tommy wanted Sarah, Kohen wanted the Hyena, and the local fighters wanted to kill as many of the criminals as possible.

Shifting his position, Tommy moved his optics to the gate and watched a convoy of two high-priced Range Rovers enter the outpost, the vehicles clouding the trail in dust. They pulled beyond the guardhouse and stopped close to the entrance of the structure. Doors opened and armed men moved into the light as others left the building, gathering around the arriving vehicles.

"Fuck, how many are invited to this party?" Elias whispered, looking through the optics of a spotting scope.

"Is it him?" Tommy whispered.

Elias shook his head. "Can't confirm, but that man to the right is our friend, Jamal."

Tommy pushed up on his elbows and pulled the optics of the suppressed SVS rifle closer to his eye. To the front of the Range Rover was the fat, bald man speaking to another man still concealed in the shadows. He let the reticle rest at the top of the Jailer's shoulders then glided it left, examining visible faces. "I don't see him," he whispered into the open radio channel.

"We don't go unless you confirm the target," came a response from Kohen on the radio.

Tommy shook his head in frustration and put the crosshairs back on the Jailer. He pulled the throat mic away from his neck and looked to Elias with his finger caressing the trigger. "What if I just pop this cat's grape?" he whispered. "Do the world a favor."

"Slow down, Tommy," Elias said, sliding closer. He leaned in and whispered, "This is a roundup; they are planning something. Nassir has to be close. We need to back off, wait."

"Repeat. It's a no-go if you cannot confirm."

Tommy kept the cross hairs on the Jailer and watched the man turn and walk away with a second man in a dark dress jacket. Together the two men approached the structure's main entrance and the door closed behind them. He shook his head in response to the radio call. "A lot of help these guys have been." He rolled to his side and pulled a pair of pain pills from his pocket and chewed them. "Elias, take the rifle. I'm moving up. Give me five minutes to get close then cause a distraction. I'm going inside."

"Tommy, listen—if she's in there and we attack, she's dead. We'd need a company of Rangers to take this place out."

"This isn't the Army. We don't have a company, Papa. There aren't any Black Hawks full of grunts inbound, and I won't let her spend another day in there if I can stop it."

"We don't even know this is where she's at."

Tommy grimaced, drawing the MK23 and screwing on

the suppressor. "I'll find out if she's here or not—" He paused and looked his friend in the eye. "If I don't come back, don't come looking for me."

"Tommy, wait," he heard his friend whisper as he leopard crawled through the high grass into the perimeter of the compound. Tommy knew the guards were undisciplined; their attention would be to the crowd at the front, not watching the canal behind them. He froze when he heard the crunching of grass ahead of him. Tilting his head up, he spotted the back of a man grinding his feet in the high grass.

Before he could ready his MK23 for a shot, he heard the wisp of the round traveling through the air. With a *clack*, the back of the man's head snapped forward. He knew Elias had taken the shot, covering his approach with the sniper rifle. Tommy crawled ahead and grabbed the body, dragging it back into the high grass before moving ahead to the outside wall of the structure. He pressed against it and rose into a squat.

Tommy steeled his mind, ignoring the commotion, and focused on the building. The walls were made of hardened bricks, the windows at least ten feet off the ground. Going to the front would be impossible so he turned toward the rear of the building, looking for a way in. He made his way along the wall and rounded the corner, entering the blind area that he knew Elias wouldn't be able to cover. Again, he squatted to listen, more shouts of men at the front of the compound.

"Tommy, hold," he heard Elias say over the radio. *"Three are coming out, and headed directly for the Range Rover."*

"A woman?" Tommy asked.

"Impossible to tell, they are moving fast and through the shadows, they just boarded the lead Range Rover— Wait the other man in the dark jacket is back; he's talking to a group near the entrance."

"Jamal?"

"Negative, I didn't see him come out."

Tommy sat motionless, trying to focus on the radio. He could hear the group of men at the front of the compound. A man was shouting instructions as the others cheered.

"Something is going on, they are cheering. The man in the dark jacket just got into the vehicle with the other three. They are leaving east on the access road."

Scenarios blasted through Tommy's mind as he tried to decide on a course of action. If Jamal was still inside, the women would also be there. An answer on what to do came to him in the form of a call from Kohen's men. *"Five-vehicle convoy headed in on the south approach, there is a Black S-class Mercedes with them."*

"What about the other Range Rover?" Tommy asked over the channel.

"They're nobody—let it go; Abdul is the target. Five-vehicle convoy on the outpost grounds. Confirmation, Abdul Nassir has exited the Mercedes. He is approaching the building entrance; we are a go."

Before Tommy could speak again, he heard the reports of AK47 rifles from the front of the compound. The attack had started.

24

F ayed sat in the back of the air-conditioned Range Rover. The driver and passenger in the front had changed; he didn't know these men. They were young and well dressed, but not the Chechens who had driven him to the Villa. Jamal was beside him, the man breathing nasally. The vehicle bounced over a section of rough road as it moved through the bombed-out village. He flinched and grabbed for a handhold above the window next to his seat. He looked down and saw the leather satchel and the suppressed pistol on the seat beside him.

Jamal caught his gaze and shrugged. "It is for the best. Sometimes you have to let merchandise go. It is not good for business to hold onto property that only causes you expenses. This property has cost us a lot, Fayed. It is for the best."

Fayed shuddered as he listened to the man speak, comparing human life to products on a shelf. The absence of the Chechens helped him relax some. For a bit, he feared he would be buried in the desert along with the women. Still he wasn't quite sure and wouldn't be until he was on a flight back to Paris. His mind scrambled for a solution; there had to be another way. "Where will we take them after it is over?"

Jamal shrugged. "That is up to you. I have no other part in this. Once you have completed your task"—the bald man pointed toward the driver—"Samir will take you wherever you wish to go. You dispose of your mistakes however you choose."

"And what about after?" Fayed said, pointing to the front seats. The men not even moving to acknowledge that he was speaking about them.

"I already said, Samir and Omar will do whatever you need them to. When your task is accomplished. They will return here, they work for you until the job is done." With the final line, Fayed observed the one named Samir nod his head.

The pair of vehicles turned onto a narrow gravel road then slowed as they crossed into a walled-in set of buildings. They drove past a hastily constructed guard shack and past several machine-gun-mounted trucks before stopping near the grounds of a tall square building. Jamal opened his door and stepped into the low-lit yard. Fayed exited on his side and moved around the front of the vehicle toward the Jailer. Jamal pointed to the front of the brick and stucco structure. "It doesn't look like much, but this outpost has served us well."

"They are inside?" Fayed asked, his voice low and steady.

Jamal looked at the inspector and saw that Fayed now had the pistol tucked in his waistband. He turned back to the Range Rover and could see the satchel still on the bench seat. He grinned, having thought it would take more to convince Fayed to carry out his responsibilities. But now the young man's face had turned hard, and there was determination in his eyes. "Yes, they are inside."

"Then let's get this over with," Fayed said, signaling for the bald man to lead the way.

Jamal obliged, stepping across the dirt path and up a set of cast stone steps. They entered a tall lobby; the room was musty and stank of smoke and gun oil. Every open space was occupied by men gathered in circles conversing over sets of stacked weapons. As the party wended through the large room, Fayed looked back and could see that Samir and Omar were following close behind them. They turned into a narrow hallway and an old woman adorned with a silver scarf greeted them warmly.

She smiled and exchanged words with Jamal before handing him a key. She then pointed to a barred door at the end of the long hallway. Jamal turned to Fayed with a smile. "It is just this way," he said, pointing to the door.

Fayed stood in the corridor, taking in the structure. To his right he saw another small room. There was no door, but the room was filled with women in black gowns; they turned away when he looked inside. The silver-scarfed woman caught the movements and rushed into the room, shouting insults at them. Jamal again laughed and motioned for Fayed to join him at the door. The Jailer turned to the guards and asked them to wait in the hall.

He then looked back to Fayed before saying, "Are you ready?"

"Yes, let's go. I have a flight to catch," he said impatiently.

Jamal dipped his chin and placed a key in the lock then unbarred the door, leaving the key in the mechanism. He led the way into the room and once Fayed was inside, he closed the door behind them. The room was small and dark, lit by a single bulb hanging from a wire in the center of the ceiling. The woman to the right was sitting, her head turning toward the sounds of the door. The second woman was lying motionless on the floor to his left. Dark hoods covered their heads. Jamal stepped to the side then turned to Fayed and waved toward the women with his open hand.

The young inspector pulled the pistol from his waist and pulled back on the slide, confirming a round was chambered. He looked down at the two figures on the floor, the end of the barrel switching between the two of them before finally settling on the lying figure. He pulled the trigger twice. The gun bucked in his hand. Even though suppressed, the gunshot was loud in the tight space. He felt Jamal jump beside him, and he heard the remaining woman begin to sob. He squeezed the pistol in his grip and turned to face the final woman.

Something clicked in his head. Something deep. It was nothing heroic or any sort of morality issue. It was purely a sense of self-preservation, something telling him that the woman was his only way out. If he killed her, he might as well be putting a bullet in his own head. Why else would they make him do it? Why would Abdul say he would be joining them at the outpost? Why was Jamal here? Surely the plan was to kill him as well.

His mind was always running twelve steps ahead. It was his intellect and instinct that he thought kept him safe and above his peers. Something was talking to him now, a plan rapidly developing in his subconscious. His finger caressed the trigger as he focused the sights on the woman's hood. He couldn't kill her, she was his way home. Without thinking, almost involuntarily, he spun and directed the pistol at Jamal's face. The man began to speak, a startled look in his eyes.

Before Fayed could talk himself out of it, the bald man lay dead at his feet. The remaining woman trembled on the floor, not speaking. He reached down and grabbed her by the back of her shirt. Changing his voice and speaking roughly, he addressed her in English. "If you want to live, you will stand and keep your mouth shut."

Surprisingly, the woman complied and with his help, rose to unsteady legs. Fayed kept her hooded and moved her to the right of the door then reached for the latch. As he pulled the door open, it pressed against Jamal's body. Fayed strained and pulled hard, sliding the dead man closer to the wall. He pushed the hooded woman out ahead of him into the hallway. He closed the door behind him and placed the pistol back into his waistband.

He found the hallway the way they'd left it—the two guards standing at the far end and the old woman nowhere in sight. He pressed the hostage toward the two guards, who eyed him suspiciously. Samir looked at Fayed and turned up his brow, looking at the hooded woman. Before he could speak Fayed ordered, "Take her to my vehicle. I will be out shortly."

The driver looked at him, confused, and his eyes drifted over Fayed's shoulder, back to the barred door. Again, Fayed spoke first. "Don't worry, that one is taken care of, but Jamal is having his fun first."

"Ahh." Samir scowled, his face showing he understood. He looked to Omar, who reached out and grabbed the prisoner. Together they turned and led her back to the Range Rover. Once they were out of sight, Fayed ran back to the door and barred it. He turned the already placed key in the lock until he felt the bolt clunk, and then he broke the key off in the mechanism. Turning back, he saw the old woman standing beside him. She looked up at him.

"It is done," he said.

The old woman nodded and turned away, returning to the second room filled with women. Fayed took in a deep breath and forced himself to walk, his hands shaking, consciously fighting the urge to run toward the waiting Range Rover. He made his way through the gallery filled with fighters, sure that at any moment, one would figure him out and shoot him dead. When he left the building and stepped outside, he came face-to-face with three armed men. They looked at him suspiciously; with his dark sport coat, he did not belong there.

Not knowing what else to say, Fayed smiled brightly and slapped the tallest of the three on the shoulder. "Make ready, Abdul himself will be joining us shortly. There will be a celebration tonight. A victory celebration!"

The fighters were taken aback, their expressions unchanged at first, before the tall man returned his smile and the others began to cheer. Men rushed inside, repeating the announcement that Abdul, their leader, would be visiting them. Fayed swiftly moved past the now cheering and jovial men, finding his way to the Range Rover. He saw the guards had done as ordered. The woman was positioned in the back seat, the hood still covering her head.

Taking another deep breath, he opened the door and dropped into the seat beside her. Fayed leaned forward and spoke to Samir in Arabic, telling him to take them east toward the city. The driver followed the instructions and sped away from the outpost. As they left the gate, Fayed spied a cloud of dust and several vehicles approaching on the road from the south. He wasn't completely lying; Abdul was on his way to the outpost, but the victory was all Fayed's.

25

W ith the fighting started, Tommy knew his time was precious; he had to find a way inside before some anxious guard decided to start killing hostages. At the back, he found a plank-wood door secured with a bit of chain but no lock attached. He stood at the edge, the air now filled with the staccato bursts of gunfire coming from the front of the compound. Tommy holstered his pistol and swung the 9A-91 forward, allowing it to lead the way as he cut into the musty building.

He stumbled into a room filled with huddling women. An old woman with a silver head scarf stood over them. She looked up at Tommy and screamed, then charged at him with a large knife. Tommy sidestepped and crushed her in the jaw with the butt of the carbine assault rifle. He felt her teeth crack as her screams were silenced. The rest of the women cowered, hiding their heads. There was a commotion in the hall and a man burst in, holding an AK47 across his chest. Tommy fired a burst, the report of the weapon deafening in the confined space of the room. The armed man fell back, his chest stitched with holes.

A shout from the hallway was followed by stomping feet. Tommy moved to the right wall, shielding himself as the women moved away from him, crowding into the opposite corner. He knew he had to act before they could close on him. Another shout and a Russian RGD-5 grenade flew into the room, bouncing off a wall and rolling toward the cowering women. Tommy acted quickly. Scrambling, he kicked the grenade with the toe of his boot, launching it back into the hallway.

Already moving forward, he dove to the brick-and-mortar wall. The blast from the hallway shook the structure, knocking out the lights and filling the room with clouds of choking dust. Tommy dropped his night vision goggles over his eyes and stepped forward. He fired at downed, yet still moving, targets on the floor. He peppered them with security shots, hitting the bodies with two- and three-round bursts, changing the box magazine as the weapon emptied.

Turning the corner, he entered a large gallery. Men were on the wall opposite him, returning fire at Elias's men out front. Rounds cut through windows, hitting the walls around him, pelting the clay bricks and showering him with debris. Tommy opened fire, cutting down two of the men before the others took notice and directed their fire on him. He dove for cover, landing hard on the tile floor and crawling back into the hallway. A heavy machine gun somewhere outside joined the fight. The walls at the building's front were now being chewed to pieces by heavy-caliber rounds. There was another explosion and Tommy was pressed back, forced to find cover.

Tommy scooted back, realizing he was in a bad position, caught in the crossfire between two opposing forces. For now, the machine gun fire prevented the men inside from pursuing him. He reached for his shirt collar and returned the audio piece to his ear. Shouts in Arabic and English filled the channel. Elias was shouting instructions to his men to flank around the side of the building. Kohen's men were moving in from the west. The men on the approach road were shouting warnings of a Russian armored convoy on the move.

Time was running out. He crawled his way back to the rear room filled with women. He snatched one by the back of the neck and stood her up against the wall. "Where is the American woman?"

She cowered away, her dead weight hard for Tommy to hold with one hand. He straightened his arm and let her fall back into the pile of women. He saw that all of them were lashed together by a long, single length of chain that looped through leg shackles and then fastened to the wall. He realized they were prisoners, the same as Sarah. All except the silver scarfed woman who attacked him. Where did she go? Tommy turned to find her, but instead felt a sharp pain in his back. He lunged forward and saw the handle of the knife sticking from his shoulder. The old woman was trying to retrieve it, to stab him again but it was wedged into the Kevlar fabric of his body armor. He spun hard, tossing her from his back. He reached with his left arm and pulled away the blade, already feeling the blood pouring from the knife wound.

He turned to find her struggling back to her feet. Locking eyes with him, she snarled and charged at him again. This time he was ready and threw a straight right punch that hit her square in the face, knocking her back. The other women pulled away, leaving her alone in a corner. She put her hands in front of still bleeding teeth. Tommy reached down and snatched her by the neck, lifting and slamming her small frame against a wall. "Where is the American?" he screamed at her.

She shook her head and spit blood in his face. Tommy ignored the warm liquid that oozed down his jaw and yanked her by the neck, shoving her into the hallway. The sound of the firefight was deafening. The rounds ricocheted, bits of plaster exploding with the impacts. The old woman tried to duck down, but Tommy grabbed her again and forced her upright, now pressing the 9A-91 against her already bruising jaw. "Where is the American?" he yelled again in Arabic.

The silver scarfed woman sneered at him with bloody teeth and pointed to a barred door at the end of the hallway. Tommy tossed her into the gallery, ignoring her screams as the gunfire intensified in the front of the building. He barely spared a glance as the old woman was cut down in the cross fire. He moved quickly toward the barred door, letting the 9A-91 hang from the sling as he drew the MK23. He put two rounds into the lock bar, destroying the hasp. He grabbed the handle and kicked the door in so hard it ripped from the hinges.

Inside on the floor he found the Jailer, the back of his bald head split by two exit wounds. What he saw on the bare floor to his front made him drop to his knees—a woman's body, her head covered in a black hood, a pool of blood formed to her shoulders. Tommy's jaw dropped and his head shook side to side, he leaned forward. "It can't be..." he choked out, reaching for the hood. Tears ran down his face as he savagely attacked the knot securing the hood to her neck, desperate in his attempt to free her. Suddenly rounds cracked over his head. He was hit in the back of his body armor, the shot knocking him to his chest and into her still-warm blood. He felt its stickiness on the side of his face as more rounds impacted the room around him.

Rage flooded his system, pushing away the despair. He clenched his fist and rolled to his back, raising his carbine. He screamed into the smoke-filled hallway, firing blind into the space to his front. He turned around and leaned back against the wall. Smoke was filling the building; the gallery was on fire. He watched a man move in a crouch around the corner, blood covering the fighter's arm and shoulder. The man was coughing as he tried to escape the flames.

Tommy fired until the carbine was empty. He dropped the weapon and went back to the MK23. He charged forward into the smoke and put several rounds into the man's chest. More fighters rounded the corner and, fueled by anger, Tommy lashed out with his fists, connecting with the first and engaging the others at point-blank range. When his pistol was empty, he let it fall to the ground and exchanged it for an AK47 from a dead man. A grenade bounced off a wall and rolled into the hallway. It exploded in a flash as Tommy leapt back into the room where the women were being held. He felt the heat now and, looking up, he could see the building's roof was on fire.

The screams of the imprisoned women filled the room as they struggled to free themselves of the chains that kept them from escaping the burning building. He turned, looking back into the hallway. He wanted to recover Sarah's body but there was no time; he couldn't leave these women behind to burn. He turned and grabbed at the long chain, finding where it met the wall. He fired his weapon and destroyed the shackle then pulled on the end. It came free, releasing the women from the bond. Once they were loose, the prisoners ran out of the room and into the darkness outside.

He felt a buzzing in his ear. Having forgotten about the radio, he cupped a hand over it as he walked from the burning building, following the path of the freed women. He stopped at a dead man and recovered magazines from his chest rig, stuffing them into his own. Shouts filled the radio channel; the code word to extract was being given, orders to retreat from the outpost.

Tommy was losing blood from the knife wound in his shoulder and there was a burning in his side where his sutures had ripped open. He didn't want to continue, with Sarah gone his will to fight died with her. His arm holding the AK47 hung slack. He turned and walked casually back across the rear yard of the building, the way lit by the flames of the building. The women were all gone now, the only sign of them being bits of their torn clothing and abandoned veils on the ground.

He stumbled across the back courtyard and looked out over the canal—nothing but water to his front, left and right, and the burning building behind him. Gunfire ravaged from the front drive and, for a moment, he considered just sitting in the high grass and waiting for them to find him. Bright lights lit the front of the outpost. Tommy turned his head; the Russians had arrived and Elias's men were all but gone. He cupped his hand over the speaker again and heard Elias calling his name over the radio.

When he went to speak back, he realized he'd dropped the throat mic somewhere in the house. He could hear them but he couldn't transmit. All he had left was the dead man's AK47. As he listened to the shouts of the fighting to his front, he decided to make his last stand there. He would kill as many as he could for Sarah and the others.

The sounds of a boat's engine turned him around. He watched a column of men running from the far side of the house, slightly obscured in smoke. Tommy strained to see where they were headed and spotted the outline of the boat in the water. He slowly moved back toward the canal and crouched into the tall grass. He watched as the men stopped and waited for the boat in the canal to approach the shore. One of the men turned, and Tommy quickly identified the man he'd seen hundreds of times in his nightmares. The thick mustache and the glistening scar across the top of the man's head confirmed it.

The Hyena was directly in front of him, alive and in the flesh.

The boat's engine roared as the throttle increased, and the group scrambled into the canal waters to board. Tommy rose with the AK47 at his shoulder. Even though firing through iron sights in the dark, he aimed at the front of the fleeing column where he thought the Hyena would be and fired. The lead runner dropped. After the first muzzle flash, he lost his night vision and was blind, but he continued to fire until the magazine was empty. He swapped magazines and he ran at the fleeing men, firing from the hip, his rounds peppering the water as the boat faded into the distance. Tommy checked the dead men on the ground and cursed when none of them were the Hyena. Rounds impacted the ground at his feet; the security forces were closing in behind him and he had nowhere left to go. He dropped the AK47 in the tall grass and disappeared into the canal. His fight wasn't over, not if the Hyena still lived.

26

Abdul stepped off the boat and moved quickly to the waiting vehicles. His jacket was ripped and his face black from smoke. Armed men surrounded him as he stopped to look back at the burning outpost in the distance. The gunfire had waned off, he could see silhouettes of soldiers walking the grounds of the distant outpost, the structures wrapped in an inferno of flame. He felt a burning fury in his chest, he wasn't used to losing and in just a few days he had lost nearly everything. "Why the hell do they continue to attack us?" He screamed pointing across the canal.

"They are dead now, all of them those women are dead—their death is on you," he cursed toward the distance. "You saved no one, they are all dead."

He took heavy steps and looked toward his Chechen bodyguards. The men stood nervously around him, their weapons up, eyes focused in the distance. He clenched his teeth and moved with them before stopping, "Contact that worthless skunk Fayed and demand that he makes this stop," he shouted to no one directly. "It stops tonight, tell everyone that the hostages are dead. Let them know there is nothing left to fight for."

The Chechens ushered him forward in the direction of the waiting Range Rovers. The villa, like a fortress on a hilltop, was a refuge for him. Ten kilometers outside the city, the only nearby village had been emptied of residents over a year ago after a desperate battle between the Syrian Army and rebel forces. The bodyguards swiftly moved him to the waiting vehicles. They needed to get him inside the walls of the villa; they were still close to the burning compound, and more fighters could be on the loose. Abdul flung the man's guiding arms aside, knocking away his guards. He moved away and stood under an olive tree, turning to watch the lights of armored vehicles responding to the outpost.

"Idiots! You fight for the dead. Join them, you fools," he shouted again at the far bank of the canal.

Covka, an older Chechen, and one of one of Abdul's chiefs of security, ushered Abdul toward the open door of the Range Rover then walked to the other side of the waiting vehicle. He looked back at the burning compound himself and shook his head before entering. Abdul turned to face him as he positioned himself in the backseat. "Get all of our people here before dawn then lock down the villa. Nobody leaves until this is confirmed over," Abdul shouted.

The elder Chechen nodded to the brothers sitting in the front, who were already dialing a mobile phone to relay the instructions. The vehicles pulled away from the bank of the canal and found the road leading them past palm groves and olive trees toward the hilltop villa.

Covka, not one to hold his tongue when it came to security, leaned in to his employer. "We should leave Syria, Nassir. Return to Europe until this ends. It would be safer there. I cannot guarantee your safety here; too many know you are in the city now."

Abdul dipped his head slightly then drew a pistol. He placed it above Covka's surprised eyes and fired, splattering his brains against the armored window.

"No. This is my city." He snarled tossing the pistol in the dead man's lap. He looked to the front, "Does anyone else, feel we should leave?"

He looked to the brothers in the front, and in a calm voice, said, "Good– Contact the man at the Vatican. Tell them that the women are dead. It is done. And demand that this is stopped or we will take and kill ten more. Demand it!"

Knowing that the issue with the women was over and that Abdul was losing control. Aslan—the eldest brother —grimaced before speaking. "I will make the contacts and see that it is done. In the meantime, we will enhance our security. I will bring in more technicals. Possibly more professionals. If you choose to stay here, it will be expensive."

"Just do it," Abdul barked as the vehicle came to a stop in front of the villa's tall gates. More men outside swung the doors open, and Abdul stepped onto the paved walkway, leaving his dead bodyguard behind. He turned one more time to watch his once proud outpost burn in the distance, before storming off toward the security of the building.

27

F ayed feigned speaking hushed tones into his smart phone then disconnected it and slid the device into his shirt pocket. He wasn't sure what the men knew, and how they reacted now would determine if he put bullets into the backs of their heads. He looked up to the men in the front of the Range Rover. "You are all about to be very rich men," Fayed said in Arabic to Samir and Omar. Omar turned his head to look at Fayed as the driver locked eyes with him in the rearview mirror.

"Aye, how so?" Omar asked.

"A last-minute deal has been reached for the safe return of this one. We will all get a share of it," Fayed exclaimed. "I hope you have papers because plans have changed. We are not returning to the city; take us north toward the sea."

The driver smiled back at him, and Fayed caught the exchange of glances between the guards to his front. He knew they would follow his instructions. It was an easy sell; money was always easy with people like this. He looked up at the men again. "I'll need your phones. We cannot risk being tracked as we cross the border."

Samir shook his head. "We are not allowed mobile devices. For the reason you just stated."

Fayed nodded and smiled knowingly. *Now to deal with the prisoner,* he said to himself.

The woman flinched and yelped as Fayed's hand brushed the fabric still covering her face. He used a knife to slice the tight knot around her neck and removed the hood. "Ahh, the American," he whispered to himself, almost disappointed that it wasn't the French woman. The American's face was bruised. Her hair, greasy and clumped, clung to the sides of her face. She looked away from him, pulling toward the closed door. Fayed held up his empty palms, showing his hands to her. Speaking in English, he said, "Miss Donovan? You have nothing to fear from me."

She slowly turned her head back toward him. Her eyes narrowing in the light. Her bottom lip quivered.

"My name is Inspector Ziya Fayed. I am a police officer with the International Police Organization." She looked at him absently as he fumbled with his jacket. She again flinched back as he pulled away the lapel. Showing her there was nothing to fear, he slowly removed his identification and placed it into the palms of her hands to examine.

Sarah took the plastic case and held it like a foreign object.

"Please, it's okay," he whispered, indicating for her to look at the identification.

Sarah took the card and slowly raised it to her eyes. She looked away then scanned the cabin of the vehicle, looking at the two men in the front and then back at Fayed. "What do you want?" she mumbled. "What do you want with me?"

"Miss Donovan, you're safe."

"How?"

"I've been able to secure your release from the people holding you. We have some traveling to do, but you are safe with me and these men. I assure you that we will get you home."

Her expression changed as she pressed back into the seat. She looked out of the side window and into the dark desert, then back at him, tiny bits of recognition showing in her eyes. "What about the others? The girl in the cell with me, is she dead?"

"No of course not, she is perfectly safe, she will be release later?" Fayed said looking to the front and seeing the grin on Omar's face from the rearview mirror.

"But–," she shook her head looking down at her scraped and bruised hands. "Where are we?"

"We are moving north toward the border then through Lebanon to the sea."

"Lebanon? I don't understand what is happening."

Fayed smiled and reached for a basket on the floor filled with supplies. He opened a bottle of water and handed it to her. She took the water and drank thirstily as he said, "Miss Donovan, I know you are confused, and it is understandable after what you have been through."

She coughed and looked up at him. "Do you have a phone?"

Fayed shook his head. "I'm sorry, but until we are safe, I cannot risk any phone calls."

She nodded and looked down at her filthy clothing.

Tears ran down her cheeks. Fayed handed her a handker-chief that she pressed against her face. He then placed a folded clean blanket on her lap. "I'm sorry I cannot offer you more, but it's not safe to stop. Once we cross the border it will be easier."

She nodded again and choked out, "I understand." The tension slowly leaving her body, she slumped back into the seat and pulled the blanket over her chest, letting her head rest with her eyes closed.

28

Tommy swam toward the opposite shore of the canal, trying to keep the fleeing boat in sight. The water shallowed near the opposing bank, the bottom becoming mucky and filled with tall grasses. He lost sight of the boat and came ashore near an abandoned neighborhood. The boat was already gone, but he watched lights move on the shore, hundreds of meters to his west. It was the only light, making them an easy target to track as the vehicles dispersed up into the hills. With the hunt over, his adrenaline rush faded, and he began to feel fatigue and pain taking hold of his body.

The air was cold, and he was already shivering by the time he pulled himself out of the dry reed grasses. Low crawling away from the banks, he saw the faint outlines of structures just off the shoreline—several homes in a tight cluster; he could just make them out by moonlight. They were far off and distant, but even closer he spotted hulking shapes to his front. He lay silent, listening for sounds of life... a dog barking, a child's cry, a slamming door, but there was nothing. The once quaint village of stone-and-clay houses was now a ghost town. Behind him he could still see the glowing of the outpost's fire on the far side of the canal and hear the roar of vehicles as they responded.

After watching from a distance to make sure nobody saw him cross the canal, he crawled to the nearest shape and found it to be the abandoned hulk of an armored vehicle. With no strength to continue, he approached it and entered through an open back ramp. He quickly picked up on the stench of death and decay, but for the moment, Tommy's pain and exhaustion overrode his sense of smell.

He crawled through the hatch and onto the cold steel floor of the armored vehicle. He'd lost his night vison goggles so he felt around the compartment by hand, finding an old cloth tool bag. He ripped it open and found a canvas tarp that he wrapped himself in. Exhausted from the escape and shivering, he curled into a ball and removed his wet clothing, kicking them out of the warmth of the tarp. Not risking building a fire, and finally succumbing to exhaustion, he drifted off and slept.

Morning came with aches, bruises, and a head filled with cobwebs. Tommy looked through the troop compartment of the fighting vehicle. He shared it with a pair of badly decomposed Syrian soldiers. One lay across a bench seat with bloody bandages attached to its chest. The other was half exposed from the turret, slumped down into a body harness.

Surprisingly, most of the vehicle was untouched. There were no obvious signs of fire or destruction to explain the death of the APC (Armored Personnel Carrier). Tommy stretched to move and was reminded of the pain in his body. His shoulder showed a deep, open gash where the old woman had stabbed him, and the sutures at his side were ripped open and oozing clear fluid. When he turned, he felt the pain in his back where he'd been shot. The round impacted his ballistic plate, but still bruised him through the vest.

There were ammo cans and weapons scattered around the compartment, but he barely noticed them as he honed in on an olive-green box that sat on the right hull of the vehicle. The first-aid box was marked with a red crescent and a star, and through the fog in his brain, Tommy strained his joints, ripped the box from its mounts, and stuffed it into his pack along with his wet clothes and the rest of his belongings.

He crawled naked down the back hatch of the vehicle and saw there were several small box shaped homes close by; he made a direct path to the closest one. Checking a back door, he found it open and tumbled inside onto a kitchen floor. Still clutching his pack, he crawled through the kitchen and into an open living space, where he rolled himself into a thick Persian rug and once again succumbed to the pain and exhaustion.

This time he woke to the sounds of roaring vehicles. It was still daylight and light shone through gaps in the drapes of a closed window. He let his head fall to the side as he examined the space then crawled from his cocoon of the Persian rug. Still naked, Tommy wandered from room to room, looking at the furniture and clothing left behind by the house's former occupants. The abandoned home was well-built and had held together tightly, the doors and windows sealed shut. In the kitchen, he found scraps of food and water, in addition to a cardboard box with meager canned goods.

He examined his burst-open stitches in a bathroom mirror; the torn flesh was red and crusted with blood and dirt. Tommy dumped the contents of the first aid kit, which included a nearly full bottle of rubbing alcohol, onto the bathroom counter. He winced as he drained the stinging liquid over his injury then slapped a bandage on the clean wound. Then he looked to the gash on his shoulder; the wound wasn't as deep and was more recent than the one on his side. He packed it with antibiotic ointment and taped it secure before leaving the bathroom to check out the rest of the house.

He entered a living space with dusty pillows arranged on the floor. The windows were covered with heavy drapes, sunlight and heat from the new day barely able to break in through cracks at the edges. He lifted his small combat pack and stepped across the room to stand beside the window. He pulled back the drapes, trying to survey the surroundings in the daylight, letting the sun warm his body.

The home was located on a gently sloping hill, one of several houses tightly clustered together. Several of the homes further away were in ruins, with the destroyed hulks of fighting vehicles flanking them. To the north, at the crest of a hill, was a large stone wall. Tommy was sure that was where Abdul fled after the night raid. He'd watched the boat cross the channel and vehicle lights climb the hill soon after.

He pulled back from the window as he heard the rumbling noise of an approaching convoy. Men, gun trucks, and equipment were moving there—lots of them.

If Tommy had to make a guess, it was that the Hyena was pulling everything in and preparing for a long stay. They would no longer be a soft target and easy to get to.

Tommy retrieved his pack and removed his wet clothes and boots. He found the satellite phone at the bottom of the pack but wasn't ready to report his failures, so he left it in the waterproof case. He returned to the kitchen and grabbed a water bottle before dropping to the cushions on the floor. Lying back, drinking from the bottle of water and wishing it was vodka, he felt his body burn from the heat of what he knew was a growing infection. He clenched his jaw, biding away the pain. He didn't have time to be sick, he had work to do.

29

A starless sky, the sea as black as crude oil. The Lebanese trawler cut through the water at a steady ten knots, the craft hardly swaying as it moved through the gentle swells of the Mediterranean. Sarah walked slowly across the deck, moving to the bow and grabbing the railing as a breeze blew back her hair. She was refreshed now, having had time in a Beirut hotel to bathe and dress in clean gowns. Still apprehensive at the strange men surrounding her, she was beginning to feel safe, knowing she was finally on her way home.

Footfalls on the planks behind her caused Sarah to look over her shoulder. Fayed was approaching, carrying two white porcelain cups of coffee. She forced a smile and accepted the cup then she turned back toward the sea. "Thank you," she said.

"My pleasure," he said, joining her at the rail.

Yellow lights in the distance moved slowly along the horizon. She focused on some, watching them fade as they moved away. Fayed followed her gaze and pointed.

"That's Cyprus on the horizon," he said and moved his hand to the right pointing at flicking lights in the distance. "We are moving through shipping lanes, those are super tankers and other vessels moving along the coast toward Turkey."

She nodded her head and looked down at the mug, sipping the hot coffee. "How long?"

Fayed smiled and looked at his watch. "Before first light of morning. We have to hold this speed and course to maintain our cover as a trawler; any faster, and military vessels patrolling these waters would grow suspicious."

Sarah looked at him anxiously. "Fayed, if you are a policeman and have secured my release, then why hasn't the military come for me? Why are we sneaking across the ocean in a fishing boat?"

The investigator laughed and sipped at his own coffee. "I am sorry, madam. Although you have been released from your captors, we are far from safe. There are plenty of dangers here. This arrangement was made directly between your Church and those that took you. Your government was not involved."

"How did you come into it?" she asked, turning her eyes back to the lights of Cyprus. "How does a policeman end up in Syria?"

"I have always been a part of it. I was assigned to your case soon after you were taken. As lead investigator for the Middle East desk, I've been looking for you nonstop. When your government failed to acknowledge your existence or negotiate with the kidnappers, I went directly to the Vatican and, with their help, I was able to mediate your release."

"I'll never be able to repay you for your kindness."

Fayed nodded and turned away. She grasped the cup with both hands and turned so that her back was against the railing. "How did you do it? I thought I would be killed."

Fayed looked at her and frowned. "Outside pressures were put on the group, forcing your release." He stared at her, focusing on her eyes. "I must ask, do you have any family at all? Anyone I could contact for you when we reach Cyprus?"

Sarah frowned. "I have a brother, but I don't even know if he is aware that I've been missing. As far as I know, he will be back in Boston."

"A brother?"

"Yes. Thomas," she said, seeing the curiosity rise in Fayed's face.

"Thomas. Tell me about him. There was very little mention of any family in your file."

She frowned. "There wouldn't be. I was an orphan, raised in a boarding school until I was of the age of emancipation. After school, I went to the convent to continue my studies."

He nodded. "And this brother of yours... Thomas. You were close?"

Sarah shook her head and looked at the horizon, searching for the proper words. "No, maybe at one time but not recently. Thomas sort of lost himself as we grew older and apart. I think he found himself once, but in recent years he has been a very lonely man."

"I see."

She shook her head. "It's not that he doesn't care. I think it would be the exact opposite, actually. He is just lost without a mission. When we were children he found his purpose in shielding and protecting me, but as I grew older and independent, he lost that. Then later he joined the military and found his purpose again—"

"But?" Fayed asked.

"He was badly wounded overseas."

"In the war?"

"Yes," she said. "Thomas was never the same after that. He never talked about it, choosing to lock himself away in his own mind." Sarah looked back to Fayed and smiled. "It's a blessing really that he didn't know of my capture."

Fayed turned his brow up curiously. "Oh? And why is that?"

Sarah bit at her lower lip and looked down at her now empty cup. "My brother isn't your average sibling. Thomas could be a dangerous man if put to it. If he knew what happened to me, he would leave a path of destruction a mile wide. He wouldn't stop until I was safe or he himself was dead."

Fayed's lips tightened as if containing a smirk. "I doubt such a man exists."

This time it was Sarah who smiled. "Yes, I'm sure it is just a little girl's fantasy clouding the image of her big brother. Do you think it would be possible to find him, to have him flown to meet me?" she asked.

Fayed grimaced and looked over the railing before nodding. "Our timeline is short, but as soon as we reach Cyprus, I will make the necessary phone calls."

30

The vehicles were readied, the men loaded. Two days after losing the outpost, he would make the meeting with the city mayor and repair his relationship with those in charge. Most of what had occurred was already being erased in the official records. There was no evidence against him, and Abdul knew the short memories of those in Washington would ensure that his funds were quickly restored. Even they knew how important it was that he return to assisting the moderate rebels in waging war against the radicals. Even if he had no intention of doing that, it was the thought that counted. He felt no guilt for keeping the funds intended for the arming and training of moderate groups to fight the extremists. Abdul was, after all, himself a humble servant.

Smiling, he walked across the cobblestone path surrounded by the well-manicured lawns and trees of his estate. The West was under perverse illusions; farmers with rifles didn't hold back the wolf. He was what held back the extremists from the region, not the Russians or the Iranians, who just motivated more of them to join the war. It was his Badawi Brigade that truly kept them away, so why shouldn't he prosper? Why shouldn't the Badawi Brigade profit from the war? His people never asked for this Arab Winter, promoted and pushed by Western politicians. The West may have started it, but it was his people who had lost more than anyone else. Yes, it was blood money, but why shouldn't it be *his* blood money?

There had been no word from Fayed or Jamal. Both of them were presumed dead in the battle at the outpost. Abdul was okay with that; it was less he had to clean up, less of a connection to the troubles he was looking to bury. The women were all dead as well, and there had been no more attacks after the assault on the outpost. The Chechens had reached out to local security forces, and there was nothing to be heard. The American operations against his forces had ceased and vanished.

Abdul would have preferred vengeance and victory over a cease fire, but he had to admit that the Americans had hurt his business greatly in a short period. Ending it the way he had gave him time to cover his losses, and once he resumed his weapons trade he would have the necessary funds to rebuild. Losing Fayed would be an inconvenience, but he would soon find a replacement and easily reestablish contacts. He would be able to get more "resistance" money from the West, and that would go even further toward rebuilding his forces.

The Russian security services may try to block him from staying in Albahr after the recent troubles, but they were more concerned with stability than what small groups did in the shadows. He could resume his trade business and bring back peace to the streets. Or at least control to the streets. Abdul stood by the front of the vehicle, waiting for his guards to open the door. He slid into the back of the Mercedes, letting the cold air conditioning soothe his thoughts. He put his head back against the leather headrest and spoke to the man next to him. "Has the meeting been confirmed?" he asked.

The Chechen flipped over the screen of a smart phone and scrolled to a table filled with numbers. He pointed at the screen, turning it so Abdul could see, and said, "The funds for the donation, were transferred in the last hour. The mayor is eager to meet with you."

Abdul grinned and nodded, money always earned him access. "And the attacks, what are the reports, from in the city?" he asked.

The Chechen dipped his chin. "We've heard nothing. The local fighters have all pulled back. Our men have reported no contacts with any resistance groups. We have leads, and tracking them is something we can discuss with the local authorities. But as for now, it looks as if the stability is holding."

Abdul sighed, rubbing the back of his wrist against his temple. "So much trouble for a few women. It'll take us years to recover from this mess."

The Chechen nodded and laughed saying, "War was so much easier in the old days."

A long, winding road led away from the fortress. It sloped down a gentle approach past palm trees and olive groves. The terrain was once a sign of pride for the previous owners, but now the property outside the gates of the hilltop estate was nothing more than overgrown scenery for the current occupant. The grasses were grown high and unkempt, making for excellent hiding places. Tommy lay in wait at the bottom of the road in a cluster of palm trees. Although the curving road with wide bends around the landscaping was designed for aesthetic appeal, it served double-duty as prime terrain for an ambush.

He was dug into the uphill slope, overlooking a sharp bend in the road that crossed a narrow bridge. A perfect choke point, where vehicles would have to slow before passing over a bone-dry irrigation stream. Two concave shaped charges, just slightly larger than dinner plates, were dug into the ground a little more than fifty feet apart. On the low side of the road, opposite the shaped charges, were the small PMN-2 anti-personnel blast mines. Russian made, they were small and easy to conceal, designed to maim rather than kill.

Farther up the winding road, closer to the walled fort, was his final surprise—an improvised explosive device— a five-gallon jerry can filled with fuel, resting atop a large ball of RDX. A steel plate sandwiched between them was buried in the road and then connected to his mobile phone. He hoped to be gone before that one was detonated, but it was still there as insurance in case he needed more time to escape.

The remnants of the armored battle field intermixed with the abandoned village had been a goldmine for someone who knew where to look and how to use the items there. Weapons were everywhere, but most important was a wooden crate of landmines. The PMN-2 mines were banned by most international agreements. But the Syrians must have made an exception, as Tommy found a trailer full of them. One of the better things about the mine, other than its ability to remove limbs, is once the cover was removed they were filled with RDX, which was a perfect ingredient for making shaped charge devices. Knowing that the Hyena traveled in armored convoys, shaped charges would be essential in stopping them.

He looked through the binoculars and watched the three-vehicle convoy approach with two black Range Rovers and the armored Mercedes in the center. This had to be what he'd been waiting for; with all the traffic in and out of the villa, this was the first time he'd seen the Mercedes. He watched them wind down the path and pass the spot where he'd buried the fuel can late the night before. He clenched his teeth and fought the temptation to trigger the IED and vaporize the Mercedes as it drove over the mark.

Destroying the convoy wasn't good enough. Incinerating the man wasn't even close to enough; he wanted to confirm that the Hyena was dead this time. He needed to see it and watch it with his own eyes. The convoy wound down the road, throwing a trail of dust behind it. He watched the lead vehicle round the final bend on the approach to his kill zone, near where the road narrowed to pass over the bridge. His heart raced and he felt the sweat roll down his forehead and into his eyes. It was almost time, and he would only have one shot to get it right.

Tommy leaned over the sights of a salvaged PK machine gun and focused on the front of the Mercedes. The weapon's barrel was rusted, and the brass of the 7.62 linked ammo tarnished, but Tommy knew it would still do the job it was designed for. Even from the distance, he could tell that he'd done his math correctly. The spacing of the shaped charges embedded in the rocks on the high side of the road were perfectly positioned to take out the lead and following vehicle simultaneously, while still sparing the Mercedes from the brunt of the blasts.

He panned left and focused on the scratched gravel. He'd placed the leaf of a palm tree over the top of the first shaped charge and he waited for the lead vehicle to cross its path. Watching the Range Rover's bumper intersect with his imaginary line, he touched a red wire to the positive post of a car battery, sending twelve volts down the line to a pair of electrically triggered detonators. In a white flash, the high explosives packed around the concave copper discs instantly converted the metal into molten, explosively formed penetrators that tore through the engine compartment of the lead Range Rover. Built up gasses blew out the windows of the vehicle.

At the same time, the second shaped charge ripped through the driver's door of the tail vehicle, killing the occupants instantly. The driver of the Mercedes reacted sharply, as a trained man should. The Mercedes cut hard right for open terrain, and the engine roared. Tommy was impressed for a moment, watching as the man cut the wheel, hardly slowing, attempting to race out of the kill zone, into the low ground of the dry creek bed.

The driver's moves were futile; he was blocked in by the burning vehicles to the front and rear. Tommy was ready and let loose with the salvaged, Russian-made PK machine gun, sending 7.62 rounds into the front tire of the Mercedes at six hundred rounds per minute, shredding the run-flat tire and incapacitating the steel wheel. The vehicle stalled in its forward movement. The tires spun and the damaged front rim dug into the soft gravel. Tommy shifted his point of aim to the driver's armored door and window, firing into the shielded glass until it was shattered beyond recognition.

He knew what would come next. Tommy had been the invoker of enough ambushes to know how the victims would respond. Although there were several variables, most ends came together the same. Most trained men reacted in similar ways when under fire, and Tommy was prepared for it. He knew some would flee and others would fight. He was ready when the doors on the far side of the vehicle flung open. Tommy rolled away from the machine gun and into a dry gulch moments before the return fire pockmarked his previous position, now easily identified by the blue smoke of the machine gun.

He moved through a shallow gulch winding among the palms, smiling, knowing what would happen next without having to watch it. The men of the ambush would continue the suppressing fire onto his previous position, as others fled with their VIP for the safety and cover of the low ground. The blast of an anti-personnel mine sealed his prediction. A lone man screamed in agony, probably having lost part of a leg.

Tommy ignored the chaos and crawled through the low ditch and into a second prepared flanking position, where he'd stashed an AK47 rifle. He cautiously lifted it into place and eased in behind it, zeroing in on the ambush scene below. Both Range Rovers were now fully engulfed in flames, black smoke roiling into the air.

A guard leaned over the hood of the Mercedes, now emboldened by the lack of return fire, possibly thinking he'd taken down the lone machine gunner. A thick man in a combat vest filled with magazines and armed with an M70 assault rifle stood upright and swept the terrain, searching.

Behind the Mercedes and in the low ground of the creek, he saw the fat man he knew as the Hyena surrounded by two more bodyguards in identical vests. Ahead of them, a fourth guard screamed on the ground, writhing, with a bloody stump below his left knee. Tommy shifted his sights back to the man at the Mercedes standing watch over the others.

Focusing, Tommy placed a shot in the man's head, the body falling back as the weapon slapped off the hood of the vehicle. Tommy turned back to the men in the low ground huddling under the low shoulder of the road. Their ears ringing from the explosive ambush, they couldn't pinpoint the shot and wrongly thought they now had cover hiding from the machine gun position in the palms, not knowing Tommy had already flanked them and now had them zeroed in the creek bed.

The ambush was effectively over, the gunfire silenced, and only pops of the burning vehicles and the screams of the wounded man still filled the air. The moment of surprise was gone and the men would soon be recovering from their shock. If given enough time they would eventually rally, and put their advantage in numbers against him. He looked over his shoulder toward the villa on the hilltop. The gate was still closed, but he knew a reaction force would be mounted soon. Looking back, Tommy saw that one of the guards had grown brave and was making a dash toward the Mercedes. Tommy raised and fired off several rounds at the running man, hitting low through the man's pelvis, causing him to tumble into the road. The injured man screamed out in what sounded to Tommy like Chechen.

Another man rose from the shoulder and fired blindly into the hillside, the rounds impacting far from Tommy's position. Tommy shifted his sights and fired several rounds, missing high before clipping the shooter's shoulder and head. Brains and blood splattered the fat man, who was now alone. Tommy watched the man crawl toward the mine field.

Tommy took careful aim and put two shots into the back of the crying man with the missing leg, killing him. The fat man yelped and changed direction back to the road. He called out to the man with the destroyed pelvis, asking for help. Tommy allowed them to exchange a few words before putting the wounded man out of his misery, leaving the Hyena on his own.

The man cowered in the gravel, attempting to crawl back to the shelter of the armored vehicle. Tommy saw a small pistol in the man's hand. He aimed for his shoulder. The round went wide, causing the Hyena to roll. Tommy fired again, this time catching the man just below the elbow, shattering the bone. The pistol flew free.

Looking back at the villa, Tommy saw that the gates were now open and a large truck was in the entrance with a smaller technical leading the way. His time was running out. He dropped the rifle's magazine and loaded another before leaving his hole. Tommy jogged down the hill, keeping his eyes on the Hyena, who was holding his injured arm and looking for a place to hide.

The man scrambled to his side as he saw Tommy approach, then clawed toward the dropped pistol with his good hand. Tommy raised the rifle and fired again, striking the downed man in the back of the leg, halting his crawl. The Hyena turned back to face Tommy and screamed at him in Arabic.

Moving closer, Tommy responded in English. "This is the second time we've met." The sound of the truck racing down the road turned his attention away.

The Hyena pointed toward the distant gate and snarled. "You should run while you have time. My men will cut you to pieces now. They'll cut you open and hang you from a pike."

With a smile, Tommy fished a phone from his pocket and dialed a number. He focused, waiting for the truck to align with a distant olive tree before pressing the send button. A large explosion rattled the earth and the technical vanished in a plume of orange-yellow flame and smoke while the larger troop truck burst into flames then careened from the road and rolled to its side.

"Oh, you mean those guys?" Tommy pointed up the hill. "They look busy."

The Hyena turned away from him, again on his belly, trying to crawl away.

"You don't remember me, do you?" Tommy asked. "It was in Syria, a decade ago. You killed my friend but not before he put that scar on your fat head."

The Hyena stopped and rolled to his back, gulping air. "That's why you are here? For an old vendetta?" he gasped.

"No." Tommy shook his head, leveling his rifle at the Hyena's face. "I came here for my sister."

"The American brother? You're supposed to be dead," the Hyena spat back.

Tommy scowled. "Yeah, so are you."

Tommy leveled the rifle and placed several rounds into the man's stomach. The Hyena convulsed and used his good hand in an attempt to hold in his guts. "I thought I'd get more satisfaction out of killing you. But now seeing you, like a hog crawling away in your own filth, I feel disappointed."

The Hyena dropped his head, the blood rapidly leaving his body. Tommy spat on the ground near the dying man's feet. He pulled the trigger, firing twice into the man's chest and then a third shot into his forehead before dropping the rifle. He turned and walked back toward the abandoned village. Rounding a corner of a destroyed building, he fell to the ground and leaned his back against the ruins. He reached into a side pocket, removed the black satellite phone case, and dialed a number from memory.

He lay back and closed his eyes tightly, listening as the phone rang several times before being picked up. He heard a groggy O'Connell struggling to form words as his head cleared. "Tommy, is that you?"

"It's over," Tommy whispered.

"Tommy thank God, I thought you were dead. Your friend Elias, had contacted me through Ali, he said you'd gone missing."

Tommy ignored the comments, his eyes pressed shut he took in a long breath then said. "I'm done, done with all of it. Sarah is dead. I'm all done here."

"No—Tommy, she isn't dead! We got her."

Tommy paused, catching his breath, trying to hold back the shock and calculate a response. He wasn't sure if he'd heard correctly or if it was the fatigue and exhaustion setting in. "It's not possible, sir, I saw her body; she's gone."

"I assure you she isn't, Tommy. We received proof of life a bit over an hour ago. A timestamped photo of her face," O'Connell said.

Tommy paused and swallowed hard, remembering the hood. He'd never seen the woman's face. "She's really alive? Where?"

"I did as you suggested and reached out to Simon Arnet. He has been very helpful. He forwarded the information about Sarah. The Vatican, the man Simon, they've managed a deal directly with the Badawi Brigade. She will be handed over to his people within the next forty-eight hours, at an undisclosed location. She wants you to be there when they bring her home—Tommy, where the hell are you?"

There was a long pause on the line as Tommy processed the information and what it would mean for his current situation. "But you're sure she's safe? I thought..."

"I know, Tommy. Simon assures me that she is okay and under armed escort. They hope to make contact and arrange her release very soon. But there's more to it."

"How much more?"

"The new friends you are making down there, the pressure you put on them—it worked, but it has to stop now. I told you it's causing a lot of problems. It all has to stop."

"He's dead, sir. The Hyena is gone."

There was a brief silence at the end of the line as the colonel considered what he'd just been told. "The Hyena? You're sure?"

"Positive. I put bullets in his brain myself." Tommy pulled the phone away and looked at his battered and beaten body. He squeezed the phone in his hand then put it back to his ear. "Sir, I need to see her."

"Get to a secure spot and call me with the location. We'll get you to Sarah."

32

The Cyprus studio apartment was decorated in ornate woods. Although of new construction, the design made it feel ancient. A balcony that overlooked the ocean connected to the main room. There was a small kitchen and a master bedroom farther in the back. Fayed paced the floor near the balcony, waiting for his mobile phone to ring. The last twenty-four hours had been hectic, but ironically, it was exactly the type of thing Fayed had been trained for. There were still plenty of things that could go wrong while he juggled several entities, but his confidence was building as the pieces all came together.

He would still have Abdul to deal with but most of his power was regional, and he wouldn't do much to go after him anyway. He could try to have him killed, but Fayed had plenty of information that would easily move Abdul to the top of an American drone hit list. Once he told Abdul that he could have the information released in the event of his death, they would rebuild a mutual trust.

And, hell, maybe one day—long from now—they would be able to work together again. And there was always the ransom money to help smooth things over. Even though far less than what Abdul had wanted, it was still better than nothing.

Early the previous evening, he'd made the phone call to his director and notified him that he would be traveling from Syria with the American girl. There was a money demand, of course, and Fayed gave them the details of a designated serial account where the funds were to be deposited early the next day. Once the money transfer was complete, Fayed would give them their address and hand over the girl.

Although highly suspicious, the director had bought Fayed's story that he had somehow negotiated his way into the Badawi Brigade and was now acting as an official liaison to assist in freeing the girl. He was there as an arbitrator of sorts, only traveling with the girl, guaranteeing her safety until the Badawi Brigade agreed to her release. The director made the phone calls and the Vatican had agreed to the ransom request.

Fayed knew there would be questions to answer, and reports to file, but his time in the apartment allowed him to plan for those eventualities. The girl was in the next room over, asleep atop the bed, a small travel bag by her side. Fayed walked to the kitchen and poured a glass of water from a stone pitcher. There were two men in the room with him—the two bodyguards that had yet to suspect anything, and so far were happy to be along for the ride. He looked at them, one smoking and laughing with the other, no concerns, as if they were on vacation. Fayed closed his eyes, tightly pushing away the tension.

The phone rang and his heart skipped a beat as he clicked the receiver, accepting the call from his director.

"Inspector Fayed?"

"Yes, sir, it's me. Is everything done, has the money been transferred? I am ready to make the exchange."

"Fayed, slow down." The director's voice was electric, far from the monotone Fayed was accustomed to. "Don't panic—but I have to ask you, are you still being escorted by men from the kidnappers' group?"

"Yes, of course, they are both here until we make the exchange."

"Fayed, listen closely. The situation has changed and you must act accordingly."

"I don't understand," Fayed said. He looked toward the entryway and could see the two bodyguards were still joking, nonchalant. They were paying no attention to him.

"Have you heard from your contact at the Badawi Brigade?" the director asked.

Fayed's heart skipped a beat as he worried that his plan was falling apart. Did they know he was lying? Did Abdul tell them that he was working on his own? He bit his lip and shook his head. No, Abdul wouldn't report him through official channels. That would be something he would take care of personally.

"No, of course not, not until I can confirm that the money has been transferred."

"Just listen. The man that we believe leads the Badawi Brigade in Syria is dead. His convoy was ambushed by militants early this morning."

"You're certain of this?"

"Yes, intelligence channels are lighting up. He was

killed in a roadside bomb this morning along with his security entourage. The Israelis are confirming the information that Abdul Nassir is dead. If the guards with you have not yet responded, then they must not yet be aware. But who knows for how long that will last. We need to get you out now. Are you armed?"

He let his hand slip to the small pistol under his left armpit. He knew that if he was really a third party working for a kidnapper, that probably would not be the case. They would have forced him to surrender his weapon. He held his breath then released it and spoke into the phone. "No, of course not. They took my weapons when I negotiated her release."

"Listen, tell us where you are and we'll come for you."

Fayed clenched his jaw and shook his head. He couldn't allow the guards to be captured; they knew too much about him. He turned away from the men. "No, if you try to enter the room, they'll kill her, and probably me as well."

There was a pause on the line before the director spoke again. "You're right, you have to do something then, anything, to get away. If they find out about the attack, we're not sure what will happen. You must act quickly— take the girl and get away. Find a public place and call in. We can't risk the guards turning... or something worse. This will be interpreted as a double cross."

"But, sir, who—how did this happen?"

"We don't know yet, but time is of the essence. You must move quickly."

"I understand," he said, ending the call and returning the phone to his pocket.

Fayed walked across the room to a large picture

window overlooking the sea. Casually, he reached into his jacket and removed the Glock 17 from the shoulder holster. Even though he knew it was the case, he pulled back the slide to confirm a round was chambered. He turned back around, now holding the pistol behind his back.

The guards were weary from the voyage. Samir now sat on a wooden chair just beside the door as Omar leaned against the frame, repeating a story Fayed had already heard several times on the voyage over.

Samir looked up as Fayed approached and smiled at him. "When will this be over so we can get some women? I'd like to see some of this island before we return," the man joked.

Without giving any indication as to why, Fayed pulled the pistol from behind his back and fired twice into Omar's head. He heard the girl scream behind him as he pivoted on the balls of his feet toward Samir, who already had his hands in the air pleading for mercy. Again, Fayed fired twice. The man's body slumped from the chair with the impact of the second round. Acting quickly, Fayed reached into the men's pockets and removed their passports and wallets.

Moving into the kitchen, he placed the wallets and passports in the stainless-steel sink and doused them with cheap alcohol before setting them ablaze. He moved swiftly through the apartment and into the bedroom, taking the woman by her arm. He looked her in the eyes and spoke methodically. "Something has gone wrong with the exchange. We are in grave danger. If you want to go free, you must do everything I say. Do you understand?"

Sarah nodded her head swiftly and rose to her feet. Fayed led her back into the main room, now filled with smoke from the burning wallets. They passed the dead men in the doorway on their way out of the apartment. In the hallway leading out of the building, they could hear shouting from other apartments, inquiring about the gunshots. In the distance, a police siren already wailed. Fayed looked at his watch and shook his head at the efficiency of the local police. He led the woman down a back staircase and into a crowded street, where they fell in among tourists moving toward a busy open market.

He walked, pulling her closer to his side to appear to be a couple, until he found a quiet café. He moved through a low fence and entered an open-air patio, smiling at a waitress as they found a small table in the shade, close to the building. He ordered espresso for them both as he watched his back trail to ensure they hadn't been followed. When he turned back to the woman, he was surprised at her composure. Instead of falling apart, she was sitting strong, sipping the beverage, looking as if she'd just had a leisurely stroll on the beach.

"What happened?" the woman asked.

"Not here, nor now; we can speak later."

Fayed sipped the espresso and suddenly began to feel great relief. Somehow things were happening in his favor. If the rumors were true, Abdul Nassir was dead, and the last two remaining men connecting Fayed to Abdul now lay dead on an apartment floor by orders of his own superior. He'd planned to kill them anyway, but this made it less complicated. He was now in the clear.

Once he turned over the girl, the case was solved. Perhaps he would be the hero. He fished the phone from his jacket pocket and dialed a number. Looking at the menu on the table, he retrieved the name and address of the café. Yes, he had succeeded once again, and again he had come out on top of it all.

The call was made and the address confirmed. Just after ordering a second espresso, he watched men in khaki pants and dark jackets enter and scan the café. The men's eyes locked on Sarah, probably having studied her photograph non-stop for the last forty-eight hours. One of the men spoke into his shirt cuff while the rest closed in around Sarah and Fayed. The men swept them to their feet just as two dark vans raced to the curb and the side doors opened.

Fayed was forced into the first van and separated from the woman as she was escorted to the second. Tourists scattered as they watched the scene unfold, completely unaware as to what they were witnessing. Only seconds after Fayed had spotted the first of the men, they were on the road and moving north toward the island's main airport.

A man looked back at Fayed from the passenger seat of the van and extended his hand. "Inspector Ziya Fayed, I presume? Congratulations on a job well done," the man said.

Apprehensively, Fayed accepted the handshake. "And who might you be?"

"Charles Davis of the US Consulate here in Cyprus. Sorry we couldn't have been of more assistance, but I was just read into the situation mere hours ago. We really owe you a debt of gratitude, Inspector. I would appreciate a full debrief when you have the time."

Fayed nodded his head and sat back against the walls

of the van. "I would like that... after I have a chance to prepare a full report, of course."

The man pursed his lips then smiled. "Take all the time you need, we're just extremely grateful to have her back."

33

T ommy was still asleep when the BMW 320 sedan
pulled onto the shoulder of the narrow road in
front of the small Catholic church on the outskirts of
Keratea, Greece. His phone rang on the seat, and startled
him awake. His eyes opened sharply and he looked
around the cabin of the car. He was alone except for the
driver who had retrieved him from the airport in Athens.
He was dressed in clean slacks and a short-sleeved polo
shirt. His wounds were cleaned and dressed, but bruises
were prominent on his face and neck. He reached for the
phone and recognized O'Connell's number before
pressing the answer button.

"Tommy?" he heard from the phone.

"Yes sir, it's me," he answered, failing to hold back a
stiff yawn.

"I'm sorry, I didn't realize you were sleeping. I had
heard you'd arrived in Greece, and I wanted to speak to
you before the meeting."

Tommy looked at his wristwatch and saw that he'd

been traveling nonstop for over twenty-four hours. He looked out of the window and could see that they were stopped on a narrow street, the only building a white stone church. Ahead of his own car were several matching dark sedans and a pair of navy-blue SUVs. "It's okay. We've just arrived at the church; I needed to wake up anyway," he said. "Any word from Elias?"

"He's safe, and I'm taking care of him."

"What do you mean 'taking care of'?" Tommy asked absently.

"I've been looking for a man on the inside. I'll make sure Elias has what he needs to keep *frying the bread*."

Tommy let out a small laugh, finally understanding. "Thank you, sir– Elias is good people."

O'Connell exhaled before continuing. "But that isn't why I called. I'm glad I got to you before you went inside. There are some things I have to tell you."

"Things?"

"Yes, Tommy. That thing you asked me to look into— about your background and people asking questions."

Tommy paused. "You found out who was helping the Hyena, who was digging into my past?"

"Yes, and you're not going to like it. His name is Ziya Fayed. He is an Interpol agent out of Paris, France. Simon was aware of his involvement, he claims that Agent Fayed was helpful even, so helpful you might owe him a favor."

"I owe him? I've never heard of him."

O'Connell chuckled a response. "Well, you are about to meet him. He is the man that brought Sarah out alive. They're making him out to be a real hero."

"And you're sure it was him, this Fayed is the rat?"

"Very sure. I'm holding a file of every record he

accessed on you. Some of this stuff goes back to your earliest personnel records with the Army. But I'm sorry, Tommy, I don't think there is anything here that we could use against the man. From all of this, it could just be he was doing his utmost to bring Sarah home, and it looks like that is exactly what he did."

Tommy paused again; he thought about the flyer with his ID card photo on it, the news of him crossing the border, and how they knew it was him so quickly. "Sir, let me ask you, did he access a military identification photo of me—it would be probably ten years or older."

Tommy heard papers flipping then stop. O'Connell laughed. "Oh yeah, looks like you were fresh out of Army basic training. You have the skinhead haircut to prove it. Why do you ask about that specifically?"

"Because a few days ago, the Hyena distributed wanted posters of me with that photo on it. That is a direct tie between this Ziya character and the Hyena."

O'Connell sighed. "It's still not much to go on."

Tommy grunted. "I'll know when I see him, I'll shake him down and get him to talk."

"No, there is something else, Tommy. You can't go after him. There is a reason this meeting is happening in a church before they fly Sarah home."

"I don't understand."

"You're a wanted man, Tommy. The Feds aren't happy; they claim you've broken a dozen or more laws. They also were not pleased to find out I was looking into Ziya Fayed and hunting for a connection between the Agent and Abdul Nassir."

"The FBI?" Tommy asked. "Why would the Bureau care what happens in that shithole."

"No, the FBI is as curious as we are now that I shook the trees for them and knocked off all the low-hanging fruit. It's the State Department and the Agency. Abdul Nassir is a known asset of theirs, and they weren't happy to find out he's dead. And yeah before you ask, I think there is a connection to Fayed and they are burying it, but—"

"But what?" Tommy asked.

"You have to let it go, son. Let it go or they will come after you."

Tommy sat speechless, trying to take in the information. They took his sister and now they want to come after him for getting her back. He shook his head and looked up as he saw Simon Arnet, the man from the Vatican, approaching his car. Tommy put the phone back to his ear. "Thank you, sir, we'll talk more about this later," he said disconnecting the call.

Opening the door, he stepped onto the sidewalk just as the Swiss Guard approached his door. Seeing him, the man rubbed his chin then extended his hand. Tommy returned the handshake and stared at the man. Tommy began to speak when Simon held up a hand, stopping him. "It's better that you don't say anything. You are here to see your sister, then we will help you leave. Nothing more, nothing less."

"Help me leave?"

The man nodded, "We will provide you sanctuary inside the church for the meeting, and we will see that you are free to leave and not be followed, but after that there is little we can do."

"But Sarah, she's here."

Simon smiled, "Yes, your sister is here."

"Does she know?" he asked, "about what happened over there."

Simon shook his head. "No, she knows nothing of the role you played, but I do, and I appreciate all of it. But not everyone does, including some of the men inside."

"You're sure I won't be arrested?"

"Not here. But you will be if you stick around."

"I understand. Can I see my sister now?"

Simon smiled. "Yes, of course."

The man turned and walked toward the church entrance with Tommy holding close by his side. They walked past the tall wooden church doors and turned a corner to a less ornate side entrance. Simon put his hand on a brass doorknob and looked back to ensure Tommy was still with him. He slowly dipped his chin then opened the door and ushered Tommy in ahead of him.

She was in the center of the room sitting on a high-backed chair. Dressed in dark pants and a long sweater, she had a blanket draped over her shoulders and her hair pulled back. She looked up at him standing in the doorway and her eyes filled with tears. Tommy couldn't remember the last time he'd seen her. He half expected her to be dressed in her usual penguin suit. He froze, not knowing what to do. He choked, holding back his own emotions until she approached him. He softened and she fell into his arms.

Both of them ignoring the pain in their bodies, they held on tight. Tommy spoke with his voice breaking. "I thought you were dead. I didn't think I'd ever see you again," he whispered in her ear, now unable to hold back the tears.

Tommy bit his lower lip and looked down at her.

From across the room, he spotted a group of men clustered in the back, all in dark blue suits but one. The last man wore a tan sport coat, his skin was bronze and when he saw Tommy's gaze, the man turned away nervously. He knew it had to be Fayed, the man was a cowered and cowards all reacted the same way. Tommy's muscles stiffened as he fought an impulse to confront him. He wanted nothing more than to fly across the room and attack.

Sarah pushed away from him, blocking his view of Fayed, and looked into his eyes. "I can't believe you traveled all this way to see me."

"I'd do anything for you, Sarah," he said, pulling her back into a hug keeping his eyes locked on Ziya Fayed.

34

Tommy didn't mind waiting. His time training as a sniper taught him to enjoy the waiting. And for this he could wait days if he had to, but he knew it wouldn't come to that. The room was dark with the blinds closed, the city lights blocked out. Night had fallen and ambient sounds of busy streets filled the air. Tommy sat in an overstuffed chair in a corner, alone in the dark, a glass of fine cognac in his hand. He wore dark denim jeans and a tight, black T-shirt. His wounds were finally healing, but he could still feel the tightness of the scar. His mind, still weary, was cloudy and visions from the past continued to haunt him every time he closed his eyes.

He sipped the liquid and felt the burn as he swished it in his mouth before swallowing. It didn't take much for him to learn everything about the Interpol agent, Ziya Fayed—the man named as the one who'd taken sudden interest in his past and arranged the miraculous rescue of his sister. Of course, he owed the man a personal debt of gratitude, and it was one he intended to pay.

Tommy had put in the time to learn everything about Fayed. Using old trade craft from his previous position, he studied the inspector's routines, his habits, where he lived, and where he dined. Most of the man's history, although well concealed, was there to be found if you knew where to look. The hard part was verifying his connection to the Badawi Brigade. That proved the most difficult. After the death of Abdul Nassir, the inspector cut all his connections to the organization. He even appeared to be going clean, putting himself on the right track.

After bringing Sarah out of Syria and arranging her transfer to authorities, he was promoted off the Middle East desk and given a meritorious promotion to Assistant Director. Fayed came from a prominent family and was considered a member of the protected class. No investigation would be mounted against him. The State Department declared him off limits and any inquiry about his relationship to Abdul Nassir was quickly met with subpoenas and cease and desist orders.

Ziya was a golden boy at home and things were looking up for the man who was already considered a fast-tracking professional. With no official interest in pursuing Fayed and State actively preventing it, Tommy relied on O'Connell for one last favor: the funding to build a case against the investigator and the last remaining link to Sarah's capture.

Of course, if you didn't turn a blind eye, all the red flags were there. The man lived above his means. When he drove, he drove the nicest cars. He traveled frequently to places often only visited by the wealthy. He made frequent trips to the conflict zones that were only loosely related to his official functions. Donovan knew from the start that this was a man corrupted by outside influences, and once the dots were connected, it was confirmed.

The counter-terrorism expert known as Ziya Fayed was dirty, and Tommy had the proof. Colonel O'Connell had funded his expedition—this investigation—and now that the dossier was complete, Tommy's work was done. The files had already been sent back to Washington to be hand delivered by courier to Colonel O'Connell the next day. Before the colonel had time to pour his morning coffee, the papers would be delivered to his front door.

It was enough evidence to confirm Fayed's connection with not only the raid on the church and the kidnapping of the nuns, but to several other crimes spanning the last half decade. Within hours of O'Connell filing the report with the FBI and the CIA, Assistant Director Ziya Fayed, the gem of Mideast investigations, would be arrested by the same agency he represented.

With the job done, Tommy was now once again officially unemployed. What he was doing now was completely off the clock. This was personal. Tommy relaxed, sitting back in the comfortable chair. He was ready to go home, even though he hadn't decided where that would be yet. In the morning, he would go to the train station and buy a ticket to anywhere—preferably some place remote, maybe the Swiss Alps or a small town in Austria to hole up for the winter. From there, he didn't know. Maybe he would finally go to the islands. He'd put away enough money to live comfortably for several years, and after that he would still have the accounts accumulating funds from his pensions. He didn't require much, he was a simple man.

He heard soft footsteps in the hallway and brought the suppressed Browning pistol onto his lap. He watched the shadows dance under the crack at the bottom of the door. He listened to the sounds of a key entering the lock and the bolt clunking home. The door opened, and a man stepped into the room. He reached for the switch and flipped it on and off again. He cursed when the light failed to come on. There was a low glow from the kitchen, and the man moved through the dark entryway and fumbled with a lamp on an end table. A click, and the room was lit. He moved toward a table and dropped his keys and mobile phone onto a porcelain tray.

Fayed froze, his body suddenly still as he spotted the uncorked bottle of Martell Cognac on the kitchen counter. The man's arms tensed, realizing his error of walking through the dark room, not immediately sensing the danger and leaving. Slowly, he turned toward the living room, where the curtains swayed from an open balcony window. A stone-cold shadow in the corner chair moved and a lamp clicked on. Fayed recognized the man instantly. His body constricted with fear and his brown eyes grew wide upon spotting Tommy Donovan in the flesh, holding a suppressed pistol pointed directly at him.

"Hello, Inspector," Tommy said in a low, calm voice, speaking in English. "Or is it Assistant Director now? I hear congratulations are in order."

"Why are you here? What are your doing in my home?"

"I think we are beyond that, you know exactly why I'm here. It's strange though; after spending the last two weeks learning all about you, I feel like we're old friends." Tommy stood. He pointed to Fayed with the pistol held in his black leather glove. "On your knees," he said.

Fayed impulsively backed away, bringing up his hands. "What is this about? I can pay you; I have a safe. I have plenty of money."

Tommy tilted his head toward a black bag against the wall. "I've already collected your money. Don't worry—I'm not stealing it. All of your money will be sent back to Syria. A friend will use it to make sure the Badawi Brigade is finished for good."

"Why are you doing this? You got her back; I helped rescue her."

Tommy smiled, showing his teeth. "You may beg if you wish. You can pray if you'd like."

"Please," Fayed said, his voice croaking. "I am an important man; they'll come after you."

"No need to show concern for me, Fayed. Now I must insist—on your knees."

Fayed's hands began to shake with the realization that he was dead. He dropped to his knees, still mumbling about being an investigator, about being able to pay for his sins. His hands raised, and on his knees, he clenched his fists in the air, pleading.

"Why did you do it?" Tommy asked.

Fayed looked up and opened his mouth, but before he could speak, Tommy rammed the pistol into his face, breaking his teeth. The last thing Ziya Fayed saw was the barrel of Tommy Donovan's pistol. Two pulls of the trigger sent two rounds bursting from the back of the man's head, splattering the room behind him.

The body collapsed to the floor. Tommy wiped down the pistol and left it with the corpse, along with a second copy of the dossier he'd sent to O'Connell.

EPILOGUE

He never pictured himself as an island man. Sure, it was always on his wish list of places to visit, but now he was slowly getting used to the life. The beaches, the slow-moving pace, and the constant attention from the local women helped him make it through his dull existence. A cool breeze blew off the ocean, light clouds drifted on the horizon. Tommy finished the last of his coffee and moved to the Tiki bar, just a short walk from his modest apartment overlooking the emerald beaches of Saint Thomas. He dressed the part now—khaki shorts and a T-shirt, a couple days' worth of scruff replacing his beard.

Once again, he had managed to hide in plain sight. He wasn't sure if anyone was looking for him, but why take chances? Tommy had no illusions that the CIA had tabs on where he was. He knew there were people in the State Department who were angry with him and people in France who would have him imprisoned for what he'd done. He also knew that groups far more nefarious in

Syria still had a bounty on his head, but those groups didn't have much resources for outside of the theater. The times of the world were changing, and he was okay with fading away into a happy existence. He slept soundly, no longer bothered by the things he'd done.

After Sarah's rescue, he made sure she had what she needed to recover, and the Church gave her a choice posting in Rome, in a small village where she would have the peace and tranquility to reflect on her life. He knew she would be okay now, and that was all he cared about. Soon after their last visit in Greece, she'd talked to Carol and discovered what he'd done. She knew most of it now, at least enough to know why he had to keep his distance from her and couldn't hang around more than a day or two at a time. Still, he snuck in a visit to her village several times while lying low in Europe. She never knew he was there, but it helped him sleep knowing she was safe and that the local security met his standards. Of course, it didn't but he put his faith in her, and trust in Simon who ensured she would be protected.

Colonel O'Connell offered him the finest attorneys, told him he would be vindicated. That he could return to Boston a free man. Tommy looked out at the ocean and smiled at the thought of never having to suffer another Massachusetts winter. There would be no forgetting the things he'd done. He quietly slipped away, using safe houses and old contacts to lock in a new identity. He was happy here, and he'd stay until he decided it was time to move on, or until something made him return.

Ordering a Mojito, she caught his eye, and before she approached him, he already knew he was in trouble. She sat across the bar from him. A white dress clung tightly to her body. She wore a thin jacket that caught the breeze in just the right way. She looked up at him then turned away in a flirtatious manner. Tommy tagged her right off for what she was. Of course, it was possible she was an attorney on vacation, maybe a bridesmaid who wandered off to find some alone time. But this wasn't a make-believe fantasy, and beautiful women don't find themselves at lonely bars before noon on the wrong side of the island. That was strike one.

He knew she was somebody's agent; he just didn't know whose yet. He toyed with the idea of allowing her to seduce him. See how far she would let him go before doing whatever it was she came here for. He smiled at her and let his eyes survey the road behind her. The lot of the small beach bar was empty, but farther up the road was a black sedan with tinted windows. He frowned. They would be her backup; there would be no seducing today.

Tommy called the bartender over and ordered the woman another drink. She took it, smiled, and stood from her stool to make her way around the bar toward him. That was strike two. And the final confirmation that he needed to know she was on the job. If he'd made the same offer to any other woman, on any other day, she'd have waited until he came to her. She walked around the bar and sat beside him and smiled.

"Are you a local here?" she asked.

Tommy laughed. "What a silly question."

"Excuse me?"

"Why would you ask if I'm a local? Do you need a place to stay?" Tommy asked.

The woman turned away from him. He knew that her impulse was to walk away. If she'd been a real tourist looking for fun, that's exactly what she would have done. But that's not what she was. Strike three. She turned back to face him. "I'm sorry if you took that the wrong way. I was just thinking this is a beautiful spot off the regular tourist paths. I was surprised to find it."

Tommy grinned and nodded. "Well done," he said.

She looked at him, confused, and he laughed at her. She shook her head, knowing she'd been made. Tommy raised a hand, ordering himself another drink then looked at her. "What are you here for?"

"Fine then, let's just get to it," she said, frustrated that her cover had been blown. She looked across the bar to see the bartender wiping down the far side with a cloth. She reached into her bag and placed a yellow envelope on the bar in front of Tommy.

"What's this?"

"It's your offer, and to be honest with you, it's the best deal you're going to get."

"What do you mean 'deal'?" Tommy said, taking the envelope. He looked inside and found a thick stack of bound cash.

"Look, I wanted to come at you slowly. I had a whole thing planned on how to break this to you, but we can do it your way. People know what you did in Syria, and you've made some fans at the Executive Branch. He calls you the Jackal Hunter."

"He was a Hyena," Tommy corrected. "Executive Branch? You mean the President?"

She shrugged, not answering the question. "Let's just say someone appreciates your ability to make things happen while staying off the radar."

"Things?"

She nodded her head and sipped from her glass. "We're tired of waiting to be attacked before we respond. We want a person like you that can go out and get things done."

"But mostly you want a person you can deny and hang out to dry if things go sideways."

"Take it or leave it, Mr. Donovan."

Tommy lifted the envelope again. "And this—what's it for? What's the job?"

"Consider it a retainer. We'll be in touch."

"And if I refuse?"

She smiled at him and leaned in, kissing him hard on the lips. When he leaned into it, she pulled away. He looked at her, not able to hide his surprise. "Don't do that, Tommy," she said. "They have enough on you to put you away for a lot of years." She stood and began to walk away before turning to look at him one last time. "You know, I had planned to seduce you... it's too bad," she said, leaving.

THANK YOU FOR READING

PLEASE LEAVE A REVIEW ON AMAZON

Click here for an opportunity to receive a free copy of the next Donovan's War Novel.

About WJ Lundy

W. J. Lundy is a still serving Veteran of the U.S. Military with service in Afghanistan. He has over 16 years of combined service with the Army and Navy in Europe, the Balkans and Southwest Asia. W.J. is an avid athlete, writer, backpacker and shooting enthusiast. He currently resides with his wife and daughter in Central Michigan.

Find WJ Lundy on facebook:

Join the WJ Lundy mailing list for news, updates and contest giveaways.

Whiskey Tango Foxtrot Series.

Whiskey Tango Foxtrot is an introduction into the apocalyptic world of Staff Sergeant Brad Thompson. A series with over 1,500 five-star reviews on Amazon.

Alone in a foreign land. The radio goes quiet while on convoy in Afghanistan, a lost patrol alone in the desert. With his unit and his home base destroyed, Staff Sergeant Brad Thompson suddenly finds himself isolated and in command of a small group of men trying to survive in the Afghan wasteland.

Every turn leads to danger. The local population has been afflicted with an illness that turns them into rabid animals. They pursue him and his men at every corner and stop. Struggling to hold his team together and unite survivors, he must fight and evade his way to safety.

A fast paced zombie war story like no other.

Praise for Whiskey Tango Foxtrot:

"The beginning of a fantastic story. Action packed and full of likeable characters. If you want military authenticity, look no further. You won't be sorry."

-Owen Baillie, Author of Best-selling series, Invasion of the Dead.

"A brilliantly entertaining post-apocalyptic thriller. You'll find it hard to putdown"

-Darren Wearmouth, Best-selling author of First Activation, Critical Dawn, Sixth Cycle

"W.J. Lundy captured two things I love in one novel--military and zombies!"
-Terri King, Editor Death Throes Webzine

"War is horror and having a horror set during wartime works well in this story. Highly recommended!"
-Allen Gamboa, Author of Dead Island: Operation Zulu

"There are good books in this genre, and then there are the ones that stand out from the rest-- the ones that make me want to purchase all the books in the series in one shot and keep reading. W.J. Lundy's Whiskey Tango Foxtrot falls into the latter category."
-Under the Oaks reviews

"The author's unique skills set this one apart from the masses of other zombie novels making it one of the most exciting that I have read so far."
-HJ Harry, of Author Splinter

The Invasion Trilogy
The Darkness is a fast-paced story of survival that brings the apocalypse to Main Street USA.

While the world falls apart, Jacob Anderson barricades

his family behind locked doors. News reports tell of civil unrest in the streets, murders, and disappearances; citizens are warned to remain behind locked doors. When Jacob becomes witness to horrible events and the alarming actions of his neighbors, he and his family realize everything is far worse than being reported.

Every father's nightmare comes true as Jacob's normal life--and a promise to protect his family--is torn apart.

From the Best-Selling Author of **Whiskey Tango Foxtrot comes a new telling of Armageddon.**

The Darkness
The Shadows
The Light

Praise for the Invasion Trilogy:

"The Darkness is like an air raid siren that won't shut off; thrilling and downright horrifying!" *Nicholas Sansbury Smith, Best Selling Author of Orbs and The Extinction Cycle.*

"Absolutely amazing. This story hooked me from the first page and didn't let up. I read the story in one sitting and now I am desperate for more. ...Mr. Lundy has definitely broken new ground with this tale of humanity, sacrifice and love of family ... In short, read this book." *William Allen, Author of Walking in the Rain.*

"First book I've pre-ordered before it was published. Well done story of survival with a relentless pace, great action, and characters I cared about! Some scenes are still in my head!" *Stephen A. North, Author of Dead Tide and The Drifter.*

OTHER AUTHORS UNDER THE SHIELD OF

FAST FORWARD

DARREN WEARMOUTH

After recovering from near-fatal injuries sustained on a mission, Luke Porterfield is offered a second opportunity to fight terrorism by a pDrivate venture. He is stored in bleeding-edge technology before agreeing to the deal, and wakes to an uncertain fate. In the vastly changed and advanced city of London, Luke is tasked to defeat a deadly and elusive terrorist group. When his mission unearths a five-decade-long conspiracy, the explosive consequences force him into a fight against the full technological power of a demented dictator. **Fast Forward** is a thrilling adventure packed with action, and technologies destined to be part of our future.

GRUDGE

BRIAN PARKER

The United States Navy led an expedition to Antarctica in December 1946, called Operation Highjump. Officially, the men were tasked with evaluating the effect of cold weather on US equipment; secretly their mission was to investigate reports of a hidden Nazi base buried beneath the ice. After engaging unknown forces in aerial combat, weather forced the Navy to abandon operations. Undeterred, the US returned every Antarctic summer until finally the government detonated three nuclear missiles over the atmosphere in 1958. Unfortunately, the desperate gamble to rid the world of the Nazi scourge failed. The enemy burrowed deeper into the ice, using alien technologies for cryogenic freezing to amass a genetically superior army, indoctrinated from birth to hate Americans. Now they've returned, intent on exacting revenge for the destruction of their homeland and banishment to the icy wastes.

DEAD ISLAND: OPERATION ZULU

ALLEN GAMBOA

Ten years after the world was nearly brought to its knees
by a zombie Armageddon, there is a race for the antidote!
On a remote Caribbean island, surrounded by a horde of
hungry living dead, a team of American and Australian
commandos must rescue the Antidotes' scientist. Filled
with zombies, guns, Russian bad guys, shady government
types, serial killers and elevator muzak. Dead Island is an
action packed blood soaked horror adventure.

INVASION OF THE DEAD SERIES

OWEN BALLIE

This is the first book in a series of nine, about an ordinary bunch of friends, and their plight to survive an apocalypse in Australia. -- Deep beneath defense headquarters in the Australian Capital Territory, the last ranking Army chief and a brilliant scientist struggle with answers to the collapse of the world, and the aftermath of an unprecedented virus. Is it a natural mutation, or does the infection contain -- more sinister roots? -- One hundred and fifty miles away, five friends returning from a month-long camping trip slowly discover that death has swept through the country. What greets them in a gradual revelation is an enemy beyond compare. -- Armed with dwindling ammunition, the friends must overcome their disagreements, utilize their individual skills, and face unimaginable horrors as they battle to reach their hometown...

WHISKEY TANGO FOXTROT

W.J LUNDY

Alone in a foreign land. The radio goes quiet while on convoy in Afghanistan, a lost patrol alone in the desert. With his unit and his home base destroyed, Staff Sergeant Brad Thompson suddenly finds himself isolated and in command of a small group of men trying to survive in the Afghan wasteland. Every turn leads to danger.

The local population has been afflicted with an illness that turns them into rabid animals. They pursue him and his men at every corner and stop. Struggling to hold his team together and unite survivors, he must fight and evade his way to safety. A fast-paced zombie war story like no other.

WAYWARD SON

JOSEPH HANSEN

His life in its late autumn years had been good if not somewhat boring, Bob Johnson is offered the chance of making a difference. Using a prototype technology to traverse gateways into alternate realities offers him a chance to change the course of history and possibly the nature of certain people, namely two young men who are becoming bad people. Bob seizes the opportunity to change those whom he had influenced and possibly rescue his own soul in the process... or quite possibly damn it. Changing those who those who are trying ruin everything he cherishes is a double edged sword yet a risk he had to take to right his inadvertent wrongs. His reality can never be the same again...

THE ALPHA PLAGUE

MICHAEL ROBERTSON

Rhys is an average guy who works an average job in Summit City—a purpose built government complex on the outskirts of London. The Alpha Tower stands in the centre of the city. An enigma, nobody knows what happens behind its dark glass. Rhys is about to find out. At ground zero and with chaos spilling out into the street, Rhys has the slightest of head starts. If he can remain ahead of the pandemonium, then maybe he can get to his loved ones before the plague does. The Alpha Plague is a post-apocalyptic survival thriller.

THE GATHERING HORDE

RICH BAKER

The most ambitious terrorist plot ever undertaken is about to be put into motion, releasing an unstoppable force against humanity. Ordinary people – A group of students celebrating the end of the semester, suburban and rural families – are about to themselves in the center of something that threatens the survival of the human species. As they battle the dead – and the living – it's going to take every bit of skill, knowledge and luck for them to survive in Zed's World.

SIXTH CYCLE

CARL SINCLAIR & DARREN WEARMOUTH

Nuclear war has destroyed human civilization. Captain Jake Phillips wakes into a dangerous new world, where he finds the remaining fragments of the population living in a series of strongholds, connected across the country. Uneasy alliances have maintained their safety, but things are about to change. -- Discovery leads to danger. -- Skye Reed, a tracker from the Omega stronghold, uncovers a threat that could spell the end for their fragile society. With friends and enemies revealing truths about the past, she will need to decide who to trust. -- SIXTH CYCLE is a gritty post-apocalyptic story of survival and adventure.